LAST MINUTE - LARGE PRINT EDITION

A Janet Black Mystery

LIBBY KIRSCH

Sunnyside
Press

Sunnyside Press
PO Box 2476
Ann Arbor, MI. 48106
www.LibbyKirschBooks.com

Publisher's Note: This is a work of fiction. Names, characters, places, and incidents are a product of the author's imagination. Locales and public names are sometimes used for atmospheric purposes. Any resemblance to actual people, living or dead, or to businesses, companies, events, institutions, or locales is completely coincidental.

Last Minute/ Libby Kirsch -- 1st ed., large print

ISBN 978-1-7337003-4-4

CHAPTER ONE

Janet Black stood back and looked at a spot on the floor near the bed critically for a long moment, then finally nodded at her boyfriend. "You know what? I think you're right."

Jason Brooks raised his eyebrows. "Well, darlin', let the record reflect that on September fourteenth, at three forty-seven in the afternoon—"

"Oh, shut up and get a stool! That should take care of the problem."

Jason's eyes lingered on her before he turned and left the room. Janet adjusted her garter belt and tapped the heel of her stiletto against the wood floor. *Ta-ta-tap. Ta-ta-tap. Ta-ta—*

"Something like this?" Jason was back, his expression betraying his opinion that it would never work.

"Yes!" Janet grabbed the stool and then eyed the bed before placing it on the floor about two and a half feet away from the edge of the mattress. "If I stand on the stool and then do a backbend to the mattress, everything should line right up—"

"What kind of tread do those heels have?" Jason's eyes narrowed and he nudged the stool closer to the bed by a few inches with his toe. "I don't know . . . if your hands slip, you'll fall to the floor." Jason crept toward her, despite his objection.

"Well, you won't just be standing there, will you? You'll be holding on to my hips!" Janet tossed her shoulder-length light brown hair back and pushed her chest out while batting her hazel eyes. At five foot six, she was too short for her original idea—but the step stool and heels combined more than made up for the height difference. "I know you won't let me fall."

The colorful ink on Jason's arms rippled as he crossed them and considered Janet's plan. He'd shed his shirt earlier and the top button on his jeans was undone. Janet licked her lips as she watched him think about doing what she wanted him to do.

She wiggled her hips and he finally reached for her.

Ring, ring.

"The phone," Jason murmured, stepping close. His day-old whiskers tickled her neck.

"Let's ignore it," she sighed, and ran her hands down his arms.

The phone went quiet, and his lips moved across her neck and up her jaw until he finally parted her lips with his tongue. Heat licked up from her core. Her legs felt like jelly.

Ring, ring.

"Damn it," she moaned, reaching back blindly for the receiver on the nightstand. "What?" She sucked in a gasp when Jason knelt in front of her, nibbling at sensitive skin.

"Uh, boss?" The woman's twangy, uncertain tone made it clear who was on the other end.

"What is it, Cindy Lou?" Janet focused on not moaning as she shifted her body to the right. Jason grinned and kept working his way up her leg.

"I think you better come in," the bartender said. "We've got—well, cops are here, and I don't know what to do."

Janet pushed back from Jason and thumped down on the bed, worry edging away all other emotions. "What do you—wait, never mind. I'll be right in."

She dropped the phone back onto the receiver. "Cops are at the Spot! I've got to go."

Jason's eyebrows knitted together. "I'll come, too."

"That's sweet, but you don't have to—"

"Janet! Of course I'm coming." He hopped up with a scowl and snagged his shirt off the ground as he stalked out of the room.

She blew out a sigh. Somehow he'd taken her offer for him to stay home as an insult.

She slipped out of the lingerie and got dressed in her usual bar "uniform" of jeans and a T-shirt. So much for being spontaneous. She picked up an envelope off the dresser and left the room. Jason's dad's mail had inadvertently been mixed in with hers, and she tossed it on the hall table on her way to the front door.

William Brooks had moved in with them over the summer, after he and Jason's mom argued their way through a messy divorce. The situation was not ideal, but Jason felt bad; his dad had nowhere else to go, so they'd been making the best of it.

On the plus side, William had been working on their kitchen remodeling project. In the minus column, he spent a lot of time moping around the house. Janet struggled to feel empathy for the man; after all, you can't cheat on a woman and then be mad when she leaves you!

"Ready?" she called to Jason.

"Let's go." He swept past her and she frowned. Every time she tried to do something nice, Jason took it as dismissive. William Brooks had brought his bad mojo from Memphis and Janet couldn't wait for him to leave.

"Bye, William. We'll be home later."

"Everything okay, Janet?" He stuck his head through the open kitchen door; drywall dust covered his hair. "I forgot to tell you I called an arborist to come to the Spot. Those ash trees need to come down—they're being devoured by emerald ash borers—"

"Fine, William, thanks so much." She turned and walked out of the house, a stiff smile plastered on her face. He needed to get his own home and business to worry over, and leave hers alone.

———

Janet stood frozen in the parking lot. The bar's Beerador, a massive seven-foot-tall, bottle-shaped refrigerator, stood guard by the door. The unusual appliance had come with the bar when Janet and

Jason had bought it years ago, but it had been taken during a murder investigation several months earlier. Why was it back?

She shuddered slightly, remembering the body she'd found, staring lifelessly out the Beerador's window all those weeks ago. A quick look behind her confirmed that Jason was still on the phone call that had just come in when he parked. She waved when he looked up, then turned and strode into the Spot. It took a moment for her eyes to adjust to the low lighting inside.

Her bar looked like it had been ransacked.

Someone had cleared a path from the door to the center of the room, forcing tables and chairs aside in an uneven mess.

Janet made her way behind the bar to Cindy Lou.

Her assistant manager, and most faithful bartender, was channeling Rosie the Riveter that day; her bleached-blond hair was tied back in a red bandana, and a short denim jumper with a plunging neckline replaced the blue jumpsuit from the poster.

"What's going on?"

Cindy Lou stared pointedly across the bar but didn't speak, only continued to prep a pile of lemons for the night ahead, her knife making *click, clack, clack* sounds against the cutting board.

"I should charge you extra for the door-to-door delivery, but I won't." The deep voice came from Janet's left. Detective Patrick O'Dell grinned from a bar stool, his green eyes sparkling mischievously. A sports coat hung off the back of his chair, and his white shirtsleeves were rolled up to the elbow. One of her regulars, Nell, an older woman with silvery-gray hair, waved, but Janet could only stare at the cop, her mouth open.

His resulting chuckle shook her tongue loose. "You're giving it back? I mean, shouldn't it go to . . . I just assumed it would be disposed of, or something—I . . ."

Janet eyed the Beerador suspiciously. She'd thought—hoped—she'd never see it again.

"Would have cost the city too much to bring it to the dump with the fees and everything," O'Dell said. "Where do you want my guys to put it?"

"Ahhh . . ." Janet grimaced. "Has it been cleaned or anything?"

"Nope."

"Son of a—"

"Biscuit!" Cindy Lou interrupted with a sharp elbow in Janet's side. "It can be just as satisfying if you say it right," she added out of the side of her mouth.

Janet snorted. Nothing could be as satisfying as a real curse word, but she bit back the one that had been on her lips, crossed her arms, and glared at the refrigerator. She'd once considered the Beerador fun—campy, almost—but now . . . Now it was a tainted vessel of death. "What am I supposed to do with it?"

"Clean it out, I guess, hon." Cindy Lou wiped her forehead with the back of her hand, then pointed at the offending appliance with her chef's knife. "I'm gettin' dirty just looking at all that fingerprint dust! I bet if we use a mixture of bleach and baking soda—"

"We'll blow up the building?" Janet popped a hand on her hip and scowled at the Beerador.

"Everything okay?" Jason edged past the Beerador at the front entrance, then stopped short when he saw O'Dell. "Oh." He crossed his arms over his chest and walked up to the bar.

O'Dell forced a grin. "Jason. Good to see you, man."

Just beyond O'Dell, Nell leaned in, her eyes flicking from O'Dell's wallet to his hand resting just inches away. Nell's dark, quick eyes—magnified through the enormous lenses of her bold, black eyeglass frames—were even then calculating the distance between his wallet and her handbag.

Janet stifled a groan; the last thing she needed just then was for their resident klepto to strike against Knoxville's lead homicide investigator. She cleared her throat. "Nell, did you need another round?"

Nell dropped her chin to her chest and tucked a stray gray hair back into her tidy, low bun. "All good here, Janet."

Janet smiled to herself, then racked her brain for how to solve the larger problem in the room. "I think . . . we should . . . turn the Beerador into a coat closet."

Cindy Lou's nose wrinkled, and her head tilted to one side. "I don't know. It wouldn't hold that many coats, would it?"

Jason didn't smile. With a scowl still etched firmly on his face, he said to O'Dell, "Now that it's here, I guess you'll be on your way."

O'Dell slid off his bar stool and laid a few bills from his wallet on the bar for Cindy Lou, then all six foot one of him tried to move past Nell. The older woman closed her eyes and leaned into the empty space between them, her puckered lips tilted up as he brushed past. Janet almost laughed out loud. Nell hated cops, but even she couldn't ignore O'Dell's broad, muscular frame and boyish good looks.

Janet met O'Dell on the other side of the countertop. "Can your guys move it out of the doorway, at least?"

"Sure." O'Dell grinned at Jason as he rested a hand on her shoulder and squeezed. "Anything for you, Janet."

Jason's chest puffed out and Janet stifled a groan. These two grown men were acting like possessive peacocks.

O'Dell tapped something into his cell phone and soon four burly men walked into the bar with a heavy-duty hand cart.

As they surrounded the Beerador, O'Dell asked, "Where do you want it, Janet?"

"Jason?" She turned to her boyfriend, but he was beyond being able to help. Waves of irritation rolled off his body like freshly applied aftershave.

She locked eyes with Cindy Lou. Her head bartender lifted one shoulder and dropped it back down, then motioned behind her. "I always did like having the bottles in there."

Janet raked a hand over her face. "I guess back behind the bar, O'Dell. We'll deep-clean it and see if it still works." Could you get the smell of murder out of a refrigerator? Seemed like a Clorox wipe just wasn't going to be enough.

As the men navigated through the bar with the heavy load, the front door opened, and a beam of sunlight sparkled beautifully off the Beerador's curved glass door.

Cindy Lou gasped, and new emotion multiplied the twang in her voice when she said, "I think she's glad to be back home, y'all!"

Janet suppressed a snort and turned her attention to the newcomer. "Come on in, don't mind the mess. Can I get you a drink?"

But the man, wearing a herringbone sports coat over khakis and a blue button-down, beelined for O'Dell. A golden badge glinted at his waist. "O'Dell. What are you doing here?"

"I'm giving that back to its rightful owners." He pointed to the Beerador, which came down off the dolly with a crash behind Cindy Lou. "I thought you were heading to a dead body call-out, Rivera?"

"I did." Rivera scanned the bar. "Now I'm here to find Nell Anderson. Do you know her?"

Janet leaned in when O'Dell asked, "What's going on?"

Rivera blew out a sigh and lowered his voice. "I just came from her daughter's house. She's dead."

CHAPTER TWO

"Oh my gosh, I mean, have you ever heard anything so terrible?" Cindy Lou said for at least the ninth time.

Janet dumped her tray onto the bar and took the dirty glasses to the sink. While Cindy Lou yammered on, she thought back to Nell, and the way her shoulders had slumped and her eyes—usually bright and sharp—had dimmed, turned dull and lifeless, when the homicide detective broke the terrible news.

Detective Rivera had said that Nell's daughter, Liv, had taken a "spill" down the stairs while carrying a huge load of laundry. It looked like a terrible accident, but they needed Nell to go to the house. She had to be there for Liv's husband and children.

Three children! Motherless now, because of laundry and a missed step.

Cindy Lou couldn't stop talking about it, and even though she was trying to tune her bartender out, Janet couldn't stop thinking about it, either.

Rivera had led Nell out of the bar. For the first time, Janet wasn't sure how old Nell really was. She'd always guessed her most steadfast customer was in her early sixties, but that afternoon's news had aged her considerably.

"O'Dell, you need another?" She pointed to the homicide detective's sweet tea.

"Nah, I gotta get back." He took another leisurely sip and made no attempt to move.

"Why is homicide involved when they think Liv slipped on the steps?"

"Standard operating procedure, Janet," he answered self-importantly. She leaned forward over the bar and rested her elbows on the countertop, staring at him expectantly. "They won't know the actual cause of death until the coroner does the autopsy." O'Dell shook the ice cubes in his glass and drained the last of the liquid. "Homicide goes to all calls with a dead body—we collect evidence, just in case."

"In case?"

He nodded, his lips pressed into a flat line. "In case it wasn't an accident. I mean, really, how many women in their thirties slip down the stairs and die?"

Janet's eyes opened wide. "Do you think—"

"I don't think anything, sweetheart, because I wasn't there, I didn't see the scene. I'm just telling you why Rivera's there, and why he's probably suspicious."

She nodded and swiped his empty glass off the bar. A throat cleared near her and she turned, then had to stifle a gasp when she found Jason on the floor in front of her, down on one knee.

"Oh my God!"

"I have a question." He leaned forward and looked up at Janet.

"Jason, don't—" She choked on the last word as panic crept up into her throat, constricting her airflow.

"Can you pass the bag of trail mix? I thought it was under here." He gestured to the cabinet by his bent leg, "But now I see it's up there by the cash register."

"Oh." Janet's face flushed and she handed him the bag. He grinned, then stood up and walked away.

Janet grabbed a piece of paper from the countertop and fanned her neck. Was it hot in here? Even the tips of her ears pulsed with heat.

Cindy Lou handed her a glass of iced tea. "You look like you've seen a ghost." She propped her hip against the nearest cooler and crossed her arms under her ample chest.

Janet took a long pull of the tea while she watched Jason top off the bowls on each table. "I thought—I mean, I worried that . . ." She tried to laugh lightly, but it came out sounding choppy and forced.

"He wants to," Cindy Lou said, tapping a finger against her teeth. "I don't know if he has the ring yet, but he's ready for the next step."

Janet turned to her assistant manager; the skin around her eyes and mouth suddenly felt too tight, and she could barely move her lips when she asked Cindy Lou, "What? Did he say something to you?"

"Yup. Asked if he should do it here at the bar or somewhere else."

When Cindy Lou fell quiet, Janet prompted, louder than she'd intended, "And? What did you say?"

The other woman jumped. "I told him that you weren't ready, of course! That it was too soon. I said that it'd be like asking for the Grey Goose after the well vodka—timing's all wrong!"

Janet felt her eyebrows knit together. "And then what did he say?"

Cindy Lou shuffled her feet. "Well, I mean, I wasn't takin' notes—"

"Cindy Lou!"

"Okay! He said, 'Sometimes you don't know you're ready until it happens.'"

Across the bar, Jason turned and winked, then stopped to talk to a customer with an easy grin.

He was perfect for her, no doubt about that. Jason was smart, funny, adventurous—but also low-key, relaxed, and easygoing. In short, none of the things that Janet could say about herself. But engaged? Married?

Janet shuddered. Thank God for Cindy Lou. She was right—Janet wasn't ready. Not for a proposal or for anything that came after. Hopefully Jason had listened.

The bartender grabbed a cloth and wiped down the bar. Then, in a quiet voice she said, "But that was months ago that he asked me about it. So maybe he . . . Well."

Janet drummed her fingers on the counter. Cindy Lou had just sent her only son off to college after raising him alone. Divorced for more than ten years, tonight she was dressed, as usual, to meet Mister Right Then. Her low V-neck and short skirt screamed, "Try me out!," not "Let's settle down."

"I can't think of a single happily married couple," she said to Cindy Lou. "Not one. Can you?"

The bartender's lips puckered while she thought, but it was O'Dell who answered. Janet had forgotten he was still sitting there until he spoke.

"My parents. Going on thirty-five years and most of them blissful—and those are their words, not mine."

"Yeah?" Janet asked.

O'Dell grinned when he heard the doubt in her voice. "Yeah. High school sweethearts, got engaged in college. Never been apart more than one night in a row. They're pretty great."

Janet tilted her head to the side as she considered being with the same someone for almost forty years. She frowned and plunged two dirty glasses into the automatic washer in the sink.

"What about you?" Cindy Lou asked. "You ever come close to finding Mrs. O'Dell?"

Janet's ears perked up, and when he didn't answer, she looked over, only to find him staring at her.

Before O'Dell could answer, an official-sounding voice at the opposite side of the bar rang out. "Janet Black?"

She pulled her eyes away from O'Dell and turned, only to find a nearly identical copy of him facing her. The stranger was also tall, with short, brown "cop hair," not quite buzzed, but nearly. He was attractive and well built but didn't have O'Dell's bright green eyes. Instead, his brown eyes squinted at her suspiciously.

"What?" She propped her hip against the cooler and raised her eyebrows.

He looked over her head and his frown deepened. "O'Dell."

"Donaldson?" O'Dell's voice was tinged with surprise. "What are you doing here?"

Donaldson's head ticked to the side and he brought his eyes back to Janet. "I am Gary Donaldson, the chief enforcer with the Tennessee Department of Commerce and Insurance." He stopped and gave her an imposing look.

"Cool." Janet motioned to the nearest bar stool. "Welcome, Chief Enforcer. Do you want a beer or a shot?"

He sneered. "Neither. I am here to issue you a verbal warning that an anonymous complaint has been filed with my department, and we are launching an investigation into you."

"A complaint?" Jason walked behind the bar and stood on Janet's right, between her and Donaldson. "Where did you say you worked?"

"The Department of—"

"What's the basis of the complaint?" O'Dell interrupted, moving from his bar stool to stand on Janet's left.

Donaldson pinched his lips together, and for a moment he looked as if he wasn't going to answer, but finally he said, "Operating as a private investigator without a license."

CHAPTER THREE

Later that night, Janet fumed silently about the inquiry with the state. Donaldson had—gleefully, in her opinion—handed over a stack of forms she would need to fill out within thirty days to refute the anonymous claim. She hated paperwork, but she hated the government's overstepping its bounds even more. The stack of papers now sat prominently on the bar by the cash register, to remind her of what needed to get done.

Cindy Lou sidled up to Janet and picked up the papers. "If you ask me—"

"Nobody did."

"—there's somethin' funny goin' on between that guy from the government and O'Dell. Did you see the way they glared at each other?" She tapped the edge of the stack against the bar until the corners were perfectly aligned, then set the papers back on the counter.

"I don't know, I mean, they're kind of on the same team, right?" Janet poured bourbon, fresh lemon juice, and simple syrup into a shaker, added a scoop of ice, and shook it more aggressively than usual. Then she strained the whiskey sour over an ice-filled rocks glass. "What I can't figure out is, who'd have filed a complaint? I mean, I may have looked into a homicide over the summer, but nobody paid me to do it. Wouldn't that be a key part of acting as a private investigator? Exchange of money for services?"

Cindy Lou looked blankly back, her mouth hanging slack, then blinked slowly and cleared her throat. "Sorry, hon, I'm downright exhausted! Been trying to go to Chip's club hockey games, but they play at eight in the mornin'! Might as well be in another country, it's that hard to get my butt outta bed at that hour." She shook herself. "Any word from Nell?"

Janet threaded a cherry through a toothpick and laid it on top of the rocks glass, then passed the drink across the counter to a customer. "No. I'll check on her tomorrow. Give her some time tonight to be with her family."

"Where's Jason?"

"He had to go home. Big account just came in from the west side of the state. He'll be busy for the next few weeks, getting everything set up."

It was eight o'clock, and the after-work crowd was thinning out. Janet wiped down a sticky splotch on the counter by the condiment tray. The only thing that could distract her from thinking about the inquiry from the state was Jason, and the more she did, the less she liked it. Jason had asked Cindy Lou about proposing to Janet months ago, but lately, he seemed reserved, almost like he was pulling away from her.

She thought back to their near-tryst in the bedroom that morning. Things had been tense since their long-term house mate moved in a month ago.

As if Janet had spoken out loud, Cindy Lou asked, "How much longer is William going to be with you all?"

Janet's lips puckered. "I guess until the houseboat situation clears up."

Cindy Lou frowned. "He'll be with you until spring?"

Janet heaved a long-suffering sigh. "God, I hope not."

"He just didn't understand how the drawdown works?"

Janet shrugged. The Tennessee Valley Authority was a well-known entity in all of Tennessee. The government agency drastically reduced water levels in lakes and waterways across the state to keep dangerous floods away over the winter months. This turned some houseboats into plain old houses, with the rectangular platforms that supported them resting at odd angles against the uneven lake bottoms until the water levels were raised again in the spring. The structures that counted on the lake water below them for plumbing were out of luck from September through March.

"William didn't realize Douglas Lake got so low when he bought the house. Anyway, he's with us now."

"What about Jason's mom?"

"We haven't seen her since William moved in. I think she's still pretty angry about the divorce, but Jason won't really talk about it, so . . ." She shrugged again and turned away from Cindy Lou, effectively ending the conversation.

The truth was, she didn't know any particulars about his parents' divorce, only that Jason refused to share his feelings about it, and William couldn't seem to stop. Janet knew every thought that entered William's head about how unjust the law was about splitting assets. And every time he opened his mouth, Jason retreated farther away. He'd barely spoken to his mother, but according to William, she'd taken everything in the divorce settlement, including the pet fish.

William was angry, Jason was reserved, but Janet, for one, was delighted. Women had to be proactive about protecting themselves, because God knew no one else was going to look out for them.

She filled a bucket from the ice maker in the walk-in cooler and lugged it out to dump into one of the beer chests. The Beerador gleamed ominously in the corner behind the bar. She'd gone over the outside of it with some cleaning wipes but hadn't yet opened the door.

"Maybe some stainless steel cleaner?" Cindy Lou said.

Janet nodded and made a note on the pad by the register.

"I'll take a strawberry margarita," a man's deep voice said off to the side. "Make it frozen."

Janet's lips pressed flat, but she couldn't bring herself to look over at the customer. A frozen margarita? And a strawberry one at that? Where did this guy think he was, Applebee's?

"Sorry," she said as she wiped a nonexistent

spot on the counter vigorously, "but we don't do *frozen* drinks—O'Dell!" She laughed out loud when she looked up to find him grinning ear to ear. "What are you doing back here?"

"Just got off my shift, and thought I'd come have a beer for once, instead of a sweet tea."

"You drink?" Janet leaned her elbows on the now-clean counter between them. "I pegged you for a teetotaler."

"Please. I'm a Catholic boy from Jersey. I started sneaking beers when I was thirteen."

She smiled and took his order. She poured herself a beer too and they clinked glasses.

"Long day?" He set his beer down neatly on a coaster after taking a sip.

She thought about Jason's pulling away, a favorite customer learning that her daughter was dead, and the new investigation into her supposedly illegal activity by the state and grimaced. "Sure feels like it. Anything new on Nell's daughter?"

"Nope. Homicide cleared the scene. Now we wait."

"On the autopsy?" O'Dell nodded. "Huh." She shuffled her feet. Cindy Lou hip-checked her from behind. After she caught her balance, she glared at her assistant manager, but the other woman looked pointedly at the stack of papers, then motioned toward O'Dell with her chin. Janet sighed but turned back to the cop. "So . . . what's up with that Donaldson guy?"

O'Dell spluttered into his beer. After he stopped coughing, he wiped his chin with a cocktail napkin and grinned sheepishly. "What do you mean?"

Cindy Lou snickered nearby and Janet smiled, too. That was a guilty reaction if ever there was one. "It just seemed as if you two knew each other."

O'Dell frowned. "I know *of* him. He's worked at Commerce for years. But we don't know each other well."

Janet tapped her fingers against her pint glass. There was more to that story, but O'Dell turned to the customer seated next to him and struck up a conversation. Janet watched him for a moment, then moved down the bar.

While she filled another order—a cosmopolitan, which was at the absolute outer limit of snobby drinks she'd mix up—she overheard O'Dell talking into his cell phone.

"Family's not taking it well, huh? Well, you just never can tell who's doing what these days. I guess it shouldn't be a surprise."

Janet unconsciously moved closer. When he tucked his phone back into his pocket she pounced. "What's going on?"

"Early notes from the investigation are in for the Birch death." When Janet raised her eyebrows, he added, "Liv Anderson Birch."

Janet nodded. Nell's daughter.

"Looks like drugs were involved. Heroin."

CHAPTER FOUR

Janet unlocked the main doors of the bar Friday morning and headed straight for the Beerador. She had to balance the books before any customers came in, but then she was going to make time to clean that god-awful refrigerator if it was the last thing she did. She planned to drop off the bucket and mop that banged against her leg with every other step and then head to the office, but before she made it behind the countertop, a jingle let her know her first customer had arrived. She turned around, surprised to see Nell making her way through the space.

The older woman's shoulders hunched forward and she crept to her regular spot at the bar. Without a word she held up two fingers. Janet shoved the cleaning supplies under the counter, clicked on the light switch behind the bar, then mixed up two vodka sodas. She fumbled with a lime, hacked off two wedges, slammed them onto the rims of the glasses, and then slid the drinks in front of Nell.

Some people didn't know what to say when a friend suffered a tragedy. But Janet was rarely at a loss for words, so she rested her elbows on the bar and waited until Nell looked up.

"I'm so sorry, Nell." The tiniest motion let Janet know the older woman had heard her, but Nell didn't speak, only raised the glass to her lips and downed half of it in one smooth gulp. "Talk when you're ready. Drink until you are."

Before she got more than a few steps away, Nell had drained the first glass and reached for the second. Janet wanted to stay close, so she decided to postpone her accounting work until later. Instead, she got her cleaning supplies ready. While the bucket filled with water in the sink, she watched Nell out of the corner of her eye.

The older woman took small sips of her drink and stared at a knot in the shiny wooden countertop.

Janet turned away and assessed the Beerador. The round shelves that were supposed to go inside the unit instead leaned up against the liquor shelves. She'd deal with them later. Her plan was to scrub the inside, then the outside, then somehow hose down the shelves with bleach before putting the whole thing back together and plugging it in.

She hefted the bucket out of the sink and carefully set it down on the floor, then plunged the mop into the warm soapy water. She wrung it out, then held her breath and opened the Beerador.

She took a tenuous, tiny breath in through her nose, expecting to smell decaying flesh or rotten blood. Only the faintest, chalky scent of ink and a light yeasty beer smell came out.

She'd just taken a deep breath and begun to lift the mop out when Nell cleared her throat. Janet dropped the mop back into the bucket and turned to face her only customer.

"Damn cops have the gall to say my daughter was using *drugs*." Nell swirled the small black cocktail straw through the ice cubes in her nearly empty glass.

Janet walked forward until the women were eye to eye and asked the question she hadn't thought to ask O'Dell the night before. "How do they know that? I heard the coroner's report won't be in for weeks—maybe months."

Nell stopped furiously stirring her drink. Her

eyes clouded and she set the glass down gently on the bar. "They found a fresh puncture hole in her arm. I guess you don't . . . you don't shoot up a prescription, right?" Nell stared straight ahead, and Janet couldn't quite read her expression.

"Do they know what kind of drugs?" Janet asked carefully, not wanting to offend her favorite regular. O'Dell had said heroin the night before, but she didn't understand how anyone could know that without the toxicology report.

Nell's shoulders pulsed slightly, and she took another sip. "I guess—well, they guess it's heroin, based off some powder they found on her—" Her lips trembled and she set the glass down and swallowed hard. "On her body."

"Does that . . . surprise you?"

Janet hadn't known that Nell even had a daughter until she died, so she didn't want to assume anything about Liv.

"I guess you never really know anyone after they reach adulthood. And certainly Liv and I weren't the kind of mother and daughter to share secrets." Janet raised her eyebrows. Nell looked down at her drink again and lowered her voice when she said, "We grew apart because of my . . . Well. She didn't like that I was taking things, and I couldn't . . . well, you know I can't just stop." Nell pressed her lips around the tiny black straw. She vacuumed the final drops of liquid from the bottom of the glass. "But I can't help but wonder why you would carry a load of laundry down the stairs after shooting up heroin. Doesn't make much sense to me, you know?"

"How do you know—"

"Clothes from the basket had dumped out everywhere."

Two splotches of pink spread across Nell's cheekbones.

Janet leaned over the bar again to get closer to her friend. "This kind of stuff is happening from suburban homes to inner cities to mansions up on the hill. I didn't know Liv at all, but—is there . . . is there a chance that she—"

"I'm not saying my family is immune to trouble," Nell interrupted, motioning for another drink. "Certainly I've proven that! Here I am, an old lady, completely and totally addicted to stealing. And not because I need anything—God, I could paper this bar with cash from my savings account. I steal because I love the rush involved in it." She flicked her head and pressed her lips together so tightly that a white line formed in the middle of her mouth. "But my Liv? She's never done laundry a day in her life."

Janet's nose wrinkled. "What? Didn't you say she's got kids? What do you mean she never—"

"Three kids! And not a single load. That was Eric's job, and she made sure of it! She would buy new pants for her waitressing job before washing a dirty pair herself." Nell went back to stirring her ice cubes. Janet walked around the bar. As she slid onto the stool beside her friend, she tried to choose her next words carefully. An unusual move for her, but this was an unusual situation.

"Nell." She waited until the other woman looked up. "I didn't have the chance to know Liv, so I can only guess here, but with a gaggle of kids and a stressful job—I mean, she sounds like someone who could have been trying to escape. Is that—is that impossible?"

"Escape. Escape from what?"

Janet bit her lip. "Look, I'm just saying, sometimes I want to escape from life. I'm so tired of finally feeling like I have things under control and then they go and flat-out change without warning! And I can't even imagine the pressure, the added strain of a big family to provide for. Could it be that Liv needed to escape?"

Nell shook her head. "Oh, Janet. Don't you know? Life *is* change, honey. To live is to be ready and willing to accept those changes and figure out how they make your life better. And if they don't, then be ready to change again. My Liv knew that better than anyone."

Janet felt a stab of uncertainty at Nell's words that pierced into her chest with surprising pain. Life was change? No, that couldn't be. Life was about getting to the place you wanted to be and then fighting to stay there, at all costs! Before she could say as much, Nell spoke again.

"Liv and Eric weren't doing well. Their marriage was on the rocks. She told me that he'd been cheating on her—and she wasn't going to take it, no ma'am. She embraced the change. Kicked him out of the bedroom and was making plans for her future."

"Maybe it was all too much for her," Janet said.

Nell shook her head. "No. She knew it was going to be a challenge, but she told me that it was one worth embracing. That's why I'm left thinking, my daughter, who's never done drugs in her life— has never done laundry in her life—all of a sudden is dead at the hands of laundry and drugs?" Nell shook her head. "No ma'am."

Janet pushed herself back away from the bar and rubbed a hand up over her temples. "What are you saying, Nell?"

Now it was Nell's turn to lean forward, and for

the first time since she'd gotten the terrible news that her daughter was dead, her eyes glittered like freshly broken glass. "What I'm saying is that someone murdered my daughter. And there's only one person who would have done it: her husband. I think Eric killed Liv."

CHAPTER FIVE

Sunday morning dawned earlier than usual at the Spot. For the first time in Janet's memory, sunlight streamed in through the windows.

The extra visibility inside the bar had necessitated a last-minute deep clean that morning, and Cindy Lou and Elizabeth, another bartender, had agreed to come in early to help her get ready for Nell's daughter's memorial. Not only had they scrubbed the floors, but they'd also had time to polish the tabletops and the kick plate of the bar.

Mel, her bouncer, manned the door like always. Only this morning, instead of checking IDs, the gruff woman directed guests to the sign-in book, pulling an endless supply of pens from the pockets of her cargo shorts when needed.

At home in any situation, Mel had traded her flannel shirt for a long-sleeve, black button-down. Her short blond hair was neat and tidy, and she nodded soberly to everyone who entered the space.

According to the obituary, Liv Anderson Birch was thirty-six years old and had died ten days ago from an unfortunate accident at home. She was survived by a husband, three children, and her mother.

Was that husband a killer, like Nell suspected? Janet had been watching him all morning. He didn't look suspicious, only sad. His brown eyes were watery and red rimmed, like he'd hardly stopped crying since Liv died. His children were much the same. Though his oldest, a girl, seemed more angry than sad. Janet didn't blame her.

"Terrible business." O'Dell came to a stop next to her, a sweet tea in one hand and a prayer card in the other.

"I'm surprised to see you here." Janet tilted her head back to look him in the eye. "You didn't know Liv, did you?"

O'Dell shook his head. "No, but it's always interesting to see who shows up to these things."

"Huh." She narrowed her eyes at the detective. "Are you saying you're investigating?"

"I'm not saying anything." His eyes scanned the room as he took a casual sip of his tea. "But we were sure interested to learn that the washing machine at Liv's house had been broken for a few days before she died."

"So why was Liv bringing laundry downstairs?"

"Exactly."

Janet raised her eyebrows. "Who told you about the machine?"

"The husband." O'Dell drained the tea and set the glass down on the closest table, then tucked the prayer card into his back pocket.

Janet shifted her weight from one foot to the other and crossed her arms. "So what's the next step?"

"Wait for the coroner to make a ruling, and that could take weeks—months even, when you're waiting on Toxicology."

"Can't your department fast-track it for something like this?"

"Maybe. Prosecutors are making drug overdose deaths a priority lately. So we'll see if he can push it through. But you know how it is, the lab is always backed up." O'Dell had been surveying the crowd along with Janet, but he turned to her with a pointed gaze. "Anything else?"

Janet shrugged. "Nell just can't see her daughter on drugs. Or doing laundry."

It was O'Dell's turn to shrug. "Drugs can take a lot of people by surprise. Family, especially, don't always see it coming." He started to walk away. When Janet reached out, he looked down at her fingers resting against his arm and stepped closer. "What?"

"I hate to bring this up again, but I get the feeling that there's some history between you and that Donaldson guy from the state. What gives?"

O'Dell raised his eyebrows, a "Who, me?" expression on his face that Janet didn't buy entirely. "We've both been working in Knoxville for five or six years; what can I say? We're not best friends. Just colleagues."

"I can't believe someone can file a complaint anonymously like that," she grumbled.

"Call your representative," O'Dell said, and his words were like a verbal shrug. It irritated Janet enough that she snatched her hand back.

O'Dell melted into the crowd with a small smile just before strong, steady hands wrapped around her shoulders and pulled her close. Jason murmured into her ear, "Need anything?"

She turned around and stood up on her tiptoes to kiss Jason on the cheek.

"I think we're good. I just asked Cindy Lou to refill the tea pitchers. The food seems to be holding steady."

Jason looked over the covered dishes and Sterno pots warming food on the bar and nodded. "I'm still surprised they wanted to have it here."

"I think it was easy—and that made it perfect." Janet had offered to host the memorial right after Liv's body was returned to the family, and Nell said Eric had jumped at the idea.

"Did you meet the kids?" Jason asked, lowering his voice.

Janet's face felt pinched when she nodded. The oldest was the angry girl, twelve, who had the knobby knees and wiry arms of someone who'd just grown too many inches in too short a time. Then there was a boy, eight, and another girl. She'd said she was six when Janet asked, holding up seven pudgy fingers, but based on her size, she couldn't have been more than two.

Liv's children stood in a group off to the side of the room, hovering near their father as the line of friends and family slowly shuffled past. Nell stood a few feet apart from them but shot furtive glances at her family. Janet could feel the distance between them was more than literal.

"Who's *she*?" Janet motioned with her chin to a

woman taking more than her fair share of time with Liv's husband and children. She had piercing blue eyes, made even more striking because of her dark brown, almost black, hair. The woman smiled at something Nell's grandson did and tucked a lock of hair back into her sleek bob. She seemed to know the children well, and took turns hugging each of them and whispering into their ears.

"Summer Hughes," Jason said. "I met her right when she walked in. She said she was school friends with Liv."

The woman was sophisticated in a way that didn't match the rest of the crowd. Liv was a waitress; her husband worked in a mechanic shop. Nell was a drunk thief happy to have her daughter's last gathering at a dive bar. The crowd that filled the room matched what you'd expect, but this woman, this friend, wore a suit and fancy heels.

"What's she do?"

"I heard her mention a family counseling practice, but I didn't catch the name." He chuckled. "She's wearing some kind of flowery perfume and it's so strong, I had to move away."

Janet turned to look at the kids again, just as Nell brushed past her son-in-law and the friend. Summer's purse trembled and Janet groaned.

"You've got to be kidding me. At her own daughter's memorial?"

Jason looked over, a ghost of a smile on his lips. "Nell just struck?"

Janet nodded. "I'll be right back." She cut across the room toward Nell, who was walking nonchalantly toward her own purse, hanging over the back of her regular bar stool. "Freeze."

Nell turned with a clear, innocent expression. She raised a hand to brush a stray silvery hair from her face and looked around the space. "Thank you, Janet, this is more than I could've hoped for. I really do appreciate you opening the bar early for us."

"Nice try," Janet said, stepping close. "What'd you take?"

"Hmm?" Nell blinked a few times, her eyes wide.

Janet had to hand it to her; she looked as innocent as a child. "I couldn't tell—was it from her purse or her pocket?"

Nell's eyes flicked to the ceiling and she blew out a slow breath. "Purse. But it's nothing." She shook her head. "Just some fancy pen."

Brendon, Nell's only grandson, stared at them from across the room, and Janet pulled her closer. "Why did you take it?"

"Why wouldn't I? I need something to take my mind off this awful day."

As Janet patted Nell's shoulder, another woman approached. "Mrs. Anderson?"

Nell pasted on a wan smile. "Yes?"

"You might not remember me, I'm Skylar Rowen? I went to school with Liv? I'm so sorry for your loss." The slight woman looked up at Nell through a curtain of long, stringy, greasy brown hair.

"Skylar? Lord in heaven above, I haven't seen you in years! So nice of you to come out today for my Livvie."

As the two women caught up, Janet couldn't take her eyes off of Skylar. She looked like the "before" picture in a drug treatment advertisement. Her pockmarked face was somehow flushed and pale at the same time, and her cheekbones cut sharply into her too-thin face. When the women said goodbye, Skylar headed right for the door.

Janet turned on Nell immediately. "You should give it back, even if it *is* just a pen."

"And *you* should mind your business."

Before she could argue the point, an older gentleman tripped over a table nearby.

"Ger-outta my way, ya dumb table!" He pushed the table roughly and several glasses and bottles slid off as it tilted dangerously to one side. He tripped again when the table crashed back down onto its heavy pedestal base, shunting him to one side.

Shards of glass crunched when he walked over the broken bottles on the floor.

Mel moved in with precision. "Sir, step this way, please." She clamped her hands around his upper arms, propelling him forward with apparent ease, then placed him in a chair at an empty table and somehow held him down without breaking a sweat.

"Oh, Sumpter, get ahold of yourself." A woman matching Sumpter in both age and demeanor stalked over and grabbed him under the arm. "Tables don't fight, you big oaf. Only drunk men do!" She led him out into the parking lot.

"Who was that?" Janet asked.

Mel read down the guest book names. "I think that was Sumpter Hamstetter and his lovely wife, Lorelai. Look like friends of Eric's."

"You need to teach me that. All of us, actually."

"How to read the guest book?" Mel asked with a grin. She straightened her collar and then rearranged the pens around the book.

"No, that bouncer stuff. Most nights we have

an all-woman staff. We should all know how to re-move unruly customers."

"Anytime, Janet. Every woman should know self-defense."

"No . . . What you did was more than that."

Mel grinned. "True. It's really offense. Some-times you've got to go on the offensive to avoid trouble." She turned back to the door when it opened and directed the new guests to the sign-in book.

Janet sized up her bouncer. She didn't know much about Mel, except that the woman had se-crets, and that was fine with Janet. After all, who didn't?

CHAPTER SIX

Monday morning dawned cool and bright, and Janet was glad she'd worn a coat. The downtown structure she approached was notable only for its lack of character. Many of Knoxville's government buildings were impressively old or impressively maintained. However, the Tennessee Department of Commerce and Insurance had been stuck in an overflow office, a nondescript, white concrete, eleven-story block that housed some government agencies, some law offices, and even a few Realtors. The space was so generic, it could have been the headquarters for a local bank. Or a white-collar prison.

Janet made her way to an office on the fifth floor.

A woman with red hair and rouged cheeks looked up from her computer screen when Janet walked in. "Can I help you?" Her voice was thick with the same Southern accent nearly everyone in town had.

"I'm supposed to turn in some paperwork in response to an anonymous complaint—"

"You must be Janet Black?"

"Oh." The corners of Janet's mouth pulled down. "Yes, I am." She looked at the other woman with a question in her eyes.

"It might be a big building, but we're a small office, dear. I heard Gary mention something about the complaint. It's pretty unusual to have an anonymous filing in the first place."

Her accent wasn't the only thing that marked this woman as a true Knoxvillian. She looked like she wished they were chatting on a front porch over iced tea as she leaned forward, her expression curious. It wouldn't take much to open the floodgates.

Janet smiled. "Gary Donaldson? Is he here?"

She laughed. "No, hon, he's not. I'm sorry, I'm Rachel, the admin here. He takes his lunch break every day from noon to one without fail. He'll be back at one on the nose if you want to wait?"

Janet shuddered. "Gah, no. I just had a few

questions about the forms he gave me—maybe you can help?"

"Sure, hon, set 'em up here." She tapped the raised countertop and then flipped through the forms and stopped at the page Janet had dog-eared. "If you sign this one here, you're confirming that you had nothing to do with any criminal investigation, and then you have to have it signed by a notary. You know . . ." She looked up at Janet over the forms, a small smile on her face. "The best way to get rid of this whole thing?"

Janet rested her elbows on the counter and looked down at Rachel. "How?"

"Just become an actual private eye. Look, the test isn't very difficult, and as long as you have no criminal record, all you have to do is pay a hundred bucks—which is half what you'll be fined if the board were to find you guilty."

"But it wouldn't matter if I become a PI now, would it? The complaint was for something that happened this summer."

She patted a stray lock back into her French braid. "Retroactive, hon. Just apply for retroactive status. All you need is a character reference from someone upstanding in the community. You know any of the local commissioners, maybe a judge?"

Janet frowned. "How about a homicide detective with KPD?"

"Perfect. Yup, that'll work." She added some pages to the stack, then handed them back over the counter. "It's all pretty straightforward, but if you have questions after reading over the application, just come on back in. If I were you, I'd try and take the test before the commission meets again. Then, instead of voting on if you should be fined, they'll vote on whether to allow you to get a license with retroactive status."

Janet stepped back and considered the woman in front of her. "Thanks for the advice."

"You'll have to apprentice, but that's no big deal. Just a few months with an established PI to learn the ropes. Of course there's the annual CE —" The admin picked up a ringing phone. "Thanks for calling the Department of Commerce and Insurance, please hold." She put her hand over the mouthpiece and smiled at Janet. "Anything else?"

"CE?"

"Continuing education. PIs need twelve hours every year."

Janet stifled a sigh. This sounded more involved than she really cared to get, in a field she had no interest in pursuing. "Do you know where the business licensing office is?"

"You won't need that for the PI license. It's all part of the—"

"Oh, I know. It's for another matter."

Rachel sat back. "Oh. Well, sure. It's down two floors. Office three seventeen."

"Thanks." Janet waved and headed back to the elevator. When the doors opened, she gasped. "Dad? What are you doing h—"

Her final word was muffled by Sampson Foster's chest when he pulled her into a hug. "Janet! I was going to surprise you down at the Spot later today after my conference ended, but you found me first." He pulled her back and inspected her face. "How'd you do it?"

"It—it actually wasn't planned! I have errands for work—I had no idea you were here."

His bald head gleamed under the fluorescent lights, and in just that first glance, she could tell he'd lost weight. The paunch that used to envelop his midsection was gone, and he looked taller somehow because of his newly slimmed-down waistline. He pulled her against his side and pressed a button to close the elevator doors. "Never mind, never mind. What a great surprise! What floor?"

"Three. What are you doing in Knoxville?"

"I'm attending a weeklong conference right in this very building. I thought I'd stay through the weekend so we can visit. It's been too long."

"Sounds great, Dad. I'll let Jason and his dad know."

"William's still staying with you?"

She kept her smile plastered on. "Yes, and he's almost done laying the cork floors in the kitchen."

"Well, at least he's earning his keep, huh? Don't worry, I'm booked at a hotel downtown."

The elevator doors pinged open. "This is me. So . . . Dinner tonight?" She stepped off the car, relieved to escape any probing questions.

"Not so fast, young lady. What are you doing here, anyway?" Sampson's foot wedged into the path of the sliding doors and he scrutinized her face.

"Uhhh . . ."

"I could ask tonight, but I'm thinking you might not want everyone to know?"

She smiled. How was her dad so observant? "Well, to be honest, I'm looking into buying Jason's share of the Spot. I wanted to find out how the liquor license transfers. Tennessee is so weird about alcohol, you know?"

"Does Jason want out?"

"Not exactly . . ." She raised her eyes to his and they smirked at the same moment. "I just thought it made sense to own my own business. Jason owns his security business, why shouldn't I own mine outright, too?" She took another step away from the elevator when an alarm sounded. The doors had been open so long, they tried closing again over Sampson's foot.

"We'll talk more about it tonight over dinner." She grimaced and he added, "Or maybe not?"

She nodded. "Bye, Dad."

The alarm cut off when the doors finally met in the middle. Janet turned and took out her phone when it pinged and deleted some spam emails, then looked up to get her bearings. A massive, impressive set of oak doors was straight ahead.

The sign above read, *Law Offices of Thornton & Brown*, and a commercial jingle immediately popped into Janet's head: "*Need a divorce, don't stray from the course. Thornton & Brown attorneys!*"

Janet backed away from the office and frowned —it was kind of depressing to think of a company making all their profit off of other people's failed relationships. She turned and walked right into a huge potted fern. As she stumbled back, she heard a familiar snort.

"What's happening here? You interested in gardening all of a sudden, darlin'?" Jason grinned and moved a frond of the fern away from her face. "Why do you look so guilty, though?" His eyes narrowed and he stepped back. "What's going on, Janet?"

CHAPTER SEVEN

Janet forced her eyes forward and tried to focus on her boyfriend, but what she wanted to do was look around to see if anyone else she knew was lurking nearby. How many other people could possibly be in this random municipal building at lunchtime on a Monday?

When Jason cleared his throat, she stuttered out, "H-how did you know I was here?"

"I didn't. My dad said you headed out to run some errands. I just tried calling you, but it went straight to voicemail. Then—the strangest dang thing—I saw your dad in the lobby, and he said you were on the third floor. And you are." His smile was stiff and not entirely happy. "Did you know he was coming to town?"

Janet's heart clenched at his expression. Was he mad again? "N-no! I mean, not until just a few minutes ago. I saw him in the elevator. I told him we'd all go to dinner tonight."

Jason nodded. "Sounds good, sounds good. So then . . .what are you doing up here, anyway?"

She looked guiltily at the door for the business licensing office and her throat constricted. Suddenly the idea of telling Jason she wanted to buy his share of the bar seemed impossible.

"What's going on?"

A flush of color warmed her cheeks and she shifted on her feet. Now was as good a time as any to start the conversation about buying the Spot, and she tried to ignore the flat feeling in her chest. It was exactly what she wanted, so why did her stomach suddenly feel like it was on the last loop of a never-ending roller coaster?

She opened her mouth, but no words came out, so she finally held out the sheaf of papers. "I just had some questions about the investigation, so thought I'd stop by Gary Donaldson's office."

Jason took the stack and rifled through the top slips. "Is this an application?" He looked up incredulously. "Are you going to become a private detective?"

Fumbling, she took the papers back, and sure

enough, the PI application was on top, not the complaint.

"Oh, I don't—I mean, it probably wouldn't make sense—" But as her eyes scanned the sheet she laughed, interrupting herself. "For God's sake, they recommend reading *Private Investigation for Dummies* to prepare for the test." She crowed again. "How completely ridiculous."

Jason motioned to some nearby chairs and as they dropped down into the seats a grin relaxed his face. "So ridiculous that you look like you're about to order the book from your phone and read it cover to cover?" He draped an arm across the back of her seat and squeezed her shoulder.

She tore her eyes away from the application. "Why are you here, anyway?"

Suddenly it was Jason's turn to shift uncomfortably in his seat. He rubbed his jaw and looked over her head. "Oh, I—I'm looking into buying old Ben Corker's restaurant."

She dropped the papers down into her lap and turned to focus completely on her boyfriend. "What are you talking about?" The abandoned building sat adjacent to the Spot and had been empty as long as Janet had lived in Knoxville.

"It's going up for auction at the end of the

month. My dad's interested in opening a restaurant."

"Right next door to us?" Janet's smile froze on her face, but Jason saw through her attempt at happy.

"Well, he, ah—he needs something to do, and he's worked in the food industry before. I don't know, it's just something I said I'd look into."

She hesitated. "This is a . . . a bad idea."

"I know, you're ready to be done with my dad—I get it. But he's—he's here for a while, it seems. And he can't work on our house forever, God knows."

How could she nicely say she didn't want Jason's father operating a business next door to her bar? She wanted William and his bad mojo to go far away. Instead she asked the obvious question. "But how can he afford to buy a business?"

"It's an auction, so he'd only bid what he can."

She fixed Jason with an unblinking stare.

He leaned forward and rested his elbows on his knees, staring at a spot on the floor about a dozen feet away. "And I can help him out. Just a little, you know, if he needs me to."

Janet rubbed the bridge of her nose. "But then he's got to operate it—buy equipment! Tables, chairs, cash registers, serving trays—"

"But there might be stuff already there, who knows what old Ben left behind? I wanted to stop into the tax office to find out."

"But . . ." Her shoulders drooped. Would they never get rid of his dad?

"So, dinner with our dads tonight, huh? Sounds fun." Jason's forced smile stayed on his face as he stood and walked the few steps across the space to the tax office. He pulled the door open and waited for her to walk through.

She hung back and let him get the information about the real estate auction, trying to work through why she couldn't seem to talk to Jason about something so important. She wanted—no, needed—the security of owning the Spot. Jason would understand, surely.

Or would he misconstrue her intentions and be hurt, just like he'd been when she offered to let him stay home while she investigated why cops were at the bar?

After he got the forms about the upcoming auction, they stood in the lobby by the elevators.

"You heading out?" Jason tapped the button for the elevator and looked up at the floor indictor before tapping the button again.

"No, I—I . . . Jason, wait."

He turned and looked at her expectantly.

"Well . . ." She didn't know how she was sup-posed to talk to Jason about a life-changing deci-sion, a major change to the way they operated as a business—as a couple—when he was staring at her like she was a scorpion about to strike. "I—I'm going to look over these forms the receptionist gave me." She held up the stack of papers. "That way if I have any questions, I can go back in and ask. I guess I'll be home later."

Jason pressed a kiss to her cheek, then stepped inside the elevator with a small wave. When she was alone again she breathed out a sigh and shook her head. What a wuss. She didn't deserve security if she couldn't even handle a difficult conversation with her boyfriend. But her brow furrowed and she dug her cell phone out of her bag. The screen was blank. No missed calls. Had he really intended to tell her about the restaurant? Maybe she wasn't the only one in this relationship who was trying to avoid difficult conversations.

————

Too jumpy to sit still, Janet headed to the Spot. It wasn't time to open, but the Beerador needed tending to, and she'd put off cleaning it for too long.

But as she reached out with her key to unlock the main door, a car pulled into the parking lot. Janet turned and waited to see who was behind the wheel.

The driver's side window of the sleek, shiny black sedan lowered, and a dark-haired woman smiled tentatively. "Janice, right?"

"Ain't nothing *nice* about me, hon. It's Janet."

The other woman's face flushed pink. "Of course, I'm sorry. I'm Summer Hughes—Liv's friend? We met at Liv's memorial."

"Oh—right, hi." They hadn't met, not really, but she remembered pointing the other woman out to Jason. Janet scrutinized Summer's car, from the shiny rims to the perfect paint job. "That's quite a ride."

Summer's dark sunglasses masked her eyes, but a small smile tipped the corners of her lips up. "I was in a car accident years ago. I understand, in a way few others do, that a safe car is a worthwhile investment."

Janet glanced around the deserted lot, then trained her eyes back onto Summer. She held a hand up to block the sun from her eyes. "We're not open yet."

"Oh—no I don't want to go in." The gravel lot absorbed the counselor's tinkling laugh as soon as it left her mouth. She propped her head against her hand and a friendly smile stretched across her face. "But I *was* hoping to find you here."

"Me?" Janet's confusion prompted Summer to take off her sunglasses and tap a button on her steering wheel that cut off the radio. "I don't suppose—I mean, you look busy, but I just thought I might be able to take you to lunch today."

"Oh—I—well . . ." The invitation was so unexpected that Janet was at a loss for words. Sitting down for a meal with a stranger was the last thing she wanted to do, but apparently her mouth didn't get the message from her brain, because suddenly she heard herself say, "I'd love to. Thanks."

CHAPTER EIGHT

"Thank you." Summer smiled at the waiter when he placed a steaming mug of hot water in front of her, and once again, Janet was struck by the contrast between the other woman's dark hair and cornflower-blue eyes. Summer unwrapped the tea bag and dunked it down into the cup. The warm, heady scent of cinnamon apple wafted up but didn't quite win the battle with her heavy floral perfume. "What a gorgeous day." Summer held the mug in front of her face with both hands. "I walk the square all the time when I need a break from the office, but I don't stop to enjoy it enough."

Janet glanced up from the menu and had to agree. Even on this chilly fall day, Market Square was hopping with activity. A half-dozen trees broke up the sea of concrete nicely and offered good shade during the hot summer months. Now wind rustled through the leaves, soothing patrons at the handful of restaurants with outdoor seating that faced the square.

"I wonder what's happening there?" Janet motioned to a tree farther away. Men in orange were blocking off part of the sidewalk, moving a cherry picker in. Another crew member marked a giant X on the tree trunk with red spray paint.

"Emerald ash borer." Their waiter was back, his order pad held at the ready, a bored expression on his face. "All the trees have to come down. They'll replant in time for the spring concert series, but the shade'll be cut in half until the new trees can grow in."

"Such an invasive insect." Summer wrinkled her nose at the trees.

"Should I come back, or . . ."

Summer nodded and he walked away, muttering under his breath.

"You said your office is nearby?" Janet asked. Summer nodded. "And you're a counselor?"

Summer nodded. "That's right—now, don't do that! You just pressed your lips together!"

Janet unpeeled them to laugh.

Liv's friend took another luxurious sip. "Don't

worry, I'm off the clock. And no one *has* to talk to me. But sometimes people need help figuring out how to talk—either to themselves or each other. You ever feel that way?"

Janet shrugged. She had felt that way, in fact, less than an hour ago with Jason.

"For example," Summer went on, "often couples need help churning through their differences and figuring out how they can make them work to their advantage."

Janet leaned forward despite herself. "What do you mean?"

"Well . . ." The other woman took another sip of her tea before focusing on Janet. "Each case is different, but any change in relationships can cause challenges—that's true for new parents welcoming a baby, or couples taking their relationship to a new level. Open communication is key!"

Janet's lip curled as she thought about how closed off she and Jason had been with each other lately. She looked away from the successful, polished woman sitting across from her, who probably had never struggled with anything in her life and her expression hardened. "Then again, other times it's best just to shut up, and not rock the boat."

Summer winced and sat back. "Well, if you ever need to talk . . ."

The waiter was back and they both placed their orders. After several long moments, Janet tried to relax her shoulders. It wasn't Summer's fault she and Jason weren't talking to each other about important life events. She cleared her throat. "So . . . how are Eric and the kids?"

"There's someone else who doesn't want to talk," Summer said, almost to herself.

"Excuse me?"

"Oh, Eric. He's—well, he's really struggling with things. The kids are, too, I mean, of course they are! He lost his wife, his life partner! The kids lost their mother. But Eric . . . well, I'm just not sure what to make of him." She turned her bottomless eyes on Janet.

"Are you—you're helping out at the house? Nell and I are headed over there later today." She bit her lip, hating that Summer had somehow coaxed her into volunteering information.

Summer's head dropped and she cradled her mug for a moment before answering. "I wish I could do more, but between work and life—you know how it is. To be honest, it's hard to be there. I can hardly stand to look at Eric."

Janet set her glass of tea down with a jolt. "Why?"

"It's no secret he cheated on Liv. I'm not one to

judge, but, I mean, of course I was on Liv's side, and she was furious! Wanted him out of the house, out of their lives. And now this . . . I mean I'm sure Nell blames him for her daughter turning to drugs. If it weren't for the kids, I'd probably never see him again. As it is I'm trying to be supportive for their sake."

Summer looked up through her eyelashes. "It's too bad Nell can't be there more. The kids just light up when she arrives. Then again, I get the impression she wasn't over a lot before Liv died? Something about a stealing problem?"

Janet made a mental note to never see Summer in a professional capacity. She was like an open tap you couldn't close down. She had to remind herself that she was in the South, where talking to strangers was an art form. But she wasn't going to be the one to parse her friend's fraught relationship with her dead daughter's family with a near stranger, so she shrugged and said, "What do you mean?"

"Oh, Liv mentioned something weeks ago, she felt frustrated, that's all. And then some little things I've been picking up at the house from Eric and the kids. I thought you might be able to shed some light on their relationship."

The women locked eyes and Janet's narrowed. "Sorry, I don't know anything about that."

Their food arrived and Janet was happy for a reason to stop talking. They fell silent while they ate, but when Summer set down her fork and took another sip of her tea Janet braced for more probing questions.

"Sorry," Summer said, taking in Janet's stiff shoulders and frown. "Job hazard. I can be charming when I think about it."

Janet snorted. "I know all about job hazards, believe me."

"Thanks for keeping me company today." She swept the bill up in one hand and stood. "I won't ask you any more questions, you're like a lockbox, and I do wonder why that is . . ." She narrowed her eyes and studied Janet before continuing. "I don't know your relationship situation, but I'll leave you with one piece of advice I give to all the couples who come into my office. If you can't be honest with your partner, you're not only doing a disservice to him, but to you and your relationship as well. If you love each other, you can find a way through almost anything."

"Almost? Well that's disappointing," Janet said, standing too.

"Everyone has a red line, Janet. Do you know yours? Your partner's?"

Summer offered a small smile and turned away. Janet watched her take care of the bill at the front desk and walk out into the cool, cloudless day.

People joked that bartenders were as good as counselors, but she was rethinking that after an hour with Summer. Just a few words from Liv's old friend had her reassessing multiple things in her life, and frankly, she didn't appreciate it.

"Red line? I'll give you a red line. Getting too personal with strangers, people prying into things they don't have any business prying into—those are *my* red lines."

"Excuse me?" The waiter was back; Janet had been so caught up in her own worries, she hadn't noticed that he was clearing the table. Now he was frozen with a plate halfway to his tray, his expression alarmed as he stared at Janet.

She headed away from the table but stopped to watch as a chain saw spluttered to life, then tore into the first of the infested trees on the square right at the red lines crossing the trunk. Sawdust flew up into the air and a fine layer of it settled onto the closest tables and chairs.

Janet rubbed her temples and turned her back on the red lines, the destruction being wrought, the mess. She would ignore it completely for now. Instead she took out the paperwork and her heart seemed to speed up, beat faster, as she read over the steps to become a PI. Here, at last, was something under her control.

She smiled as she walked to her car and ordered a few books from an app on her phone before she cranked over the engine. The books would be here by the weekend. Plenty of time to soak up all she needed to know to ace the test.

CHAPTER NINE

Janet pulled up to the small house on Knoxville's east side and tapped her horn.

Beep beep.

It sounded low and sad, but maybe that was Janet's imagination, knowing who she was picking up and where they were headed.

Just as Janet was deciding whether she should properly park the car and get out, the front door opened and Nell emerged. The older woman buttoned up her overcoat, then set a small purse primly on her arm before turning around to lock the door.

"Thank you so much for doing this," Nell said as she pulled the door open. After buckling up, she turned to Janet. "I hate that I don't want to go over to the house on my own, but I just don't trust Eric."

Janet eased the car away from the curb and snuck a glance at her companion. Her conversation with Summer had piqued her interest on several fronts. "What was your relationship like with Liv and her family before she died?"

Nell pressed her lips together and stared out the window before answering. "We managed." Her eyes flicked over to Janet. "Liv wanted me to get counseling, wanted me to stop the stealing, but I . . . I just couldn't do it. And things were strained because of that."

"How so?" Janet turned to look Nell full in the face at a stoplight.

Nell's cheeks pinked slightly and her lips pressed together again. "She never said as much, but I think she worried that I would be a bad influence on the kids. As if I'd steal from my own family!" Her eyes flicked over to Janet's again, and she flushed a deeper shade of red.

"Not once?" Janet asked. "You never once stole from Liv, her husband, or your grandchildren?"

"W-well, I mean nothing important." Nell turned her face away from Janet. When she spoke again, her voice was softer, all the defensiveness gone. "I should've listened to her. She thought getting help would be good for me, not her. She had my best interests at heart, and I should've listened."

A different person would have reached over to pat Nell's hand, but Janet just drove, and she hoped that Nell knew there was no judgment in the silence.

"Make a left up here." Nell pointed the way, then turned in her seat to face Janet. "You know, there's one more thing that's been bothering me. About the drugs? So let's say Liv was using. Let's say my straight-as-an-arrow, always-do-the-right-thing daughter was using drugs. Where did she get them?"

Janet shrugged. "Where does anyone get drugs? Corner store, someone at work, family member?"

Nell nodded encouragingly. "Exactly. But not just any family. I mean, those damn police didn't find any other drugs in the house. No sign of previous drug use, no pills, no hidden stash of anything anywhere." Nell shifted in her seat to face Janet. "And as far as I know, they didn't even find the needle she'd supposedly used that very day. And why not?"

Janet raised her eyebrows and her shoulders.

"Because Eric covered it all up, that's why! *If* she used drugs, it's because of him! He's responsible for my Liv's death. I can't stand to look at him!"

Janet flicked on her blinker and changed lanes. As far as she was concerned, there wasn't an "if" about it. The police had found trace amounts of heroin on Liv's body, found the puncture hole where she'd used the needle. All they were waiting on was confirmation from a blood test. But Janet set that aside for now as she turned to face her friend. "Nell. That's a very serious accusation to make about the father of your grandchildren, and you have no evidence to back it up."

"Yet."

"What do you mean?"

"I mean I don't have any evidence yet, but I'll be looking. I did some research online last night. If Eric is the one who brought the drugs into the house, he can be held liable for Liv's death. Legally, he can be charged with a drug-induced homicide." She looked triumphantly at Janet. "And that's why he got rid of everything before calling the cops when Liv died." She turned to face forward again, her shoulders set resolutely. "So I just have to prove that Eric brought the drugs into the house."

Janet's right eye started to twitch and she

pressed the heel of her palm down on the socket. "Even if that's true, the police didn't find any evidence. What makes you think that *you* can find—"

"Slow down."

The women had been getting louder to talk over each other, and Nell's last words echoed in the small car. Janet pulled over, took a deep breath, and lowered her hand from her face. "I'm not the one jumping to conclusions, here, Nell, you are."

"No, I meant slow down the car. That's their house. We're here." She pointed across Janet's line of sight. "Let me do the talking, but keep your eyes open." The older woman climbed out of the car and strode across the street. "The black truck is Eric's, that old Taurus was Liv's, but I don't know who owns the red Firebird. It seems indecently happy at a time like this." She drew her eyebrows together and glared at the car before squaring her shoulders. "We are about to find out though." She buzzed up the front walk and knocked sharply on the door. Brendon answered.

"Hey, Grandma Nell."

"Brendon. Why are you home?"

The boy only turned to yell over his shoulder, "Grandma Nell's here!"

Janet followed Nell into the house but hung

back in the entryway, taking in the children's art-work hung crookedly on the wall with blue painter's tape as Nell continued to fuss over the boy.

"Give me a hug, Brendon. Have you eaten to-day?" Brendon only grinned self-consciously, and she tried another question. "Your dad home?"

"Yeah, but he's napping."

"Then who's cooking chicken?" Nell raised her nose in the air and sniffed delicately. "Smells like my recipe, too."

Brendon ducked away from Nell and backpedaled to the couch. Two women walked out of the kitchen, ignoring everything but each other, their voices raised but controlled.

"I think it's time you left, Skylar."

"Like I said, I'll wait for Eric."

Summer's face was tight, but she forced a smile when she saw the new guests. "Oh, Nell, Janet, hello. I was just telling Liv's old friend Skylar that Eric is sleeping, and it's probably best she be on her way."

Skylar shook out of Summer's grasp. "I brought a casserole over for the family. I just wanted to make sure it makes it *to the family*."

Summer scowled. "I'll make sure it does. Thanks so much for stopping by." She looked pointedly at the door and with a huff, the other woman stalked through the room.

"Mrs. Anderson." She nodded stiffly as she passed. Nell tried to reach out, but Skylar slipped by without a backward glance, her body rigid. The drawings taped to the wall danced in the wind as the door slammed, and Janet's hand shot out to catch one piece of paper as it fluttered down toward the ground.

She pressed the tape back against the wall and smoothed out the sheet. A strange jumble of letters written in bold black print filled the page—it must have been written out by the youngest child, because there wasn't a single real word, just a series of letters grouped haphazardly together, though the writing was sure and steady. Strange. Janet turned when Nell spoke.

"What happened?"

"Oh, that woman just makes my blood boil!" Summer said, still breathing hard. "Coming in here, after the way Liv d—" She blanched, then cleared her throat. "Brendon? Why don't you wake up your dad, tell him your grandma's here." After Brendon bounded away, Summer cleared her throat again. "I don't think Liv would want that woman coming here. She's still using by the looks of her, and she needs to get her own life together before she comes knocking into their lives." She pressed her fingertips into her temple.

"Using?" Nell asked. "Skylar Rowen? Never."

Even Janet had to force the look of disbelief from her face. "Oh, Nell. She's in a bad way, and has been for a while by the looks of her."

Nell harrumphed and then took a step toward Summer and lowered her voice. "Why isn't Brendon in school? I thought it might be a good distraction for him to get back there."

Summer shrugged. "He thought he needed some time at home, and Eric said it was okay." She dropped back a step and led the way into the kitchen, holding the swinging door open for the other two women.

Janet paused when she saw two overflowing laundry baskets of dirty clothes leaning next to the couch, and a third by the steps that led down to the basement.

The steps.

Janet couldn't blame anyone in the family for not wanting to tackle the exact thing that had led to their mother's death. Was the machine fixed finally? Would Summer start up a load after she cooked the chicken?

"It's been stressful, of course it has been," Summer said, and Janet snapped to attention and slipped into the kitchen after Nell. "But these kids are resilient. You always read that that's the case, and I'm watching it in real time. They're just amazing."

A pan of hot oil shimmered on the stove, and steam rose up from a paper-towel-covered plate of fried chicken. Summer saw her studying the food and smiled. "I know we just ate a few hours ago, but I'm starved again, what about you?"

Before she could answer, Eric banged into the small room, rubbing sleep from his eyes. His well-worn jeans hung from his thin frame. In the main room, Brendon leapt from a chair to the couch, and over to another chair.

Nell's hands fluttered between the water Summer had set in front of her and her lap, her lips set in a thin line—angry, but unsure how to proceed. She suddenly stood. "Excuse me, I have to use the bathroom." She sent a knowing look toward Janet, but before she could sweep out of the room, Summer cleared her throat.

"Nell, you'll need to use the upstairs bathroom. Somebody decided to see how many Crayons they could flush down the toilet." Summer frowned. "Five was too many, in case you were wondering, too."

Nell shot a victorious look at Janet before she

disappeared behind the swinging door and Janet had to bite her lip to keep from smiling. Having a legitimate reason to go upstairs was much better for snooping around, and Nell was delighted with the unexpected news.

Eric groaned and then dropped down into the open chair next to Janet. "Do I need to call the plumber?"

"I already did," Summer said.

"Thanks."

Summer nodded, then after a moment, he turned to Janet with red, watery eyes. "Who are you?"

"You remember Janet, Nell's friend from the bar?" Summer said.

Eric grunted out a greeting and dropped his head into his hands.

"Eric told me that Bonnie's just been sleeping terribly these last weeks." Summer pulled a bag of corn from the refrigerator and started shucking it over the sink. "Long nights make for long days, that's what Liv used to say, anyway."

His head nodded in his hands and he muttered, "It's nothing new, I'm just not used to dealing with it."

Janet's lips pursed. He'd been a father for twelve years but wasn't used to dealing with kids waking up at night? She guessed that meant that Liv had been on night duty for more than a decade.

"Anything else keeping you up?" With Nell gone, it was up to Janet to ask probing questions, and she was ready.

Summer's eyebrows shot up and she stopped mid-shuck to look over, but Eric didn't seem to catch her tone.

"Just everything. And nothing. That's the worst." Eric shuffled to the fridge and pulled out a soda. "Everything and nothing." Air shot out of the can when he pulled the tab. He took a long drink.

Brendon streaked into the kitchen to grab a bottle of water. He ran back out in time with the door swing and, once again, leapt from the floor to the chair. But this time, when he skipped over to the coffee table, the surface quaked, and all the adults froze at a splintering crack of noise.

"Brendon! What did I say about jumping on the furniture?" Eric roared. He flung the door back open. Brendon stood frozen on the tabletop. He took a tentative step, then another. When the table didn't collapse, he breathed out a sigh. "Sorry, Dad!"

He landed on the carpet lightly and then threw himself onto the couch and picked up the remote.

Eric's hand fell to his side and the door swung toward him, faster than he'd been expecting. He caught it just before it smacked him in the face as Nell marched into the kitchen, a small, round plastic trash bin in her hands.

"What is this?" Her eyes locked onto Eric's, the trash bin held out between them, her body stiff, a red flush creeping up her neck.

"A trash can." Eric's brow furrowed and he stepped away from his mother-in-law.

"Not the can, what's inside it? Huh? Where did it come from, Eric?" Nell's voice shook with emotion, and Janet leaned forward to get a better look.

But when Eric squinted over the rim, his whole body went rigid. "I—I don't . . . I mean, what . . ."

Nell's lips turned down into a disgusted frown. "How long have you been using, Eric?" She slammed the trash can down onto the table. "Did you pressure my Liv to use? But why? Why would you do that? She was a good girl, she didn't deserve any of your crap—not your cheating, not your drugs, none of it!"

"It's not—it's not mine, I swear it!" Eric stumbled back a step and reached behind him for a chair. "Where did that come from?"

"Where did it—what do you mean where did it

come from? It was sitting right there in the bathroom where *you* must have put it!"

"But the kids—the kids use that bathroom all the time!" Eric gasped, passing a hand over his face. "What if they'd—"

"Not the kid's bathroom—this was in your bathroom! The master bathroom!"

Eric's face twitched as he considered that Nell had been in his room. Janet stood to lean over the plastic receptacle. Peeking out from the bottom folds of the plastic liner, a small, silver hypodermic needle glinted in the overhead light.

After a beat of silence, Nell peppered Eric with more questions.

"Who's your supplier? How long have you been using? How in God's name did you convince Liv to try it?"

Eric's eyes hardened and he clenched his jaw so tightly that when he answered Nell, his lips barely moved. "I'm telling you that's the first I've seen of it."

In an instant, the atmosphere in the small kitchen changed. The exhaustion and irritation that had been exuding from Eric was gone, replaced with a simmering anger that left Janet breathless. She moved away from the table; even

Summer dropped the ear of corn she'd been holding and stepped back.

The hot oil on the stove popped and the older woman dropped her voice. "*Whoever* this belongs to"—her tone made it clear she thought it was Eric's—"it should be sent to the police. They'll want to test it."

"I agree. They've been asking questions about Liv's habits, and frankly, I didn't have any answers for them. I'm sure they'd like to test it. I'll call them about it right now. I'm sure you can see your way out." He stormed out of the room and they heard him pound up the steps.

Nell's shoulders slumped and she swayed unsteadily on her feet, then leaned against the table, and her hand trembled when she reached up to rub her eyes. "It's time to go."

They left Summer standing, frozen, in the kitchen, and made their way through the family room. Janet's only concern was getting her friend into the car before she collapsed.

However, as they walked down the path toward the street, she turned to look back at the house. Framed in an upstairs window, Eric clutched his chest. The only word that could describe his crumpled face was "anguished". Though it seemed that he had lashed out at Nell in anger, maybe the emotion that came through was powered by something else. Because the person she was staring at now was a devastated man. Maybe seeing the needle in the trash can had made him angry at Liv—for using, for leaving him alone, for dying.

How could she, or Nell, ever know the truth of what had happened?

CHAPTER TEN

"Ready, Janet?"

She jumped, then shook herself and flicked a stray wisp of hair from her eyes. "Yup, let's go!" She turned from the hall mirror and joined Jason at the front door.

Jason squinted briefly, and Janet thought he was going to say something, but he only held the door open. "My dad's going to meet us at the restaurant, he's wrapping up some business downtown."

"What kind of business?" She waved to Kat, Mel's partner, just returning to their half of the duplex from the grocery store, and a surge of excitement flooded her veins. "Now that he's done with the kitchen floors, is he going to move on to cabinetry?" They'd been without a kitchen at the house since they moved in over a year earlier. Janet was no chef, but she longed to make coffee without having to partially fill the carafe under the short bathroom sink twice in order to brew a full pot. Even home-boiled pasta would be a nice change from their daily fare of takeout and microwavable meals.

"It's about his restaurant."

"His restaurant?" Janet tried to keep her voice pleasant, but Jason's shoulders tightened at her tone. "Have things moved forward since this morning?"

"I guess I should just tell you. He was in talking to Cindy Lou about coming on board as his manager."

"*What?*" Jason's jaw clenched, but Janet pressed him. "He's going to steal my employees without even having the courtesy to ask me first?"

"*Our* employees," Jason corrected her, but frowned. "And I know. I talked to him about boundaries."

"Did he hear you?"

Jason shook his head. "Probably not. He's like a dog with a bone with this new idea."

"Well he can't take Cindy Lou." She climbed into the truck and slammed the door, fuming.

"It could actually be a really good move for

her." Jason got into the car and kept his eyes on the road as he backed out of the driveway. "Better hours, probably better pay—I mean, she'd draw an actual salary, wouldn't be so reliant on tips."

"That's just—I mean, she'd never—how can you even—"

"Calm down. Nothing's happened yet."

She turned away and glared out the window. This was exactly why she wanted to be the sole owner of the Spot. You just couldn't trust anyone anymore, including your own boyfriend's family. Hiring employees right from under her nose! Ridiculous. She cracked her knuckles, then flexed her fingers and turned back to Jason. "What did *she* say?"

"She said she was going to talk to you about it."

"Well she hasn't!" She huffed out a breath and crossed her arms over her chest.

"Wonder why." His eyes flicked over to her but he held his tongue, and they drove in silence the rest of the way to the restaurant. After Jason thanked the valet he reached for her hand. "Can we just have a nice dinner with our dads tonight? Figure this out tomorrow?"

She didn't answer. He held the door for her, and she breathed out a sigh when her father stood up from the bar to greet them.

"Janet, Jason! Lovely to see you both."

Sampson stepped back, surprised, after she gave him a particularly warm hug. Hating the misty feeling that tickled the back of her eyeballs, she turned to the waiting bartender and ordered a drink.

In the mirror, she saw Jason and Sampson exchange a look, and she hurried to sit between them. Sampson was *her* father. Even though they'd only known each other for a few years, she was confident that he'd be on her side.

"How's the conference?" She turned her back on Jason to focus on her dad, still amazed, three years after connecting with Sampson, that she had one at all. When Janet was growing up, her mother had claimed that her father left when he found out she was pregnant with Janet. Sampson had tracked her down several years ago, insisting it was her mother who'd left *him*, and had never even told him she was pregnant. By then, her mother—the only one who could refute his story—had been dead for years, and Janet had slowly adapted to—and secretly loved—the new reality of her family.

"It's great, really interesting stuff on tort reform at the federal level. I won't bore you with the details, but I'm glad to see such interest from a broad range of federal judges in attendance."

"Hey, y'all! Sorry for the delay!" William squeezed between Jason and Janet and motioned to the bartender for another round.

Sampson canceled the order for his drink refill. Janet, meanwhile, downed the rest of her existing drink in one gulp and reached for the second as soon as the bartender set it down.

Ignoring Jason's pointed look, she turned to look his father square in the face. "William, I heard you're trying to hire Cindy Lou out from under me?"

William ducked his head good-naturedly. "I got found out, huh? All I did was talk to her about the idea of coming to work for me, just to gauge her interest."

"And?"

"She didn't leap at the offer, but she didn't send me packing, either. I think she wanted to talk to you before she really considered it."

"It does seem the appropriate order of things, doesn't it?" She glared at William over the rim of her glass.

His brow wrinkled, but before he could answer, Sampson broke in.

"What's the new business going to be, William?"

Janet ignored Jason's peeved expression and focused on her drink. If he wasn't going to keep his father in line, she had no problem taking the reins.

"I'm thinking about opening a restaurant next to the Spot. Just small at first, with the ability to expand as business does."

"Restaurants are hard work. Very difficult to turn a profit."

"You sound like my wife." William waved his hand. "It's all a matter of proper planning and good employees . . ."

Janet's mind wandered as William recited his business plan. Liv had probably thought she'd planned well, but she'd been one cheating husband away from having to figure out custody arrangements and alimony. Jason's mother had had to take her ex to divorce court to protect herself when the schnapps hit the fan after twenty-two years of marriage.

She smirked to herself; now she was fake-swearing in her own head! Cindy Lou would be proud.

Her lips pressed together and she swallowed hard against a sudden aching in her chest. Janet didn't want to find herself in the same situation. One breakup away from the welfare line, no control over her own life. She would find a way to make Jason see her side; her desire to own the Spot had nothing to do with him—it was all about her taking care of herself. How could he not understand that?

She tuned into her father's conversation with William again, only to find Jason staring at her, his expression unreadable.

She smiled thinly as William said, "I just think you miss the signals, and all of a sudden you're out on your ass, without a leg to stand on legally."

"Well, I'm not sure about that." Sampson grimaced, then motioned to the bartender for another drink. "There are plenty of laws in place to protect everyone's rights in a divorce. Then again, Tennessee is an 'at-fault' state. So if you cheat . . . well, all bets are off."

The bartender set Sampson's new drink down and smirked when William said, "One random lay hardly constitutes losing half my 401(k), though, right?"

Sampson took a long pull of his new drink instead of answering, then the bartender was back, this time with a sizzling appetizer for the group. He lowered the platter onto the counter in front of Janet. Delighted to have something else to focus on, she smiled and scooped up some of the seven-layer dip with a sturdy chip, then looked up when Jason chuckled.

"What?"

Jason only shook his head.

"Another round?" William asked, his hand already waving for the barkeep's attention.

Her father looked just as relieved as she felt to end the conversation.

CHAPTER ELEVEN

"Okay, crew. I want everyone to face me, wide stance, hands out." Mel's white sneakers stepped apart and she waited for the rest of the bartenders to mimic her.

Cindy Lou yawned but set her glass of tea down and bounced slightly on the balls of her feet. Her yellow hair was curled and ready for a night out, not a hands-on tutorial on taming unruly patrons, but that was Cindy Lou's way. She'd wear high heels to the gym.

Elizabeth, meantime, had pulled her long blond hair back into a ponytail and set a textbook down reluctantly on a nearby table.

"Janet?"

Janet jumped. She'd been so busying studying

her employees, she was holding up the demon-stration.

"Wide stance. Got it."

Mel surveyed the small group of women. "Great. Now, what you want to do is be ready with quick fingers"—she wiggled her outstretched digits —"to call the police."

Cindy Lou groaned and Janet crossed her arms. "Mel."

Janet's neighbor raised her eyebrows. "Ladies, let me be clear. Getting involved with a drunk, combative person is not a good idea. Your first line of defense should always be to call the cops if someone is acting dangerous or violent."

Janet perched against the nearest table. "Mel, no one is under the delusion that Cindy Lou—or I," she added hastily when Cindy Lou glared at her, "are going to take out a three-hundred-pound drunk, belligerent man. What we need to be able to do is neutralize the threat before it gets to that stage."

Mel frowned but nodded and pushed back her sleeves. "I agree, which is why I'm here. But I want to impress on you that I've had years of training, and even I—"

"Where?" Cindy Lou cocked her head to the side and fixed Mel with an unblinking stare.

"Huh?"

"Where did you have years of training?"

Elizabeth focused fully for the first time on the meeting and even Janet leaned forward with a finger tapping her lips. Mel was a mystery, and even the tiniest nugget of information would double what they knew now.

"Everywhere," she answered with a small smile. "But the main takeaway in all my training was always try and deescalate first. If that fails, then take 'em out." She stepped behind a table like it was a podium. "To deescalate, you want to try several things. First, be friendly and confident. These assholes can smell fear, and you don't want to give them a reason to prove their power. Always approach from the side—never give them a direct line of attack from the front. Your advantage in this bar will be that you're sober and they're drunk! Don't lose that advantage by giving them a clear shot . . ."

Elizabeth paled at the words, but Cindy Lou's eyes narrowed and her head bobbed, like she was soaking it all in to try out later.

Suddenly Janet wasn't sure this training was a good idea. She bit her lip just as Mel called everyone up to the front to do some practice moves.

After an hour of learning about elbow strikes, bear-hug holds, and other basic safety moves, the group broke apart.

"Pressure points, huh?" Janet grinned up at Mel.

"Cindy Lou will have the advantage on all of you there."

"What do you mean?" Janet's nose wrinkled. She was certain she could take someone down. As long as they were smaller. Or already passed out.

"A foot stomp, with those heels? She'll lay anyone out flat and break about ten bones in their foot. Look out."

Cindy Lou grinned and took a sip of her sweet tea. "Thanks for the lesson."

Mel's smile faded. "Honestly, we'd probably be better off arming everyone with pepper spray, but it's always good to know the theory behind the moves, at least." The bouncer looked doubtfully at the staff and Janet frowned. She hoped Mel wasn't lumping her in with Cindy Lou and Elizabeth.

"I've got to jet, Janet!" Elizabeth called from the door, her backpack heavy with textbooks.

"We miss you, E. How are classes going?"

She leaned against the door frame. "They're good. I just have to finish up these core classes before I can apply for a transfer to UT. I'll be able to pick up more shifts after the fall semester ends."

"You just let me know when. We can always use more help behind the bar."

The young woman headed out and Janet sighed. She was glad Elizabeth was getting her studies in order. She wanted to become a veterinarian, but Janet hated to think about hiring a new bartender to fill the hole in her schedule with Elizabeth's class load taking priority. She mentally added "post job opening online" to her to-do list.

Cindy Lou draped an arm across her shoulder. "I miss her, too."

Janet turned to look at her. Would she have another spot to fill if Cindy Lou left? Her assistant manager dropped her arm and her cheeks flushed, but she stayed quiet. Janet sighed and pushed a spray bottle toward her. "Let's clean this mess up before the regulars get here."

Cindy Lou fiddled with her dangly earrings and opened her mouth, but then snapped it shut when she met Janet's eyes. "Whatever you say, boss."

———

Janet dunked a rag into a sink full of clean soapy water, then wrung it out before approaching the

Beerador. Cindy Lou had finished deep-cleaning the outside of the refrigerator unit, and now Janet had to tackle the inside.

She cracked her neck and mentally rolled up her sleeves. It was just a refrigerator. If you thought about it, what she was doing was nothing new. Really, blood had to be cleaned out of refrigerators all the time—if a package split open and liquid seeped out. She gulped. It was just usually blood from *animals*.

But just as she reached for the handle of the Beerador, the bell over the main door jangled.

She frowned at the happy sound and dropped the dishrag down to her side. It had been Cindy Lou's idea to put the bell over the door, so of course it was cheerful. She wished there was a different-sounding bell they could get. One that was less "Hey, y'all, thanks for coming" and more "You sure you're supposed to be here?"

She plastered a smile on her face to welcome the customer and it turned cautious when she recognized the new arrival. "Hey, Summer."

Liv's friend strode toward the bar and dropped her bag onto a barstool, her expression distressed. She had appeared just as shocked as anyone else at the turn of events in Eric's kitchen the day before, but Janet wasn't sure where her loyalties really lay, or why she'd come to the Spot now.

"Such a disaster at the house yesterday. What are we going to do? How is Nell holding up?"

"She's—well, she's pretty torn up about it all. Eric called her after we left—told her not to come back to the house again. I mean, I know he's angry, but I don't know what he's thinking! He's got to work full time; how's he going to take care of the kids without Nell's help?"

Summer sighed. "He asked me to step up, but I'll be honest; it's more than I can really handle at this point. I mean, I've never had kids—even an hour with them is fairly exhausting."

"I feel that way about ten minutes in," Janet said.

Summer's smile at Janet's words turned indulgent. "They're amazing, though. I try and think about their future when I get overwhelmed. They're going to have great lives, those kids."

Janet absently wrung her cloth out over the sink. Tiny droplets of water dribbled down and hit the metal basin with a quiet *tap-tap-tap*. "You're there at the house a lot—do you think Eric's using? Or do you think that was Liv's needle and the police just missed it?"

Summer's hand fluttered to her neck. "I've

been asking myself that very question since you and Nell left yesterday. Liv mentioned that finances were tight, and I'm sure that's stressful, but stressful enough for that? From him? I just . . ." She blew out a sigh. "I don't know what to think."

"Well, I mean, how well do you know Eric?" Janet asked.

"I met him in college but didn't really know him well."

"Eric went to college?" He was a mechanic; Janet had imagined he'd gone to trade school, not college.

"Well, he started, anyway. That's where he met Liv."

Janet dropped the rag down onto the counter and leaned forward. Finally some backstory on all the players. "Were you all friends back then?"

"No, Liv and I just realized the connection recently. We all started at Community around the same time, but none of us finished there. I think I'm the only one who got my bachelor's." Summer turned away from Janet and her eyes wandered the bar again. "Well, I've got to go, I'm running late. But I just wanted you to know that I'll talk to Eric today about letting Nell back into their lives. Something's going to have to change." When she reached the door, she stopped and turned back, one hand behind her resting on the handle.

"I almost forgot—is there any chance I left a pen at Liv's memorial?"

"A pen?" Janet remembered the nice fountain pen that Nell had lifted from Summer's purse at her daughter's memorial gathering, but she kept her expression flat. Pointing out Nell's problem to the one woman who might have influence with Eric didn't seem right. She opened her eyes wide and said truthfully, "Nothing's been turned in."

"No," Summer said slowly, "I wouldn't expect that it would." She let out a loud breath through her nose just as Jason walked out of the office, the sleeves of his shirt stretching tight across his biceps.

"I'll stay through the beer delivery," he said to Janet, "then I've gotta head home to get some work done."

Janet smiled at Jason, then her grin widened when she caught Summer standing halfway out the door, staring at her man. "Well, nice to see you again, Summer. Have a good day!" she called, watching with satisfaction as Summer jumped guiltily.

"Oh, ah . . . Yup. Yes, I'll talk to you soon." She smiled brightly at Jason and left.

"What was that all about?" Jason asked, resting his elbows on the countertop and leaning across the bar toward Janet.

Janet explained what Summer had been looking for, and they laughed together for the first time in days. A knot she didn't even know had been wound tightly in her chest relaxed just a fraction at the normalcy of their interaction.

"Wonder if Nell still has it." Janet shrugged and he reached across the bar to tuck a stray lock of hair behind Janet's ear. His fingers trailed slowly down her jaw, his eyes never leaving hers. "Are you happy?" he asked.

Janet's brow furrowed. "Aren't you?" She tilted her head to the side and stared into Jason's soulful brown eyes. There was some emotion reflected back that she couldn't name: not quite worry or concern, but something wasn't right.

Instead of answering, he asked her another question. "Do you ever think about starting a family of your own? Of our own?"

She took a calm, steadying breath and ignored the urge to run screaming from the room. Instead, she laced her fingers through Jason's. "I think that sounds nice, someday. But I'm not ready for it today." She hesitated, then asked, "Are you? Ready for it today, I mean?"

He looked past her, but Janet didn't think he was seeing the rest of the bar.

"Your dad coming in today?" he asked mechanically.

She must have stopped breathing for a moment, because the next sound she heard was her own sharp inhale. He'd avoided her question, just like she'd avoided his a moment earlier.

Was neither of them prepared to have a real discussion about their relationship? Were they both worried it would end if they did?

He finally brought his eyes down to meet hers and she attempted a smile. "Not sure. His conference wraps up with some kind of dinner tonight, but he's being cagey about what he wants to do this weekend."

"Cagey, huh?" He smiled, but it didn't quite reach his eyes, and Janet felt an underlying edge to his words.

"How's your mom? Have you talked to her lately?" In the divorce, Faith had gotten the Memphis house, the fish, and a major anger problem when it came to her ex. "I mean, have you talked to her at all?"

"She's not happy that Dad's here, you know? She feels like I picked his side."

"Did you tell her you didn't?" He dropped her

hand, and she pressed it to her chest. The knot was back and tighter than ever. "Is everything okay?"

"It will be." He pushed back from the bar. "I think I hear the truck." He headed into the office to sign for the beer delivery, and Janet stared after him long after he'd left.

After the driver carted the cases into the walk-in cooler, she waited for Jason to come back in. Instead, she saw his pickup truck drive past the front window.

She tossed the rag she'd been clutching into the sink and let out a breath she didn't even know she'd been holding in, then kicked the Beerador. The huge, heavy appliance didn't wince, but she did. "Daa—" She grimaced, trying to think of a good word to substitute for the one she wanted. "Daiquiri!" But as the bar settled into quiet and her toe continued to throb, she slumped into a stool and dropped her head into her hands. Why did life always have to throw curveballs? Couldn't there be one or two easy pitches over the plate?

CHAPTER TWELVE

"Any update on your grandkids?" Janet slid a drink across the bar to Nell. "Are they all back at school finally?"

It was three thirty on a Saturday afternoon—more than a week since Eric and Nell's showdown —and customers crowded in for the happy-hour specials. Nell wore all black, as she had since Liv died. Today a black scarf wrapped around her neck, blending into her black button-down top and black leggings. The only bits of color were the sparks of light that glinted off Nell's silver hair.

"I don't know." When Janet raised her eyebrows, Nell looked down at her drink and swirled the ice around clockwise twice, then counterclockwise, before answering. "I haven't spoken to Eric or the kids since . . . since last week."

Janet frowned, remembering how shaken Nell had been when she'd discovered the needle. "Do you think he called the police after we left?"

"Doesn't matter."

Janet leaned close, studying Nell's satisfied expression with confusion. "Why not?"

"Because I did. Rivera was very interested to hear what I found and said his people had specifically checked all the trash cans the day Liv died, and hadn't found anything. He said they would send someone out to the house to collect the evidence and run some tests, but I haven't heard anything since."

"You think it wasn't there the day she died?"

Nell set her drink down onto the bar and leaned closer. "That's exactly what I think! I think Eric's the drug buyer and main user in that house, and if my Liv used, it's because she got the drugs from him!"

"I don't know, Nell—"

"And then he tried to cover his tracks!" Nell interrupted. "It makes sense! After Liv died, Eric realized he could get in trouble! We've all seen those officials talking tough on the news lately; about how they're going to crack down on suppliers! So

Eric got rid of the evidence and then hoped no one would notice the heroin in Liv's system, but they did. After it came out that Liv had the puncture mark on her arm, he realized he'd made a mistake, so he put the needle in the trash can for me to find."

Nell had gone from abstract, baseless claims to very specific ideas on how her daughter had died. But were there any facts to back them up?

"If he's using, it could just be another needle, though."

"Rivera said they can run tests on it—see who used it. And then we'll know. *Then* we'll have some facts." Nell pursed her lips and looked away.

Janet grabbed a glass off the shelf and filled it with ice. "Also, other people have been at the house between Liv's death and when you found the needle." Nell waved her hand dismissively but Janet pressed on. "Skylar." She tilted her head to the side and waited until Nell looked back over. "We know Skylar's using, and she's been at the house. Why are you so sure it was Eric?"

"Eric found Liv in the basement. Eric called the cops. Only Eric had a reason and opportunity to hide the needle."

"He doesn't *look*—" She'd been about to say that he didn't look like he was using drugs, but the words died on her lips. He was skinny—too skinny —and had ever-present dark circles under his eyes, stark smudges against his sallow skin. Janet had chalked it up to grief over Liv's death, stress from single parenting. But what if it was more? What if he *was* using?

"Aha! Coming around, finally?" The small, victorious smile that had lifted the corners of Nell's lips flatlined within seconds. The older woman turned to the side and rested her elbow on the bar, so Janet could only see her profile. "I know Eric had a hand in what happened to my daughter, and I will make sure he pays for it."

Janet sighed and poured vodka over the ice in Nell's glass, then swiped a lime wedge across the rim. "So what happens next?"

Nell's shoulders relaxed marginally and she turned back toward Janet, but the vigor that had powered her words earlier had left her body. She slumped over the bar, her glass dangling from her fingertips at eye level, her face pale. "Rivera said they'll be in touch if there's anything to report."

"And until then, you don't get to see your grandkids? Oh, that just really burns me—"

"Nell? I thought I'd find you here." Liv's widower, Eric, sat down next to Nell. Those dark circles lay under his eyes like crescent moons, and his wrinkled clothes had grease stains down the front.

"Eric." Nell barely inclined her head in greeting, and she tucked her elbows into her body, her frame rigid, her back straight.

"Nell, I'm sorry about—about everything." He stared at the edge of the countertop. "I got upset at the house, and I shouldn't have lost my temper with you." He looked up and searched Nell's face. "You have to know I never wanted any of this to happen."

"Nor I." Nell focused on her drink. The set of her lips let Janet know she wasn't about to help Eric with an encouraging word.

"I know you're upset with me, and I—I can't blame you."

"Eric, you cheated on my daughter, you are responsible for her death, and now you've cut off access to my only grandchildren. You have no idea what I'm going through. You—you didn't love her like I did."

Eric flinched, but leaned toward Nell and dropped his voice. "I did love her, Nell. We'd just been going through a rocky patch. I knew we'd work it out, it was just going to take some time. The other woman—she meant nothing to me. It—

it was a mistake, and I knew it. I was working for forgiveness. There was hope for us, there was."

Janet pressed her lips together but slid a beer to Eric across the bar. He grabbed it like it was a lifeline and swallowed a few gulps before turning back to Nell. "The kids—they miss you."

"How are they?" Nell asked, turning to look Eric in the face for the first time.

"Brendon seems to be bouncing back. And the baby is confused, but she'll be okay. It's Andrea I'm worried about. She heard about the drugs, and she just can't make sense of it."

"That makes two of us," Nell said archly.

"Three of us," Eric said, lifting the bottle to his lips.

Nell shook her head in disbelief, but Janet jumped in with a question before the other woman could ruin the possibility of a truce and a chance to see her grandkids again.

"Has anyone found where she kept the drugs?"

Eric looked up when he realized that Janet was talking to him. "Excuse me?"

"Nell's been telling me about the case. I just wondered, where did Liv keep her needles? The drugs? Most people don't start with heroin. What else was she using?"

"Nothing. She was perfect. She always was."

Nell shook her head. "When I searched the bathroom, except for what was in the trash can, I only found hairbrushes and makeup."

Eric frowned. "It must have been her first try. It doesn't make sense, but it's all I can figure."

Nell's mouth pressed flat. "How does a first-time user even know where to find heroin unless it's already in the house?"

Eric flinched again, and again Janet tried to stave off an argument with another question.

"Didn't you pick up anything in the weeks before her death? Did she seem depressed? Sad?"

"She'd just found out I cheated on her. We weren't really on regular speaking terms."

Nell fixed Janet with a meaningful look, then pushed away from the counter. Her chair screeched against the tile floor as she stood. "I have to go. Janet. Eric." She carefully set her purse on her arm and tottered out of the bar.

Eric took a long, deep breath after she left and drained his drink in one gulp. "Another," he said, then added, almost as an afterthought, "please."

Janet assessed him over the taps as she pulled another draft. "Was it Summer?"

He spluttered into his drink. "What?"

"Your affair. Was it with Summer?"

"Oh, God no. Summer was Liv's friend. I actually don't think she likes me very much—but she's been a huge help since Liv . . . since she . . . Well." He cleared his throat and took another sip, slower this time. "She spends as much time with the kids as I do these days. But no . . ." He stared at the lip of the bottle. "It was a mistake. Just a dumb mistake with a near stranger, and I . . . Kids are hard, you know? Don't get me wrong, they're amazing, and life changing—but they're *life changing*! You're tired all the time. Do you have kids?" Janet grimaced and shook her head as she set his beer on a coaster in front of him. "Then don't nod like you understand. You don't. You can't! It's bone-weary exhaustion. And you stop communicating as a couple and just talk to the kids, and soon you're living separate lives and sleeping with a customer who needed a new fender."

"Wow." Janet slid two dirty glasses into the dishwashing sink. "How did Liv find out?"

"I told her. I—I had to tell her! She didn't say a word. Just took the kids and left. I—I didn't know if she was going to come back when I left for work that day. And when I came home she was there, but I was on the couch. She didn't talk to me again. Not a word. She didn't even let me explain—not that there's any explanation! But she wouldn't even let me apologize, and I was gone. Out of the bedroom, out of my own life as I knew it . . . out of my mind, really."

The spinning dish brushes buzzed through the soapy water and then Janet dunked the glasses into the cleanish water in the next sink over.

"I didn't give drugs to my wife."

She looked up to find Eric's penetrating glare fixed on her.

"I know that's what Nell thinks, but I didn't. I don't—I wouldn't even know where to start with buying drugs. But it is my fault she's dead."

"How do you figure?"

"The affair, the way I handled it? It must have driven her out of her mind. If she used drugs like the cops are saying—then it's because I drove her to it. And I'm angry—so damn angry when I think about it, and then so s—" He broke off, his eyes shone brightly, and he shook his head hard, as if to shake off the sudden emotion. He looked away from Janet and cleared his throat. "I'll never forgive myself. Never."

His words had the ring of truth to them, but it wasn't her job to absolve him. He drained the beer and made to stand up, but Janet had one last question.

"What happened to the other woman?"

He snorted. "I have no idea. I don't even know

her name." He rummaged through his wallet and Janet struggled to make sense of the situation. She didn't know him well, but he didn't seem the type to pick up a stranger without even knowing her name—only to tell his wife about it right after. There was something else going on, but she didn't know what.

He tossed a twenty down on the counter, then snorted again. "I'm a mess."

"I'm sure it seems that way now, but things will work themselves out." She was thinking that if he had killed Liv, he'd eventually pay for his crimes, but he seemed to take solace in her words.

"Thanks, but I mean literally, I'm a mess. The washer's still broken. No one's done laundry since Liv died." Air snuffed out his nose and he held up his arm: a streak of grease ran from his wrist to his elbow. The stain wasn't new; the edges were lighter, the fabric stiff. "It's not so bad for the kids, but I'm a mechanic. This is my last clean shirt, and it ain't so clean anymore."

"I'm guessing it's just as bad for the kids. How old is Andrea?"

"Sixth grade."

"Old enough to be worried about clothes." Janet sensed an opportunity. "I can . . . I mean, I'd be happy to take it all to the Laundromat. I could probably get all the loads done in an hour." She didn't know why Summer hadn't offered, but she didn't care. She was going to help Nell find her way back into her grandkids' life in spite of how she felt about her son-in-law. And if that meant doing ten loads of other people's laundry, it seemed a small price to pay. "Why don't I follow you to the house, and I'll just load it all up in my trunk. Nell will make sure it gets back to you in the morning. Then she can take the kids to the park and give you a break."

"Oh, no, I'm sure we'll—"

"Does anyone have any clean clothes left at all over at your house?" Janet asked.

Eric had the grace to blush. "Well, no. Andrea tried to do it the other day; poor thing didn't know the washer was broken and ended up crying in the basement, laundry in the machine, nothing working. Summer's done so much, I just hate to ask her, and honestly by the time I get home from the shop and take care of the kids, I'm done. We aren't quite sure what to do without Livvie. She was the happy one, you know? The solid, caring, giving one. The one—"

"So I can come get it right now," Janet interrupted. She didn't want to hear a posthumous love story from a definite cheater and possible killer.

Eric's eyes glazed over, and Janet bet he was still thinking about how Liv had been the lifeblood of his family, but he nodded and pushed his stool back. "Okay. Yeah. Thank you."

Janet motioned to Cindy Lou that she was leaving. The other bartender gave her a look that meant she'd have a lot of explaining to do later.

Janet gave the same look back to Cindy Lou and the other woman flinched. Her assistant manager hadn't yet mentioned William's employment offer. Janet had given her enough space and time to make Jason happy, but the clock was ticking. She would bring it up on her own terms soon. Apparently, she'd have the time to figure out when to confront Cindy Lou while she was at the Laundromat.

CHAPTER THIRTEEN

Eric carried a stack of laundry baskets out to her car, then with a sheepish grin said, "Give me a few minutes, and I'll bring out the rest."

"The rest?" Janet muttered under her breath, unsure where any additional laundry would fit.

By the time she drove away, there was barely room for *her* in the car. She made her way through town to a Laundromat she'd passed before.

At four thirty in the afternoon, thankfully business was slow. Janet hauled in all the baskets, set them on top of a dozen washers, and inserted a twenty-dollar bill into the change machine. The initial surge of excitement that hit when the quarters rained down ended when she counted the coins. "Shorted a quarter already?"

"Fancy meeting you here," a deep voice said as a hand touched her lightly on the elbow.

She bit back a smile as she turned around and then narrowed her eyes at Detective Patrick O'Dell. "I'm beginning to think that you're following me." He grinned sheepishly and she added, "I'm pretty sure that's against the rules in detective-land."

"I was thinking the same thing of you," O'Dell said. "I've been coming to this Laundromat for four and a half years and never seen you here. What gives?"

"It's kind of a long story."

He grinned charmingly. "I think we'll have twenty-seven minutes to kill as soon as your baskets are in. And your story sounds better than this old magazine I found on the table over there." He held up a sports magazine, at least three years out of date.

She nodded and said, "I'll meet you at the vending machines in . . ." She looked at her wristwatch. "I'm betting it'll take me ten minutes to get all these machines up and running."

O'Dell lifted his own laundry basket from the ground and nodded. "It's a date." They locked eyes and he turned and walked away with a grin on his face.

Don't be stupid, Janet told herself. She had a good thing with Jason; just because they were having trouble now didn't mean it was time to cut and run, and take off with someone else. Nevertheless she found herself humming a happy tune as she put quarters in the first machine.

By the sixth machine that happy feeling had disappeared entirely. Two machines had eaten her quarters, and a third one just flat-out didn't work, which, of course, wasn't clear until *after* she loaded the laundry and detergent into the machine. When she tracked down the manager he shrugged and said, "Oh yeah. That one's broken."

Another twenty in quarters later, she finally closed the last lid, then hurried down the line to check her first one. She had eighteen minutes until she'd start all over again with the dryers.

She glanced over at the vending machines and gulped. O'Dell waited at a table, a soda and chocolate bar beckoning from the empty seat across from him.

Her stomach felt pleasantly hollow as she walked across the room, his eyes taking in her every step.

This was clearly not a good idea.

Janet sat down with a smile.

"Dinner of champions," he said with a grand

gesture at the food. "I tried for the pretzels, but the machine ate my quarters."

"I know the feeling." Janet looked darkly at washing machines seven and nine.

O'Dell shifted on the hard plastic bench. "So what's with all the laundry?"

Janet filled him in on Nell's family situation. When she finished, he whistled low.

"Sounds like a lot of drama."

She leaned forward. "Any new developments with the case?" O'Dell's open face shut down almost imperceptibly, so Janet leaned closer still. "Nell told me she called Rivera about the needle and he can't figure how his people missed it the day Liv died."

The cop looked at his watch briefly, then leaned toward Janet. "Rivera had the needle tested, and here's where things get strange. It had been wiped clean."

Janet's brow wrinkled. "What—no fingerprints at all?"

"Exactly. Rivera asked Eric to submit to a drug test but he missed the appointment at the lab. But if we take him out of the equation, and go with the theory that Nell found Liv's needle, the needle that delivered a fatal dose of heroin, then we're supposed to believe that she shot up, then took the time to wipe down the needle before heading downstairs to do laundry?"

"Doesn't make sense."

"No, it doesn't," O'Dell agreed. "That's someone else's needle."

"So what are you doing about it?"

"Rivera is out sick with the flu. He asked me to clean out Liv's locker at work. You want to come along?"

"When are you going?"

"Right after we're done here. You should join me." As the words left his lips, his gaze deepened, and Janet felt heat rush to her cheeks. *Pfffft.* She looked away as she cracked open the can of soda, then took a long, slow sip, and only when the cool liquid reached her belly did she turn back to the Knoxville cop. His hand rested an inch from hers on the table. If he moved even slightly, their fingers would touch.

She gulped. "I wouldn't miss it." They held each other's gaze for a long moment. Things were about to get interesting.

———

When the dryers were full and another fistful of quarters gone, the pair sat back down at the table.

"How are you, Janet?"

She tried to smile but could only force one side of her lips up. Everyone was asking that lately, but no one really wanted to know the answer.

"Great. Your name came up the other day."

"Why's that?" he asked, looking pleased.

"Turns out the best way for me to avoid this whole investigation of your pal Donaldson's—"

"He's *not*—"

"—is for me to become a legit PI. And to do that, I'll need a character reference." Janet leaned forward with a grin. "Guess who'd be perfect for the job?"

"Me?" O'Dell chuckled. "Oh, boy. That would be a challenging letter to write."

"Hey!" Janet said, but laughed. They fell silent and stared at each other until Janet looked away.

O'Dell leaned forward. "But really, how are you?"

"Fine. I'm fine, thanks."

His eyes narrowed. "I can tell things are tense for you at . . . at work, and I just wanted to make sure you're okay." Her lips pressed together and he chuckled. "Don't make that face at me. I'm worried."

"Oh, you're worried, huh?"

"Okay," his gaze intensified. "I'm interested and worried."

She sat back and folded her hands together on the table. "O'Dell, I'm not who you're looking for."

He leaned back too and tried to look casual, but his words cut to the heart of the matter. "What if you are?"

"I guarantee I'm not. You're looking for steady, consistent, law-abiding . . . and probably kid-loving?" His face remained impassive. "I'm—" She struggled to find the right words. "I'm in my first long-term relationship in my life and I'm thirty-one. And I'm still learning. You probably had your first serious girlfriend when you were twelve."

She raised her eyebrows and waited until he made eye contact. "Thirteen." He grinned sheepishly.

"Exactly! I know what you're looking for and it's not here."

He frowned but ignored her last statement, asking instead, "What do you mean you're still learning?"

"Oh." Her cheeks flooded with heat and she looked away, under the guise of checking the time on her machines, but when she turned back he was still waiting for an answer. "Well. It's a tricky balance, isn't it? Between the you that's alone, and the you in a couple?"

"Tricky? How so?"

She fiddled with the pop top on her can. "I mean, I can barely make 'me' work, so how in the world can I make an 'us' work?"

His eyebrows drew together and a lopsided smile crossed his face. "If the relationship is good, then whatever makes you great also makes the couple great. The two things aren't mutually exclusive! Just the opposite. A relationship succeeds because both halves benefit the whole."

Janet's nose wrinkled and she stood. "That's my machine." She unloaded the warm, dry clothes and got to work at the folding table, keeping her eyes resolutely on the job at hand, but she felt the weight of O'Dell's stare until his own machine buzzed.

If being stronger on her own was supposed to make her relationship with Jason stronger, then she was doing something wrong. Because it didn't feel that way at all.

CHAPTER FOURTEEN

O'Dell parked at the far edge of the parking lot.

Janet cleared her throat. "You got a problem with any of those closer spots?" She pointed to the hundred spaces between them and the door of the restaurant.

"I'm not getting boxed in over there. We can walk." He climbed out and slammed his door. He might have chuckled, too.

It was dark now, and cooler. Janet wrapped her sweater around herself and crossed her arms over the light fabric to keep it tight. O'Dell stepped closer, and her body warmed considerably.

She knew she should step away.

She didn't.

"Are they expecting us?" she asked as they approached the main door to Plaza Eats.

"Rivera told the manager not to touch her locker until we got here, so in a way, yes, they're expecting us." He pulled open the door. "After you."

She walked in first and blinked in the sudden light. The diner-style restaurant had dark coverings over its windows, but the fluorescent lighting overhead was like daybreak on the beach in North Carolina—blindingly bright.

A chipper young girl behind the hostess stand pulled menus from a slot on the wall. "Hi, welcome to Plaza Eats. Table for two tonight?"

O'Dell flashed his badge. "I need to speak to your manager."

The girl's eyes opened wide and she yelled through the open kitchen door without looking away. "Dad! I got some cops out here to see you!" She leaned against the stand and lowered her voice. "Are you here about Liv?"

Before O'Dell could answer, a burly, bald man walked out of the kitchen, his apron tied haphazardly around his expansive middle. He stared pointedly at his daughter. "Poppy, didn't I ask you to walk over and *get* me if you need me? The customers don't need to hear you screaming across the restaurant, do they?"

He turned, wiped his hand on a white towel that was folded over his apron string, and then stuck it out toward O'Dell. "Paul Monte."

"Are you the manager?"

"Manager, owner, cook, sometimes busboy, yes to all of that."

"I'm Detective Patrick O'Dell, Knoxville PD. I need to clear out Liv Birch's locker."

Paul shook his head. "Bad business, real bad business." He looked past Janet and O'Dell, and in a more cheerful voice, said, "Welcome to Plaza Eats, folks. Poppy here will get you a table." Then he turned to O'Dell. "Follow me."

He led them through the kitchen into a small employee area by the dishwashing bay. A short, pale, skinny man barely glanced up as they passed, too busy sending a plastic crate full of glassware through the large, steamy dishwashing machine.

"Mrs. Trestle was in. Make sure you get that lipstick off her glass," Paul called as they walked past. The dishwasher grunted, and Paul raised his eyes to the ceiling. "Good help! Hard to find. And even when you think you've got it, they go and die on you. Poppy said Liv was doing drugs?" Paul frowned and looked at O'Dell for confirmation.

"How did Poppy know that?" Janet asked. The girl didn't look more than fifteen years old.

"She used to babysit over there. I'd have never let her if I thought . . . Well. Poor thing was all torn up, I mean, of course she was, but heroin?" He shook his head. "It's everywhere these days. I had to call the paramedics just a few weeks ago, some yahoo passed out in the bathroom here. Damn needle still in his arm."

"Did he die?" Janet asked.

"Nah," Paul answered. "Paramedics showed up and revived him with that naloxone stuff. What an idiot, though, shooting up in a restaurant bathroom? Jesus, what is the world coming to?"

O'Dell cleared his throat. "Which one was hers?"

"Top right. She'd been here the longest—well, except for me." He smiled wistfully. "She's going to be hard to replace. She was a great employee. Knew her customers; they came back just to see her, some of them anyway." He shot a dark look over his shoulder at the dishwasher. "Not everyone is so dedicated to their job."

The dishwasher mimed a guitar riff to match the solo he was singing along with from an old nineties song, which was playing so loudly through his headphones that Janet could hear every note.

She recognized the tune but couldn't name the song. A crate of steaming, clean glassware neared the end of the conveyor belt.

"Oy!" Paul shouted. "Dave! The dishes?"

The dishwasher grabbed the plastic crate just before it would have tumbled over the edge.

Paul grimaced. "He's lost four crates of dishes since I hired him a month ago. Idiot."

"Thanks, Paul. If you can just unlock the locker door here, then I'll let you know when we're done," O'Dell said, dismissing the owner.

Paul reached forward with a key.

"Anyone been in here since she died?" O'Dell asked when the small door swung open.

"Nope. I have a master key for all the lockers, but each employee makes their own code with the dial."

O'Dell snapped on a pair of blue latex gloves as Paul walked away. At first glance, the contents looked pretty basic: a can of hairspray, a mirror, some makeup items. While O'Dell started sifting through everything, Janet turned and saw the dishwasher looking their way with interest.

She walked over. "What are you listening to?" She read his name tag, then pointed to his earphones. "Dave, is it?" From afar, she'd pegged him as a twentysomething, but as she got closer, the crow's-feet around his eyes and mouth came into focus. He looked like he was about her age but dressed like he was a decade younger. His entire rear end—covered with blue, paisley-print boxer-briefs—was exposed above the belt that cinched his jeans tight against his thighs.

He pushed his headphone away from one ear. "Just some old hair band. You a cop?"

"Nah, just hanging out with one tonight." She wrinkled her nose. "Paul said you've lost some dishes?"

"One slippery crate when I first started and you'd think I damaged a Picasso." Dave rolled his eyes. "Paul ain't happy unless he can shout at someone."

"Is he mean?" she asked.

"Nah. He's cool." Dave shrugged. "Just loud, ya know?"

Janet nodded. She'd known some yellers in her time working at bars and restaurants. She glanced over her shoulder. O'Dell had pulled a small metal table close to the lockers and was cataloging all of Liv's belongings in an orderly fashion. "Did you know Liv at all?"

"The dead lady? Sure." Dave pulled at his waistband, then moved another rack of newly cleaned dishes off the machine's conveyor belt. "She was nice." He started loading dirty dishes into an empty rack but looked up at Janet. "I didn't know about the lipstick thing at first." At Janet's blank stare, he elaborated. "I mean, this machine gets everything hotter than hell, but it don't touch lipstick. You gotta scrub that shit off by hand." He held up a water glass with a smattering of rose-colored lip prints. "I didn't notice that at first, so Liv had to bring a bunch of glasses back. But she was real nice about it. She told me to remember that rain don't wash everything away, only the stuff on top, you know?"

"Did you know that she was using?" Dave pressed his lips together. His eyes flitted over Janet's head and she stepped closer. "Did you see something?"

"Hello, officer. How are you tonight?" Dave said very formally, looking to Janet's right.

O'Dell stood by her elbow, looking at them critically. "Janet? I'm done here. Did this kid know Liv?"

"Nah. I mean, do you really know the people you work with? I'm just passing time here until I can afford college, right?" Dave slid his headphones over his ears and turned his back on them both.

"That's gonna take a long time," O'Dell muttered.

"What'd you find?" Janet asked as they made their way back through the kitchen.

"No idea, yet." O'Dell patted a bag at his side. "But there's plenty to look through at the station."

Janet glanced back and found Dave staring at her, his expression tinged with concern. He knew something but didn't want to say it in front of O'Dell. She wondered if it was important. She'd have to come back alone and find out.

Poppy's eyes followed them as they walked through the main restaurant. "Did Dad tell you that Liv was interested in buying the restaurant from him?"

"Poppy!" Paul stood up from behind the counter and glared at his daughter. "Go clean table twenty-two."

She flounced off in a huff.

"Is that true?" O'Dell asked.

Paul sighed. "Yes and no. Liv wanted to buy into the restaurant—a fifty percent stake."

"When?" Janet asked. "When did she tell you that?"

Paul leaned in and lowered his voice. "It was right when she found out that Eric had been cheating on her. Said she'd been saving up to help him open a mechanic shop, but—well—things change."

"Were you going to do it? Sell?" O'Dell asked.

"I was considering it. We took a hit when this strip mall changed ownership last year. Never really recovered after the Target moved out. Liv said we couldn't do it until the divorce was finalized, otherwise Eric would own half of her half, ya know?" He shrugged, then crouched back down behind the counter, rearranging cleaning supplies.

O'Dell pulled the door open for Janet. She walked backward toward his car so she could keep her eyes on his face. "Sounds like Eric was about to lose more than his marriage, huh?"

O'Dell lifted one shoulder. "Maybe. But we don't know if he even knew about Liv's plan."

"You going to ask him?"

O'Dell's shoulders lurched back and his chest swelled. "Yes I'm going to ask him."

CHAPTER FIFTEEN

O'Dell insisted on following Janet back to the Spot after he brought her back to her car at the Laundromat.

"I need a beer, anyway," he said, trailing her into the bar.

Mel waved them through the crush of people by the door and Cindy Lou shouted, "What is going on?" when she saw O'Dell. Janet forced her way through the standing-room-only crowd and leaned over the bar.

"Shut it," Janet said from between mostly closed lips.

"Jason is here," Cindy Lou replied from a similarly clenched jaw.

"Shit," Janet muttered.

Cindy Lou furrowed her brow, then her eyes lit up and she said, "Shiraz!"

Janet started to laugh, but it died on her lips when she saw Jason's expression as he walked out of the office.

"Gary Donaldson has been waiting for you. We didn't know you were with O'Dell." He frowned at the police detective. O'Dell grinned carelessly back.

"I wasn't *with* O'Dell," she said, recognizing the lie only after it left her lips. "I was at the Laundromat."

"Why?" Jason asked, momentarily sidetracked. "Are our machines broken?"

"No, I—I offered to do Nell's grandkids' laundry."

Whatever Jason had been expecting her to say, it clearly wasn't that, because he stared at her wordlessly for a moment before shaking his head and motioning to Donaldson.

"Well, here she is. What did you need to say?"

Donaldson couldn't tear his eyes away from O'Dell. Finally, he cleared his throat, but it took another moment before he spoke.

"I am required to inform you, via section eleven seventy-five dash oh one of the Tennessee Private Investigation and Polygraph Commission, that the review board has voted unanimously to move forward with investigating the complaint filed against you."

"What?" Janet exclaimed. "My thirty-day response period isn't even up yet!"

Donaldson's gaze moved from Janet to O'Dell and then over to Jason. His jaw tensed, and he shook his head as if he'd reached some internal decision. "You'll need to attend the next meeting to answer questions from the board. It's on the first of the month, or the next Monday if it falls on a weekend." He sent one final glare to O'Dell before turning on his heel and stalking out of the bar.

Jason crossed his arms and stepped between Janet and O'Dell. "I think it's time you leave, too, O'Dell. There's nothing for you here." A casual listener might have assumed he was talking about the menu, but Janet knew otherwise, and she was incensed.

"Jason! Don't be ridiculous. You can't kick out a customer for no reason!"

"No reason? N-no reason?" Jason spluttered. "Janet, this guy's got to go. *Now.*" His jaw, shoulders, and fists clenched; his entire body was strung tighter than a harp.

"Jason—"

"I'll go. It's not as relaxing in here as I'd

wanted, anyway." O'Dell stepped around Jason and lowered his voice. "Donaldson's crossing lines. You need to get the city code, make sure he's following the law. He can't skip steps in this process." He put his coat on and touched Janet's elbow. "It's not fair for Donaldson to target you like this, Janet. I'll see what I can do on my end. I promise I will."

Jason smacked his lips together in disgust, but Janet nodded.

When he was gone, Jason dropped his arms. "I canceled the trip to Blackberry Farm. It doesn't seem like the right time to go, you know?" He pivoted and walked back to the office.

Janet stood shell-shocked for a few moments before Cindy Lou tapped her arm. "Uh, boss? You okay there?"

"Uh-huh."

"When were you supposed to go to Blackberry Farm? Isn't that the place down in the Smokies? The really fancy one?"

Janet cleared her throat. "Uh, yeah. We'd planned to celebrate our anniversary there, but . . . it's—I mean, he's right, it's probably not a good time."

Cindy Lou propped her hip against the cooler and studied her nails. "I've heard of so many people getting engaged there."

"Really?" The last thing she wanted was to get engaged, so why did her stomach drop uncomfortably when the office door slammed and Jason disappeared from view?

"It's all for the best," Cindy Lou said, parroting Janet's own thoughts, as she swiped at the outside of the Beerador with a towel. "You said you weren't ready to get engaged anyway, right?"

Janet nodded woodenly and walked blindly down the bar toward the beer taps. She pulled herself a pint and leaned against the counter. Jason was slipping away, and she didn't know why.

She was used to relationships ending—in the past, because she'd dated unsavory characters who weren't smart enough to hold her attention. Jason was different, and it would be hard to let him go, especially because she didn't really understand what was happening between them.

She shook herself. The time to dissect her relationship with Jason was not now, in the middle of her bar during a busy night with customers crowded around the countertop shouting drink orders. She squared her shoulders and took one order, then another.

Janet shoved a twenty into the cash register and as she mentally counted out the change, she was distracted by Cindy Lou's low muttering nearby.

The other woman poured liquor and mixers into a shaker, her eyes glued to the task, her voice oddly singsong as she muttered at the stainless steel. "Sounds like he just saved you from having a difficult conversation, huh?" She clapped a glass over the shaker and rattled the drink back and forth, then continued muttering as she poured the liquid over ice in two waiting glasses. "And we all know you don't like those tricky chats, just not your cup of tea, right? So when people think about moving on, you'd rather just let them think about it on their own terms instead of trying to convince them to stay, ain't that right, sugar?"

Janet frowned in confusion, but just as she reached out toward her assistant manager, Cindy Lou passed the drinks across the bar and took another order.

Janet blinked. Was Cindy Lou upset that she hadn't confronted her about William's job offer? The only reason she hadn't was because Jason had told her to give the woman some space. Her eye twitched and she felt like chugging liquor directly from a bottle.

Instead she grabbed the ringing phone behind the bar.

"The Spot, we're open." Janet tucked the receiver between her shoulder and ear while she took change out of the register and passed it to a customer.

"Janet? It's Nell."

She pulled out two beers and slid them across the bar, then turned away from another customer shouting his order to press the phone tighter to her ear. "Nell! Where are you?" Even though the woman was on the phone, Janet glanced over to her usual spot and saw that her seat had been taken by a regular named Bill, an older man with a beer belly and twitchy hands.

"I'm at home, but the strangest thing happened today, Janet. I'm coming straight in. Will you wait for me?"

CHAPTER SIXTEEN

Business was so brisk that Janet didn't think of Nell again until the older woman tottered into the bar over an hour later. Nell stalked to her seat and stared at the gentleman sitting there for a good thirty seconds before he turned to her with a question in his eyes.

"Yes, thank you, I do need to sit." Nell leaned against the back of the chair. When the surprised customer didn't budge, she stepped in between him and the bar and set her purse down on the countertop, pushing his beer out of the way. Janet rubbed a hand across her forehead when her favorite regular customer then proceeded to back into the still-occupied seat. She hefted herself up onto the lower rung of the stool, and when her hindquarters came into contact with the seated man's belly, he scrambled off the stool with a surprised, "Hey!"

"Thank you, dearie, my back is just killing me tonight." She looked up at the stranger. "You know, they say that Southern manners are dead and gone, but look at you! Gave up your seat for a little old lady. Your mama'd be proud."

His stunned face softened a bit at her words, and Janet said, "Next one's on the house, Bill. Back booth is open. I'll have Cindy Lou bring you another round."

He smiled, and his buddy slid off the stool next to Nell and they trooped to the back of the room.

"You know that isn't *your* seat. If someone else is there, you have to pick another spot."

Nell flicked her head. "You'll never guess what happened tonight!" She dropped her voice and leaned in close; her lips smacked together and she eyed the wall of liquor behind Janet. "Can I have a vodka soda, hon?"

Janet stifled a laugh and poured Nell a drink. After the older woman took a pull, she carefully set the glass down on a cardboard coaster and motioned Janet closer. "Eric called earlier tonight, just after you picked up the laundry, in fact, to see if I could help with the kids." Nell's eyes narrowed.

"And something became so clear to me when I heard his voice. He took my daughter from me. I'm not going to let him take my grandkids, too! I'm going to take whatever time I can get with those kids and let the police worry about Eric. And if I happen to find something that they would be interested in, I'll be in an excellent position to pass it right on to investigators . . ." She stared into her drink with a grim smile, then shook herself. "Anyway, I went over, and the kids were doing what kids do—" At Janet's blank look, she added, "You know, faces buried into their devices, blindly eating chips out of a bowl—when I saw a huge pile of mail on the table." She lowered her head with a small smile. "I was just going to toss all the junk mail, really, but when I saw this...well..." She dug into her purse, pulled an envelope out, then plucked a paper from inside and slapped it onto the bar between them.

Janet wiped her hands on a towel. The letter was addressed to Eric Birch. "You took Eric's mail? I think that's a federal offense."

"Nonsense. It's about my daughter, and I was at their house watching their kids. I think I can look at something about my own daughter!"

"What is it?" Janet asked.

"It's information about her new, huge life insurance policy." Nell's bitter voice broke and she cleared her throat and leaned in closer. "I'm telling you, Janet, Eric must have decided she was worth more dead than alive."

A single tear streaked down Nell's pale, wrinkled face and she didn't even wipe it away, just took a long, slow pull from her drink and set the glass down on the coaster carefully.

Janet slid a pen under the corner of the paper to turn it around so it faced her. She wasn't taking the chance of getting her fingerprints on a piece of stolen mail, especially with a PI test coming up.

"A million dollars? That's—well, I agree, it's certainly a lot of reasons to kill . . . but, I don't know. He seems pretty torn up about Liv's death. Not like a man who knows he's on the verge of easy street!" Janet looked over the letter from the insurance company. It explained that since the children were the named beneficiaries, the payout would go to the parent or guardian of Liv's children after the investigation into her death wrapped up.

"Then why don't the police know about this? No. He's a dirtbag," Nell said with finality.

Janet crossed her arms. Family life at the Birch house had been strained in the days before Liv's death. If Liv had taken the policy out recently— say, after finding out Eric had cheated on her, and while she was planning on leaving him, as her former boss had explained—would she have told him about it? Would Eric even know about the policy?

One look at Nell told her that the older woman, at least, considered this piece of information to be the smoking gun that would convince the police there had been foul play.

Eric seemed genuinely distraught over his wife's death, but . . . She shook off a sense of horror at the thought that Eric would have killed the mother of his children for money.

Jason moved past her. "Love all this business!" He grabbed six bottles of beer from the fridge and headed back around the bar with a grin. She tried to smile back, but the expression got stuck halfway, her lips settling into a straight line.

You never knew who you could count on or for how long. Best to take care of yourself first. Always.

CHAPTER SEVENTEEN

An hour later, the bar was quiet. Only a few patrons remained, spread out across the space, and
Cindy Lou and Mel had already started the closing
routine.

"Janet?"

Janet stopped scrubbing the inside of the sink
basin to look up at Nell. The older woman hadn't
moved more than her arm since tucking the insurance letter back into her purse earlier that night.
Now the older woman shook her empty glass and
Janet slid a cup of ice water over. Nell grimaced
but took a sip through the straw.

"There's something else."

Janet looked up again, this time dropping her
sponge and crossing her arms over her chest, wait-

ing. Nell's prolonged silence piqued Janet's interest, and she looked critically at her friend. Under the increased scrutiny, Nell's eye twitched. "Nell, what did you do?"

"Nothing illegal."

"I guess that's a good place to start."

The older woman blew out a huffy breath and looked away. "I *might* have taken something—but I wouldn't even consider it stealing. More like pre-cleaning, really, so I'm sure he'd thank me in the end."

Janet waited and Nell's cheeks colored slightly. "It's just a scrap of paper."

"Oh." Janet barked out a laugh. She'd been expecting something more dramatic—a diamond ring, Eric's driver's license. "Well. What's the big deal about that?"

Nell frowned. "Eric said he'd been relying on Summer too much, and he felt bad, that's why he asked me to watch the kids tonight. But I slipped this out of his wallet after he came home tonight." Her eyes opened wide. "What? He set it down on the counter right next to me and then went to check on the kids! It's almost like he was inviting me to go through it . . . so . . . when I saw this note scribbled down, I thought it needed looking into."

"What's on the paper? Let's see it." Janet held

out her hand with a "Give it here" motion, and Nell handed the scrap across the bar.

A phone number was scrawled across the page in red pen, along with the words *Dino can help.*

"You took this out of his wallet?" Nell nodded. "Who's Dino?" A shrug this time. Janet picked up the phone in the bar. "The Spot's number is private —comes up 'unavailable' when we call out." When Nell nodded, she punched the digits into the phone.

It rang twice and disconnected.

"That's weird." She dialed the number again, and, again, the line disconnected on the second ring. Rolling up her sleeves, she punched the numbers in one last time. When she looked up, she found Nell staring at her. "Third time's the charm," she said with a smile.

"It sure is," a man's voice answered back. The phone hadn't rung on her end at all, so she was momentarily confused. Then the voice said, "You got me, now what can I get you?"

Janet frowned. What the hell was going on? Intrigued enough to keep the conversation going, she said, "How . . . uh, how much you got?" Nell gave her a funny look, and she shrugged.

"Why is every bitch bein' so crazy tonight! You want it or not? I ain't got time for games."

Indignant, Janet snapped, "Then, bitch, I ain't got time for you!" In her peripheral vision, she saw Nell's jaw drop.

After a long pause, the man on the other end of the line chuckled. "Touché, bitch. It's late. Tomorrow okay?"

"Sure." Janet wondered what she was agreeing to.

"Text me an address tomorrow. I'll meet you at . . . eleven a.m. okay?"

"Uh-huh."

He disconnected and she looked up at Nell. "I think I just made plans to buy drugs tomorrow morning at eleven."

Nell gasped as Janet dropped the receiver back in the cradle. She rested her chin on her palm as she leaned across the countertop.

"I knew it!" Nell pushed her glasses up her nose and thumped against the back of the bar stool. "I knew he was using." Her eyes narrowed. "But now we *know* it!"

"Do you want to call the police?"

"No!" Nell covered her mouth and leaned back toward Janet. "At least not yet. We need to investigate this ourselves, first. I mean, if Eric's involved with a drug dealer they might—they might try to take the kids!"

Janet's face softened. "Nell, honey, if he's convicted of providing your daughter with the drugs that led to her death, that's going to happen anyway."

Mel stopped pushing the mop and leaned against the handle. "If the state gets involved, the kids could be in government custody for weeks while they sort out who gets them. That's what happened with Hazel, anyway."

"Have you seen her lately?" Janet asked. Mel and her partner had fostered a baby for several months earlier that year.

"Nah. The birth mother isn't too happy with how things went down."

Nell drew herself up. "That mother should be kissing your and Kat's knuckles! You stepped in and saved her child when she couldn't do it herself!"

Mel frowned. "Not everyone can be a good parent all the time. Kat and I were glad to be there to help when the state came calling—but you know not every child is so lucky." She laughed bitterly. "And some would probably question whether Hazel *was* lucky—sent to live with a lesbian couple? Some Bible beaters down here would think that's a fate worse than death!"

"That child probably had the best two months of her life when she was with you," Janet snapped.

"And how sad is that?" Mel's eyes grew bright. "And how sad to sit by now, idly hoping her mom stays clean—and if she doesn't that she thinks to bring Hazel to us?" She pushed the mop forward. "When all goes according to plan, the kids stay safe, they stay together. But that doesn't always happen. Did Liv have a will?"

Nell's face paled and she leaned unsteadily against the counter, her eyes trained on Mel as the bouncer mopped her way across the room. Finally, she turned to Janet. "We haven't found a will. What's going to happen to the kids? What are we going to do?"

"I guess we're going to meet with a drug dealer tomorrow at eleven a.m."

Nell nodded. "We can ask him some questions —find out how long Eric's been using, if he sold Eric the heroin that killed my Liv."

Janet frowned. "I don't think this guy's going to sit for an interview, Nell."

"Well we have to at least try! For Liv's sake!"

Nell was clearly shaken, and when her glazed expression didn't clear, Janet said, "Do you want me to call you a taxi?"

"No, dear. No. I'm fine. I'll see you tomorrow."

Janet watched her walk out, then turned when she heard Cindy Lou tut-tut under her breath. "What?"

Her bartender patted the sides of her hair and tucked a stray yellow strand back into the loose French twist. "What *the fudge* is Jason going to say when you tell him you're going to meet with a drug dealer tomorrow morning?"

"Why in the fudge would I tell him?" Janet said, avoiding Cindy Lou's glare and wiping down the counter. Despite her glib response, she was unable to shake off a sense of foreboding that slid down her spine and settled into the base of her belly. But what could she do? Nell had to protect her grandkids and her daughter. Liv certainly deserved as much.

CHAPTER EIGHTEEN

Janet held a perfect plank position in bed over Jason. He murmured in his sleep, and she lowered herself down slowly and shifted, until her body pressed against his side. She draped a leg over his lower half, ignoring the way the thin strings of her lingerie dug uncomfortably into her waist. It would be worth it when she saw Jason's face.

One eyelid blinked slowly open. He moaned. "Wicked, wicked woman!" After thoroughly exploring the lines of her slinky garment, he saw the clock. It was just before nine. "I love that you woke me up this way, but why in God's name are we up so early?"

"Are you saying it's too early for this?" Janet moved his hand to her chest and sighed.

"You know it's never too early . . . or too late . . ." Jason's hands roamed lazily over her body and she sucked in a sharp breath when they reached under the G-string and lingered. "But it seems lately you're more disposed to sneak out of the bedroom than wake me up to make love."

Janet moved his hand to the left and moaned, "I don't sneak!" She flopped back against the pillows. Jason propped himself up on his elbow and a slow grin came over his face while he cataloged her body. She sighed. "I don't think we've ever had trouble connecting, Jason Brooks."

"Mmm," he agreed, and ripped his boxer shorts off in one swift motion. "So true."

———

Janet crept out of bed and showered off, then pulled her clothes on and tiptoed toward the bedroom door.

"Busted."

She stumbled back at the sudden sound. "I thought you were asleep, I—I didn't want to wake you."

Jason threw an arm over his head and assessed Janet from the bed. "You didn't seem to mind waking me an hour ago."

She grinned. "True. But that was for fun. I thought you could use some recovery sleep."

He chuckled. "Where are you sneaking off to, Janet? Bar doesn't open for another few hours."

"Oh, uhhh . . ." She looked sideways at the door. "Just . . . uh . . . I told Nell I'd help her with something this morning."

"Not laundry again?" Jason's eyes narrowed as he asked, without asking, if she was going to see O'Dell.

"Nope. Something else. I'm supposed to pick her up at ten thirty, so I've really got to get a move on." She smiled and took another step toward the door.

"Why don't you let me help?" He jumped out of bed. "She's my friend, too, you know."

"Oh . . ." She watched him pull on his jeans and bit her lip. This wasn't going according to her plan at all. "This should probably just be me and Nell.

Jason stopped the search on the ground for his T-shirt and stepped closer to his girlfriend. "What are you up to, Janet Black?"

"What do you mean?" Her eyes widened, but Jason wasn't buying it.

"Now I know something's going on. Spill it, darlin', before I fill in the blanks with something much worse."

"Okay, but it's not a big deal, so don't act like it is, okay?"

Jason stepped closer and rubbed his hands over Janet's arms. "Officially worried now. But go ahead. Tell me." It was almost a command, and his hands were obviously placed with precision, keeping her locked in his grip.

Because she had no other choice, she told him about the scrap of paper, the phone call, and the plan to meet at eleven. Each time his expression darkened further, her voice grew harder, tighter, and she could barely snap out the final words.

"You're meeting with a stranger?" Jason asked incredulously. "A stranger that you believe—with good reason, I might add—is a drug dealer? Janet!" He dropped his hands like she was suddenly too hot to handle. "What are you thinking? And Nell is on board with this?"

She nodded silently. There wasn't really anything else to say, but she stood there as if she were waiting for Jason to approve of the plan. Not likely.

"Why not call O'Dell?"

The words were so unexpected that Janet's shoulders dropped from their tense position and she said, "What? Why?"

"Don't you think he could find out who the guy

is? Surely he's got friends in the drug unit—they could trace the number somehow."

At first, Janet couldn't believe she hadn't thought of that, then she cringed anew, imagining O'Dell's reaction to the plan.

"Aha. You don't want O'Dell to know you're acting like an idiot either, huh?" He crossed his arms over his chest and nodded. "How could you consider doing something so rash without discussing it with me?" She didn't answer, and her silence seemed to galvanize him. "Are we or are we not a couple? Are you willing to entertain the idea that we are together, or is even *that* too much of a commitment for you?"

"Jason, of course we're together! We live together, we own the Spot together. We have sex together. Yes! We're together."

He took a step back. "Is that how you'd describe us?"

"No—I was just—I was answering your question! Jason, this has nothing to do with *you and me*. It has to do with me. This is something I can do. I don't need anyone else's help."

Her answer did the opposite of satisfy him. "Something you can—what are you talking about? No, darlin', you can't investigate drug dealers—and you *shouldn't* investigate drug dealers."

His words echoed in the small space. They'd both been shouting.

She unclasped her hands and stepped back toward the door. In a quiet, controlled voice she said, "I'm going, Jason. I'll be careful."

He snorted and threw his hands up as he stalked to the door. "It's nice to know where I stack up for you, Janet. My feelings come somewhere after Nell's and O'Dell's, but before . . . uh, that's right, I'm not sure who I come before. Huh." He headed through the main room, muttering about his "stubborn damn woman," and disappeared into the kitchen. Footsteps pounded down the stairs to the basement and his office door slammed with finality.

She took a moment to compose herself, then stepped out of the bedroom. William leaned back from his work station in the kitchen.

"Morning, uh . . . morning there, Janet." His expression was pained, as if he was embarrassed to have to talk to Janet after hearing her fight with his son.

"Morning, William." She didn't even try to sound happy. This was her house, and if she wanted to be morose, it was her damn right!

She shuffled past the kitchen and slipped her feet into her shoes. She didn't intend to say anything, but she could feel William staring at her; his eyes bored holes into the back of her head.

"What?" she said, feeling only slightly guilty when William flinched at her tone.

"I just wanted to say, hang in there. You're like a magnet to him, he just can't stay away."

The slightly encouraging words were tempered by his disapproving expression. It was almost enough to break her. Before she could turn away, he pushed up from the floor, his bones and joints creaking and popping painfully. "I know it's not easy having a houseguest, and I'm going to make some changes so this doesn't happen again, you know, during the drawdown next fall."

She swallowed hard. This was William's not-so-subtle way of telling her he was going to be with them until the spring, when the TVA would raise the water levels and his houseboat would be floating again. She had to work hard not to break down in tears at the news. "We're glad to have you, of course, William. I just wish . . ." This was her chance to flesh out some information on Jason's mother, and even though she was running late and emotionally wrung out, she had to ask. "I wish Jason's mother wasn't so upset about you being here."

"Pfft." He flicked his hand and smiled. "She'll

be fine. A divorce is hard on everyone, but at least she's got all of our stuff to keep her company." The bitterness in his voice couldn't hide behind his lopsided smile when it was just the two of them.

"What *really* happened between the two of you?" Janet asked, picking up her car keys from the hall table but keeping her eyes on his face.

This time he flicked his head dismissively and turned back to the kitchen, picking up the drill and engaging the trigger. The tool whirred, then stopped. He knelt back down by the base cabinet he was placing and said, "Someone's got to be in charge in a relationship. I don't care what everybody says nowadays about fifty-fifty. That doesn't work. Never has." His head disappeared into the cabinet and the drill spun to life again.

Janet stared at his feet silently, waiting for a more forthcoming explanation. Just as she gave up and turned to the door, though, his voice floated out of the cabinetry.

"If you're the one who's in charge in a relationship, you gotta stay in charge. Can't go changing the rules halfway through the game is all I'm saying."

She frowned as she walked through the door into the crisp fall day outside. It sounded like Jason's father had wanted life to stay the same, and his wife had wanted something to change. Was that so bad—to want things to stay the same? Much as she hated to admit it, she understood William better than she liked after their short conversation.

Her shoulders drooped. If only she could understand her Jason as easily. Something was going on with him, and she couldn't figure out what. They would have to talk later—if she had to force the issue, she would.

It wasn't until she climbed into her car that she realized Jason was gone. He must have left through the basement door after their fight and driven away. Maybe they wouldn't talk later after all.

CHAPTER NINETEEN

Janet pulled away from the curb too fast and had to slam on the brakes at the stop sign at the end of the street. Her car swerved and a woman swore loudly from her porch that Janet should slow down. She did, but not before swearing back at the woman.

Using an actual string of curse words instead of Cindy Lou's fake ones put a smile on her face, and she drove with more restraint the rest of the way to Nell's house.

She tapped the horn when she pulled up to the small structure, and Nell popped out the front door. Janet smothered a laugh.

Nell wore a prim black headband in her silver hair, a black turtleneck sweater, and black leggings.

A pair of black Keds finished the outfit, and her usually jaunty, colorful, beaded bag had been replaced that day with a nondescript black backpack.

"Oh, good, I think we'll fit right in driving your car." Nell tapped the hood of Janet's beloved, beat-up clunker with a satisfied smile. When Janet climbed out of the car she added, "I see you dressed for the part, too."

With a frown, she turned away from Nell and pulled the first of the baskets of clean and folded laundry out of the backseat. She'd done no such thing—she was just wearing her usual jeans and a navy blue T-shirt—but supposed that Nell didn't need to know that. "Is your car unlocked?"

She shuffled the baskets into Nell's car, then climbed back into her own.

As she backed out of the driveway Nell said, "So what's the plan?"

Janet, still stung by Nell's assumption about her outfit, took her time answering. "We'll meet the owner of the phone number. If he is who we think he is, then we'll pump him for information."

"I'm certain he won't know my Livvie. No," she said with certainty, "he knows Eric."

"But here's the thing, Nell. Why would Eric have his number written down? Wouldn't he just have it stored in his phone?"

Nell harrumphed and they were quiet for a few blocks. "Well, it's not her handwriting," Nell said slowly.

"What?"

"On the scrap of paper. That's not Liv's handwriting." She took the paper out of her handbag and held it in front of her face. "It's not . . . it's not Eric's chicken scratch, it's not Andrea's beautiful script, it's not Brendon's terrible penmanship, and it sure as heck isn't Bonnie's. So who wrote down the number?"

Janet bit her lip. "Maybe the dealer did? I don't know."

Nell's eyes narrowed. She opened her mouth but snapped it closed before she said what was on her mind.

"We'll find out soon, anyway," Janet said, motioning to the clock on the dash.

Nell sniffed loudly and looked out the window. She swiped at her face roughly with a tissue. "We are going to get some answers."

Janet's stomach clenched. Couldn't Jason tell that this was important? Helping Nell wasn't the same thing as putting him last. She could be his girlfriend and a good friend. It didn't have to be either/or.

"We're here."

"Why are we at the Spot?" Nell said suspiciously.

"I told him to meet us in the parking lot. The bar's not open yet, so there shouldn't be any prying eyes, and it's a dodgy enough area, I figured we'd blend in."

Nell guffawed and settled into her seat. "So. I guess now we wait." She took a set of knitting needles out of her bag. "I told Bonnie that I'd make her a blanket for her lovie. Might as well start now." Soon, the only sound in the car was her needles' clacking in a regular rhythm.

Janet tapped her finger against the steering wheel, her eyes constantly scanning the street. Should be any minute now.

"Do you think I'm a bad influence?" Nell asked.

Janet turned to look at the older woman. "What do you mean?"

"Oh, it's just . . . you know, now that I'm spending more time with the kids, I guess I just worry . . . that I'm not good enough."

"What's got you talking such nonsense?" Janet took off her sunglasses to look her friend in the eye. "Did something happen?"

"No . . . well . . ." Nell set her knitting needles down and sighed. "I like to think that no one knows when I take little things."

"You're smooth, no doubt about it, Nell."

"But last night, for example, as I was putting the kids to bed, I may have collected some . . . items."

"You mean apart from the phone number and mail?"

Nell's cheeks flushed. "I wasn't really going to take anything else, but sometimes I just slip things in my pockets, and then into my bag. Just because."

"So what happened?"

"Well, after I'd cleaned up the kitchen and sat back down, everything was gone."

"Gone from where?"

"From my bag."

Janet bit her lip. "Are you saying one of the kids is stealing from you?"

"Here's the crazy thing: everything I'd taken was back in its proper place in the house."

Janet grinned. "One of the kids is recovering items from you?" Nell's eyebrows drew together but she nodded. "I think you can file that under the 'good influence' column. Someone knows that taking things is wrong, and they're trying to keep you in the right column."

Nell smiled and picked up her needles again.

Just as the urge to chuckle almost overcame her, Janet saw movement on the street. "Here we go."

A low-rider Chrysler Sebring crept into the parking lot and pulled up next to Nell's open window.

A deep voice said, "You looking to score?" Extra-large wheels with blindingly bright, two-inch whitewalls pumped the other car up enough so that Janet couldn't see the other driver through the open window. She didn't want to blow their cover by looking overly interested, so she let Nell do the talking.

"Mm-hmm. Are you Dino?"

The dealer chuckled. "Not Deeno. They call me Dynamite, Dino for short. How much you want, Gramma? I got a ten or a twenty." He spoke with a slight lisp on his T sounds.

"H-how much?" Nell asked, her fingers still working the yarn in her needles.

"Yo, this is some crazy shit right here." He leaned closer and his lower jaw came into view. He rubbed it and grinned. "I am freaking out right now. Old lady needs heroin. I just can't *even*."

An old nineties rock song wafted from his speakers into Janet's car. It was the second time she'd heard it in two days.

Janet lowered her head to get a better look at the driver and gasped. "Dave?"

The driver squinted. "Who's askin'?"

"Dave, the dishwasher from Plaza Eats?" Janet leaned over Nell's lap so that she could see him better. "What are you doing out here selling drugs?"

"I—I'm not—is this some kind of sting?" He glared at Janet. "You said you weren't a cop! I thought you were cool, man!"

"No—no cops." She motioned behind her. "This is my bar, not a sting. We're totally coo—" She looked at the knitting needles and bit her lip. "We're cool," she said with conviction. "What are you doing out here, what about college?"

"I don't give my permission to be recorded!" He craned his neck around so he could look into Janet's backseat.

Janet looked at him critically, the gold chain around his neck, a gold front tooth that hadn't been there before. "You look like you watched a movie on how to be a drug dealer and then copied it. When'd you get a gold tooth?" Janet looked accusingly at the dishwasher.

"Yo. I ain't need your permission—"

She raised her eyebrows and he frowned, then spit something out of his mouth into his hand. He held it out through the open window. It was a gold tooth cover. "It makes me look legit. That's all it takes for some people to not screw you over, you know?"

"If you say so."

"If you ain't stinging me with the cops"—he looked warily around the parking lot—"then why did you call me? Old lady don't look like my regular customer. Neither do you, at least, not really."

"I am not an old lady," Nell said, bristling. "And I could certainly do drugs if I wanted to."

"Do you?"

"Yes," Nell said. She threw a twenty into his car. "How much can I get for that?"

He laughed. "A hit. You really want a hit?" Dave looked at Janet. "She really want a hit?"

"Don't talk over me, boy. Just give me the goods."

He chuckled again and then wrapped something into a package and handed it to Nell.

Janet frowned. "Liv died from a heroin overdose. Was she your customer?"

Dave tsked. "Shit, no, she wasn't my customer. I don't deal at work, okay? That's separate."

Janet raised her eyebrows. "Do you know Eric?"

"Who's Eric? He dead, too? Look, just because Liv died of an overdose doesn't mean it was from *my* smack." He put his car back in gear and it lurched forward. "My shit is good, okay? She musta got some bad shit." His car crept forward a few inches.

Janet was struck again by the endless contradictions that made up Liv's coworker. He didn't want to care about anything, but something was bothering him about Liv, she could tell. He acted young with his pants and his music, but he was Janet's age or older. He spoke of college—but likely it was just a place to do market research for his drug business.

Before he rolled out of sight, he slammed on the brakes and backed up. "Hey, how'd you figure out my password? Who gave you my information?"

Janet looked at Nell and both women shrugged. "What password?" she asked, avoiding the last question.

"You know, call twice and I hang up, then on the third time you say, 'Third time's the charm.' Who you been talking to?"

"Your *password* is to have someone call you three times, then say 'Third time's the charm' when you answer? It was dumb luck." He looked at her uncertainly. "You should make the secret phrase 'First time's the charm' on the third try. That way no one will accidentally say it."

"Yo, but that shit don't make sense!" Dave glared at her.

"Exactly."

He peeled out of the parking lot, leaving a cloud of smoke and the smell of burnt rubber behind.

"That was a waste of time," Nell said, putting her knitting needles away.

"It was worse than that. Now we have heroin in our possession, and you're out twenty bucks."

"You take it, Janet. I don't know what to do with it. I just couldn't have him calling me Grandma, like I couldn't handle heroin."

"But you can't! You can't handle heroin!" Janet exclaimed. "And that's nothing to be ashamed of. I mean, no one can!"

"But he didn't have to say that to my face!" Nell set the tiny blue balloon full of heroin down on Janet's dashboard and climbed out the car. "Come on, can you open early today, Janet? I need a drink."

Janet looked at the contraband on her dash and dropped her head. No kidding. So did she.

CHAPTER TWENTY

When Nell was settled with a drink, Janet called her boyfriend. At least, she hoped Jason was still her boyfriend. He didn't answer, so she left a message explaining that she was still alive, then stared glumly at the phone for several long moments before picking up the receiver again. This time, she dialed O'Dell.

"You did what?" His next series of swear words was muffled, and Janet could picture him putting the phone down and walking away during her explanation of the events that had taken place that morning. "Jesus H. Christ, Janet! What were you thinking?" His voice vibrated the phone, and it rankled Janet enough that she started shouting, too.

"We thought we might get some information, O'Dell, that's what we were thinking!"

"Information on what? How to buy drugs?"

"No, on Liv's death!"

A noisy sigh echoed through the line, and when O'Dell spoke again he'd lowered his volume, but his voice had no less venom than before. "I should arrest you. God, I only hope you didn't buy yourself a felony."

"First of all, *I* didn't buy anything, okay? Second of all, your department isn't doing anything about Liv's death! What are we supposed to do? Just . . . wait?" She snorted.

O'Dell pounced. "This isn't a joke, Janet. People die at the hands of these dealers. Liv did. Now you're putting an old woman—a grieving mother, the only granny those kids have left—in harm's way, too? I—" He sighed again, then said with finality, "I thought you were smarter than that. You mentioned a reference letter? Never."

Click.

He'd disconnected.

Shit. What was she supposed to do with the drugs?

She rubbed her chin and stared at the bar, then resolutely snapped on a set of disposable latex dishwashing gloves and marched the balloon to the bathroom. Over the toilet she snipped open the edge and watched the brownish-yellow crystallized powder sprinkle down to the basin.

Water swirled down the bowl with a whoosh. She pushed the lever a second time, then got out the toilet cleaner and scrub brush for good measure.

She took off the gloves and stared at them uncertainly. They might have heroin residue on them, but how to destroy the evidence?

Nell pushed open the door, and before she could react, the older woman grabbed the gloves, threw them in the toilet bowl, and pushed the handle down to flush.

"Wait!" Janet lunged toward the toilet but stopped short of reaching into the water to retrieve the gloves. She held her breath, hoping the gloves would make it out of the bowl and down the pipes without blocking the line and causing a backup.

They disappeared with a gurgle.

"That toilet is twenty years old! They don't make 'em like that anymore. You could probably flush an entire pint glass down without a problem." Nell brushed her hands off on her pants and left Janet gaping after her.

After she drove Nell home, all she wanted to

do was get to Jason and grovel, apologize, beg for his forgiveness. But when she was finally alone in the car, her dad called.

"Hey, kiddo. Can you still pick me up? I—I have a bit of a deadline—can call a cab if you're not going to make it."

She clapped a hand to her forehead. Her dad! She'd forgotten that they'd made plans to see each other that day. "No—sorry, Dad, I'm on my way. Be there in ten minutes."

She spent the drive downtown rewriting the last day of her life. Even after Jason's silence and O'Dell's anger, if she could have done it all over again, she still would have brought Nell to meet the dealer. She only wished that she'd pressed Dave for more information. He knew something.

When they'd first met at the restaurant, she thought that he was on the verge of telling her something before O'Dell butted in, and then today there had been a spark of . . . "guilt" wasn't the right word, but maybe regret. When she'd mentioned Eric's name some emotion had crossed Dave's face that she needed to explore further. And she was going to. Right after she spent some quality time with her father.

———

"Janet!" Sampson Foster crossed the sidewalk and had the door open and his seat buckled before she'd really come to a complete stop.

"Where to, Dad?"

"Head south on the Alcoa Highway." He fidgeted in his seat so much that Janet checked to make sure the seat heater hadn't accidentally flipped on.

"Down toward the airport? Where are we going?"

"There's a nice little walking trail I thought we could manage, and . . ." His eyes flicked to her face before he cleared his throat. "Kaylee flies in later this afternoon. I want you to meet her."

She stared at him for so long that Sampson grabbed the dash. "Watch the road!"

"I am," she said, still leveling him with a stare. She blew out a loud sigh and pulled her eyes away from her father. Kaylee. Sounded like a four-year old, not the name of a grown woman close to retirement age. "How'd you meet her again?"

"We've run in the same circles for years. Finally connected."

"What do you mean 'finally'?"

He shifted in his seat and stared ahead. "She got divorced recently, and—"

"Dad! Did you break up her—"

"No-I-did-not-Janet-Black-now-keep-your-eyes-on-the-road."

His admonition came out sounding like one long word and it was enough to make her smile. "You really like her, huh?"

He didn't answer, and when she finally risked a peek to see why he was so quiet, she found him inspecting the dash of her car. The exact spot where the heroin balloon had rested just hours ago.

Did her father somehow know? Rationally she knew there was no way he could, but when he reached out to touch the surface, her stomach clenched. That was dust on the dash, wasn't it? Just regular dust?

"Janet," her father began, an underlying edge to his voice that was impossible to ignore. He dragged a finger across the dash. "Listen here, kiddo—"

"Dad, I messed up, okay?" The whole story poured out of her: Nell's daughter's death, the insurance policy, the motherless kids, the cheating husband, the broken washing machine, even the drug buy that morning.

When she finished, her father reached over and squeezed her shoulder. "Janet, pull over. We'll figure all this out, but not if we die because you're not paying attention to the road."

She took her foot off the gas and eased to a stop along the shoulder. "How did you know?" Janet asked, wiping her nose on her sleeve.

"I was going to admonish you for letting your car get so dirty. There's a layer of dust on the dash so thick my allergies are already acting up. But that's just dust, Janet. Not heroin. Thank God."

Even though she and her father were barely more than strangers, she was glad he was there. She was glad to have someone firmly on her side.

She calmed down and started driving toward the hiking spot again. Sampson cleared his throat. "I want to hear more about the case, and more about your plans moving forward, but I also want to say that you're being reckless." He held up a hand to stop her from interrupting. "It's okay to take chances, but you have to weigh the risk with the reward. Did you get valuable information you need from this Dave character? Yes? Then it was worth it. But, Janet, aside from being reckless with the drug dealer, you were reckless with Jason and his feelings, too. If you're not careful you'll end up just like me. Or even worse—" His face scrunched distastefully. "—you'll end up like William."

Janet bit her lip. The turn to personal matters was so unexpected, she had to force herself to keep her eyes on the road. "End up like you?" she repeated. "Sign me up. A successful federal judge with the respect of an entire community and job security you can't even buy anymore?" She smiled wanly. "Yes, please."

"No, Janet." She looked over in time to see Sampson smile ruefully. "You'll end up sad and alone, pining for the family you never got to enjoy."

"You're sad?" she asked, his words wedging down into her heart in a way she'd never experienced before.

"I was. But Kaylee . . . well, one of the reasons we planned this trip is because I want you to meet her. She makes me happy in ways I never thought possible. And . . . well, I guess there's no reason to keep it from you. We're engaged."

Janet forced herself to smile and say the proper words at her father's surprise announcement, but inside she crumpled a little, because her sense of security had just been blasted apart in seconds. Her dad wasn't there to save her. He was there to tell her he was moving on, and she was on her own after all.

CHAPTER TWENTY-ONE

"You want another layer?" Cindy Lou asked with a barely suppressed smile.

Janet wore her usual work clothes, which consisted of jeans and a black T-shirt, but then, because of the task at hand, she'd added a long-sleeve T-shirt and two layers of rubber gardening gloves, and topped the whole thing off by pulling her hair back in a ponytail and then covering her head with a baseball hat.

"I thought an oxygen mask would be overkill." Janet stood halfway inside the Beerador with a spray bottle of cleaning solution and a sponge. A box fan pointed at the entire setup to carry away the fumes. "Why don't you get the outside one last time. I thought I still saw some black smears by the side window." Cindy Lou grumbled and Janet smiled. Served her right for mouthing off.

After her near breakdown in the car with her father, she'd begged off going to the airport with him to pick up Kaylee. Instead she'd dropped him off, with assurances that it was no problem for the pair to take a taxi back to the hotel and meet up with Janet later at the Spot.

With unexpected time on her hands, she was determined to get the Beerador up and running. Before she'd suited up, Janet had topped off the drinks of the two customers in the bar, and now she and her assistant manager worked quietly. Cindy Lou hummed a nameless tune, and Janet's mind wandered to her relationship with Jason.

She and Jason had been dating long enough now that they'd worked through all but a few of their issues. She supposed that was how it went in any long-term relationship. You came to accept most things about your significant other, but one or two things would always irritate you. For her, that seemed to include Jason's desire to talk about every damn thing she wanted to do, and for him, it was her need for independence and reluctance to report everything she was doing to him.

Really, they were two sides of the same issue. Could there be any way to resolve it?

She was delighted when the bell over the door tinkled, saving her from scrutinizing her own shortcomings. She dropped her spray bottle and stepped out of the Beerador, coming eye to eye with Cindy Lou.

"I've got it—"

"You keep working, I'll—"

They burst out laughing, and Cindy Lou snapped her gloves off first. "I'm on it, boss!"

But as Janet picked her spray bottle back up, Cindy Lou groaned. "Never mind. You take it. He's here to see you, anyway."

Janet's heart leapt. Jason! She looked over with a smile that froze on her face when she came face to face with O'Dell. "Oh. It's you." Disappointment slid down her throat like bitter beer.

He crossed his arms. "Not you, too? I expect that greeting from others here, but not you."

She shook her head and remembered her last conversation with O'Dell. "What can I get you?" she asked woodenly.

"Now, don't be like that. I came to—well, not apologize, really, because I stand by what I said on the phone. Did you take care of it?"

"Yes." She set the spray bottle on the bar and snapped off her gloves. "I just—"

"No, no—nope." He covered his ears. "I don't

want any details. At all. I just want to know that it's gone."

Janet nodded mutely.

He blew out a breath. "Good, good. Okay, then." He tilted his head to the side. "Like I said, I'm not going to apologize, and I'm certain you're not either, so let's just move past it. We can have disagreements and still be friends. Right?" Most of what he said sounded like a rehearsed speech, but his last word came out as a real question.

Janet relented and smiled faintly. "Of course. We're fine, O'Dell."

"Okay." He smiled too. "Okay if I stay and have a beer?" She nodded and pointed to a stool, then cocked an eyebrow. He drummed his fingers on the bar and said, "I'll take that new one you've got on tap."

When he was settled, Janet got back to work. After another fifteen minutes, she decided the Beerador was as clean as it was ever going to be.

She climbed out, pulled off her gloves, and wiped her forehead with the back of her hand. Cindy Lou handed her a tall glass of sweet tea, and Janet smiled at the other woman before taking a long sip. The sugar, caffeine, and cooling ice had an immediate impact on her outlook on life, and she felt herself perk up.

"Let's get those shelves back in and we'll be ready to load her up," Janet said. She and Cindy Lou wrestled the heavy, circular metal shelves back into the unit, then started loading beer bottles into the refrigerator.

Janet was so focused on the task, she'd blocked out all the other noise in the bar, but when the dull job of adding bottles to the shelves was nearing an end, she heard O'Dell talking with someone about an old case. She glanced over. Detective Rivera sat on his right with a beer. They must have planned to meet up .

"I just hope she can do it, man." Rivera ran both hands down the sweating glass in front of him. "You know that not many cases really stick with you, but this one did."

O'Dell popped a pretzel in his mouth from a nearby bowl of trail mix and grunted. "Those are the worst. And the best, huh?"

Janet gently lined two more bottles up next to each other on the second shelf from the top, eavesdropping on the cops without remorse.

"Exactly." There was a long pause while both men drank. Janet continued to move bottles around, although now with much less thought behind the process.

She willed O'Dell to ask about Nell's daughter.

It was as if he knew what she wanted, because he said, "Autopsy back yet on the Birch case?"

Rivera grunted. "Yup—we asked them to fast-track it because of that thing I mentioned earlier."

Janet grimaced. What thing? She turned her head to the side to hear better.

"It was heroin laced with fentanyl in her system, like we suspected. She probably died minutes after it entered her system. So glad we rushed through the tox screening. You just never know these days."

"No kidding," O'Dell said. He lifted his beer to his lips, then pulled it back without taking a sip. "Homicide?"

"Coroner hasn't finalized it yet," Rivera answered. "But prosecutors'll want us to go all out, find the dealer, see if they can make charges stick."

O'Dell's eyes drifted up to meet Janet's. "Family thinks a few things don't add up."

Rivera rooted around in the snack bowl, finally plucked out a cashew, and popped it in his mouth. "They're right about that. We'll probably bring the husband in. See what he *really* knows. He's skipped two drug tests now. All voluntary, but still. Looks bad." He wiped his hands on a napkin and turned toward O'Dell. "You know how these things go. It'll be hard to prove she didn't buy the drugs herself. These idiots mess around with heroin . . . I mean, they kind of know they're playing roulette, ya know? Roulette with a syringe, and everybody loses."

Both men fell quiet, and Janet turned to get two more bottles to add to the Beerador. She glanced at O'Dell and he lifted his eyebrows. Had he asked those questions just for her? She smiled slightly and he nodded, then turned to Rivera. "How 'bout that game last night?"

Janet finished filling up the Beerador and then grabbed Cindy Lou's hand. She held her breath as she plugged it in. The lights across the bar dimmed, then came back up to full as the old refrigerator sucked wattage from the entire building to start up. The unit hummed and Cindy Lou patted it on the side with affection. "This crazy thing is glad to be home, ain't that right, baby?"

Janet's mind buzzed, too, as she took off her protective layers and pulled her hair out of the ponytail. Heroin laced with fentanyl. A killer dose. And not long after Liv died, her mother had found the phone number for a heroin dealer scrawled on a scrap of paper in Liv's husband's wallet.

Who was responsible for Liv's death? Dave? Eric? Or Liv herself? Her phone buzzed in her pocket and she checked the screen. A stab of dread hit her in the stomach when she read the text from Jason.

Meet me at our spot in thirty minutes. We need to talk.

She gulped. It wasn't as bad as a breakup text, but it didn't seem far off. Was he asking her to meet him at their favorite fountain at the park so he could break up with her? No way, not on her watch. She texted him back one word, *No*, and then resolutely turned off her phone.

She must have made a distressed sound, because when she looked up, O'Dell stood in front of his stool, one hand extended toward her. "Are you okay, sweetheart?"

Before she could answer, another voice called her name. Mel strode over, a folded piece of paper in her outstretched hand.

"Some guy just dropped this off for you." She nodded to O'Dell and slapped the note down on the bar.

"What is it?" When Mel shrugged, Janet dragged the slip of paper across the counter and unfolded it. *Meet me tonight in the alley behind Plaza Eats. 8 p.m. Dave.*

She gulped, and her heartbeat quickened when she looked up at the two Knoxville cops sitting nearby.

Mel noticed O'Dell's interest and leaned in and lowered her voice, effectively cutting the cops out of their conversation. "The guy was nervous. Said it was important that I get that note to you immediately. Is everything okay?"

"I don't know." Janet looked at the door and grimaced. "I guess I'm about to find out."

CHAPTER TWENTY-TWO

If meeting an unknown drug dealer in broad day-light outside of her own bar had sounded insanely dumb to Jason, she hated to think of what he would say about her current situation. She eased her car next to the Dumpster in the alley behind Plaza Eats and turned off the engine. It was dark, but a low-wattage bulb over the back door of the restaurant cast a faint glow over the alley—until it clicked off without warning, plunging the area into complete darkness.

"Well, shit." She sat as still as a statue in her seat, feeling very much like a bunny frozen when a predator is near, hoping the threat would slide by without noticing her existence.

A gentle tap on the passenger window might as

well have been a gunshot for how she jumped. Dishwasher Dave's mouth moved, and his muffled voice came through the glass.

"You gonna let me in, or what?"

Cold fingers of fear scraped at the sides of her stomach, and she nearly said no. Instead, she reached across the passenger seat and unlocked the door.

She inspected Dave from head to toe as he climbed clumsily into the car. His gold tooth was gone; so was the gold chain. He smelled of lemon-fresh dish soap and tangy sweat, and despite the cool night, he wore only a short-sleeve T-shirt and the same style of low-rider, baggy jeans as he had on their first meeting. A sweatshirt dangled from his hand, and he shoved it down on the floorboard as he climbed in. He could have been hiding a gun, but it wouldn't make sense to kill Janet tonight. Not with Mel's knowing about their meeting.

"Didn't think you'd have the balls to come," he said, sucking on his teeth.

"Didn't think you'd be dumb enough to ask me to." He flinched, and Janet knew that she wasn't the only one worried.

"I've been thinking," he said.

It wasn't the start of a thought, it *was* the thought. Janet waited for more to come, and after several long minutes, she prompted him. "About anything in particular?"

"Yes. There was a bad shipment." His eyes flitted to Janet's, then back out his window. "It was a while ago. But there were some deaths."

She searched back in her mind, remembering a news story. "Eight, ten months ago? The two men at the library?"

"Mmm."

News coverage of the deaths and investigation had been thorough. Two men, less than two days apart, had been found dead in study cubicles in the back of a little-used area of the downtown library. The employees had been heartbroken and the city passed a resolution to provide staff at all city buildings with naloxone, a drug that could reverse the deadly effects of heroin if administered fast enough. After one day of celebrated news stories, the backlash struck, with a minority of the library board of directors against the plan, as they worried about the risk to their employees of trying to treat drug-addicted, unpredictable people in crisis.

"That was you?" Janet turned to look Dave full in the face for the first time.

His breath came out heavy and loud. "It wasn't *me*. It was a bad shipment, okay? Once I found out,

I contacted all my customers. Got most of it back. Everyone got a freebie for the mistake."

"Oh, well, that was nice of you," Janet said drily. "The customer's always right, unless they're dead, something like that?"

He hissed and moved farther away from her in the seat. "Do you want to hear this or not?"

"Yes, please. Go ahead."

"Obviously I didn't get it all. Some people didn't call me back—and I never heard from them again. Don't mean they're dead," he added defensively. "Just means they left town, or got clean or whatever. But I wonder if someone saved some. Somehow gave it to Liv." He'd slowed down by the end of his thought, so that the final words came out like a funeral dirge.

"Who would do that?"

He bit his lip and looked out the window. Something was holding him back from sharing everything he knew with Janet. Something—or someone.

She took a different tack. "How did you know it was yours back then, anyway?" Janet turned to look at the dealer.

He squirmed uncomfortably in his seat. "I always thought I'd want to know if my shit was bad, okay?" His words spluttered to a stop. Janet leveled a glare across the seats, and he coughed and started back up again like an old motor on its last ride. "So I tinted my product."

"What do you mean?"

"It's a simple process, just a drop of this, a bit of that," Dave said dismissively. "But my point is, back then, I tinted it orange." He looked beseechingly at Janet. "Do you know if the heroin Liv used was . . . was it orange?"

Janet shook her head. "I'm sorry, I don't know." Her eyes narrowed. "But the drugs I flushed down the toilet today were brown."

He rubbed a hand across his jaw and turned to stare out the window. "Yeah, well I don't tint mine anymore. Turns out I don't want to know if it's mine."

Janet's eyebrows drew together as she looked at Dave. This drug dealer, who must surely have delivered people to their final moments on a weekly, if not daily, basis, was racked with guilt.

"There's something else," Dave said when Janet remained quiet. "Liv's husband was in tonight."

The way he said "husband" pulled her out of her own head.

"You don't like Eric?"

"You know, a restaurant is like a big family. Liv was pretty torn up when she found out he cheated on her. She lost some weight, seemed to really be out of sorts just before she died." He turned back to look out the window. "Anyway, he came in to clear out her locker. Really lost his shit when he found out the cops had been there first."

The news surprised Janet. "Why?" she asked. "What was his problem?"

"I don't know," Dave said, turning to Janet. "But he ripped through her things like something was lost. Like something important was missing. Then he threw out almost everything."

Janet blew out a sigh and then looked at her watch. It was too early to feel as tired as she did just then. She saw movement from the corner of her eye, and when she looked over, Dave was polishing a silver compact mirror with his thumb. "What's that?"

"She used it to touch up her lipstick every night. Hey, I took it out of the trash, okay?" Janet bit her lip at his defensive tone. She hadn't meant to look at him with judgment. "It's real silver. Probably worth a lot of money," he added in a harder tone, but Janet didn't miss how he carefully placed it in the breast pocket of his T-shirt and patted it, before pulling his sweatshirt from the floorboards and shrugging into it.

"Let me know if you find out anything." He climbed out of the car.

"Hey, Dave," Janet called, and the drug-dealing dishwasher turned to look down at her. "Stop dealing. If Liv did die from your drugs, she's certainly not the first and won't be the last. Do good, okay?"

He frowned and looked down his nose at her. "Who are you to talk, lady? You run a bar, right? You're serving up alcohol to people to numb the pain from their sad lives. I do the same thing, you're just making them suffer a slow painful death."

Janet flinched when he kicked her door before turning away. She sat in the dark for a while, then finally turned her phone back on. It vibrated with notifications of four voicemails and a text from Jason.

Don't avoid me, Janet. I'll find you.

Nell's son-in-law might have killed his wife to cash in on her insurance policy. Meanwhile, here she was, hiding in an alley at night to avoid having Jason break up with her.

She started up the engine and flooded the dark alley with her headlights.

Ain't love grand?

CHAPTER TWENTY-THREE

Janet drove back to the Spot. She certainly wasn't going to risk running into Jason at home—the quiet privacy of their house was too scary a proposition just then. Surely Jason wouldn't break up with her in a crowded bar, their place of business? Yes, the Spot was home base that night—safe for Janet while she figured out what she was going to do.

She stepped inside, and when her eyes adjusted to the low lighting, she recognized her father at the bar. To his left an older woman looked nervously around the space. Could it be the dreaded Kaylee?

Turns out in life, there aren't any home bases. Just time bombs waiting to go off at every turn.

Mel tapped her arm. "Jason was in looking for you," she said apologetically. "He wants you to call him a-sap."

She squared her shoulders and walked through the room, then ducked behind the counter. Cindy Lou caught sight of her when she turned to get clean pint glasses from the shelf. "Oh, hey! Jason was just in looking for you."

"Yeah, I heard." She crossed her arms and stared darkly at her assistant manager.

Cindy Lou pulled two beers from the taps. "What?"

"Did you—are you going to go work for William if he opens a restaurant next door?"

One of the beers slipped out of Cindy Lou's hand and crashed to the floor. Broken glass scattered everywhere and cheap draft beer slicked under the rubber mats.

"Son of a biscuit!" The bartender jumped away from the pool of beer and slid the remaining full glass across the bar. "Sorry, Billy, just give me another minute on that other one."

Mel hurried over with the mop and Janet picked up the dustpan and sweeper. Within minutes the floor was clear and Billy's second beer was delivered.

Cindy Lou's back straightened and she crossed

her arms as she turned to Janet. "He offered me a pretty good position, but I haven't come to any decisions. Yet."

"I guess here's where I'm supposed to say that I want you to do what's best for you . . ." Cindy Lou screwed up her face and started to turn away before Janet added, "But in all honesty, I don't. I want you to stay here with me, and if we need to talk about giving you a raise, switching your schedule around, then that's what we'll do." Janet nodded gruffly and pivoted, but not before seeing Cindy Lou's lips lift in a grin.

She was going to keep orderly whatever part of her life she could just then, no matter the cost.

A hand reached out across the bar to cover hers, and she snatched it back reflexively, then let out a low chuckle.

"Oh, hey, Dad. I didn't see you th—"

Sampson wrapped his arm around the woman sitting on his left. "Janet, this is Kaylee. We've been waiting for you."

Her vision blurred, narrowing down to tubes of elongated color surrounded by black on all sides. The woman smiled tentatively, and she found herself shaking hands and asking—her voice too loud, overly friendly—how Kaylee's flight was.

The woman must have answered—her lips certainly flapped—but Janet only heard blood rushing through her ears, her heartbeat thundering in her chest. Her father said something, he touched her hand again, and she looked down at their fingers. Sound roared back unexpectedly.

"Where'd you sneak off to tonight?" From behind her father, O'Dell materialized out of thin air. Sampson Foster turned to assess the newcomer, and he didn't seem to like what he saw.

"Hey there, fella, a little space, please?"

O'Dell rocked back a step. Cindy Lou's elbow dug into her side and Janet muttered, "Yes, I see. Drunk."

"So unexpected." Cindy Lou's voice was low.

"What was that?" O'Dell swayed as he looked between the women.

Rivera put his hand out on O'Dell's shoulder and reached past him to set an empty water glass on the bar. "Come on, big guy. Time to get home." Rivera grinned at the group. "Haven't seen him drink more than one beer in a night in the five years I've known him."

"Big deal," O'Dell said with a sly wink. "So I had two beers."

"Two beers?" Rivera asked.

"Okay, fine. Four, big deal."

"With shots in between, and now you're closer

to the truth." Rivera held up his credit card. "Can I close out my tab?"

Cindy Lou found the slip and ran Rivera's card. O'Dell wedged past Janet's father and leaned across the bar, motioning Janet closer.

"What?" she asked warily.

"Come here." He grinned boyishly.

She took a step forward and smiled, likening O'Dell's expression to that of a four-year-old caught rummaging through the candy jar in the pantry. "What is it, O'Dell?"

"If you leave him, I'm ready."

She laughed. "Okay, I think it's time you take that ride home."

His eyebrows knitted together and he lowered his voice. "I'm serious." His lips moved in an exaggerated fashion, each word getting full enunciation. "I'm ready for you, when you're ready for a change. Whenever, okay? I'll be waiting."

"Oh, boy. O'Dell, say good night to the pretty ladies. Sir," Rivera said, looking at Janet's dad, "don't mind us, we're on our way. Home," he added when O'Dell looked back hopefully.

"G'night, y'all." O'Dell waved to the bar in general, and Rivera pushed him out the door.

"Hey! Rivera?" Janet hustled out from behind the bar and caught Rivera just before he got to the door. "Can you not tell O'Dell what I'm about to ask you?"

His lips turned up at the corners and he nodded. "Did we go back to middle school? Passing notes in study hall? Okay, shoot."

"Is there any way to tell if the heroin in Liv Birch's system was tinted orange?"

Whatever he'd been expecting Janet to ask about, it wasn't a dead body investigation. He shook his head, and his eyes, which moments earlier had been crinkled at the corners with a smile, lasered in on Janet with a sharp, cutting focus. "What?"

"When you were out at Liv Birch's house—was there, by any chance, heroin that had been tinted orange?"

He checked O'Dell's progress in the parking lot through the glass door, then turned back and squinted at Janet. "I can't discuss an open investigation with you. But . . . what's going on? Do you know something about . . . something?"

Janet glanced back and saw her father staring at her, his face a mask. "I just . . . I heard that some bad heroin made the rounds a while ago that was tinted orange. I wondered if the heroin that killed Liv could have been from that bad batch." Rivera's eyes narrowed to slits and her heart rate accelerated. His cop stare made her feel guilty and she rushed to add, "It just made me wonder how a new user, like Liv supposedly was, got her hands on heroin that hasn't been sold around here in over six months."

Janet jumped when O'Dell pounded against the door. "Rivera! Let's go, man. Or let's stay. But let's not do neither."

She barked out a laugh before Rivera's glare silenced her.

"Come see me tomorrow. We have things to discuss." He gave her his card and added, "Nine a.m. sharp, Janet."

"Shit," said Mel from her post by the door as they watched the pair of cops walk to Rivera's car. "You're in it now, girl."

"I always am," Janet said with a frown. "I always am." It was approaching two in the morning, and Janet felt like she'd been awake for days. Her father and Kaylee left with promises to meet for brunch the following day. She bused a table and deposited the dirty glasses by the sink. When a new customer approached, Janet forced a smile. "Hi, hon, you got here at the last minute tonight. We close real soon. Probably time for a shot, but not a drink."

The woman bit her lip and leaned over the counter. "Are you Janet Black?"

The skin on the back of her neck prickled. "Who's asking?"

"Dave told me I could find you here. There's something you should know about Eric Birch."

"Cheese and rice," Cindy Lou muttered, then reached up above the cash register to ring the bell. "Closing time, folks. Everyone clear out!"

CHAPTER TWENTY-FOUR

When the last customer left, Janet pulled two pints of beer from the tap and walked them over to the corner booth.

"Hayley, thanks for waiting."

The other woman fiddled with her earring but made no move to take the beer, so Janet set it down in front of her, then slid into the bench seat opposite.

She took a sip and waited, but the other woman didn't move. "How do you know Dave?"

Hayley barked out a laugh. "We're not friends, if that's what you're asking. I'm a—well, I was a client."

"A client?" It sounded like too classy a way to

describe a heroin dealer and his customer. "How long you been clean?"

"A while."

"What happened?"

She pushed the beer aside. "Can I get a water?"

"Sure." Janet called to Cindy Lou. When the assistant manager delivered the drink, Hayley held up the beer to trade. "Sorry, I didn't realize—"

"It's okay, I'm in a bar, why would you know? When I quit, I just decided I might as well make a clean break from everything. Well," she added, her brow furrowed, "I still drink coffee, but I'm thinking about switching to herbal tea."

"Because of the caffeine?" Janet made to take a drink from her beer, then thought better of it. She turned to place the pint glass on the empty table behind them and Hayley smiled.

"Yes. I tend to go to extremes. I'm just happy this time it's extreme sobriety." The women sat in silence while Hayley collected her thoughts. "It used to be just the opposite. I—I took whatever I could get my hands on. Beer, vodka, Everclear, then the hangovers were too much, so I moved on to pills, Oxy, Vicodin, whatever I could beg, borrow, or steal."

"What happened?"

"It got too expensive—"

"No, I mean, what happened to make you turn to drugs?"

"Oh." Her cheeks colored. "It's a long, boring story, and not the one I came to tell you about tonight."

Janet nodded. Her fingers twitched for the pack of cigarettes she'd given up eighteen months earlier. "So you started using heroin?" The woman sitting in front of her looked just shy of PTA president material.

"It wasn't supposed to be my path." Hayley took on a faraway look. "Sometimes you can pinpoint exactly what went wrong. Which path you shouldn't have gone down. That's what it's like for me, anyway."

Janet rubbed at her temples. There were many forks in the road she wished she'd never chosen, but none that left her shooting up heroin in the bathroom at a diner or a library study cubicle, thank God. "What was it? Which path?"

Hayley shook herself. "There were too many. But I'm choosing the right paths now; that's why I'm here. I'm going through the steps—righting my wrongs. But this one . . ." She worried her upper lip and rubbed her arm with enough force that Janet looked for a spark. "It's not even my—I mean, I guess I should have gone to the police when I heard about it, but it was after the fact, so . . ."

Janet's left eye twitched and she pressed the heel of her hand against the socket. Her staff had finished their closing chores, but Mel lingered by the door, staring at Hayley while she pushed the mop around the same stain that had been there for years. Cindy Lou wiped a stretch of counter slowly. Everyone was waiting for Janet to wrap things up with this stranger. "What can I do for you, Hayley?"

"Dave called me tonight—I didn't recognize the number or I wouldn't have even answered." Her accusatory glare landed on Janet. "I should have blocked his number months ago, but I deleted it from my phone—it felt more freeing, you know? Like, I'm deleting you, you don't hold any power over me. Big mistake." She glowered at her glass.

Janet turned to trade a look with Cindy Lou and blew out a breath. She didn't have time to be this woman's drug counselor. "And uh . . . why did Dave call?"

"He said I needed to tell you what happened earlier this year."

Janet's hand moved from her eye to her temple. "Why me?"

"I don't know, he said if I didn't come talk to you he'd make trouble for me."

"Hayley, why don't you tell me what happened, and together we can determine if it's important."

"Okay, but—keep me out of it, if you can. I—I don't want . . . I mean I worry that—"

"What happened?" Janet's patience was running thin.

"So most people try to get sober a dozen times before it sticks, did you know that? Took me one try. That's how determined I was. But I have bridges to rebuild. Twelve-step programs to take. And unfortunately debts to repay."

"Hayley." Janet's eyes flicked to the clock on the wall. "I'm sorry if this sounds cold, but I have an appointment at nine o'clock—*in the morning*—and that means I need to get home and have a long-postponed discussion with my boyfriend as soon as possible, so I can get to bed at a reasonable time." She was aiming for head-on-pillow at three but would probably have to settle for four. "So what did you do that has you eyeing the beer behind me like it's a goblet of water in the desert?"

Hayley stopped licking her lips and tucked her tongue guiltily back into her mouth. "*I* didn't do anything. But my—my friend"—she winced —"made some bad choices. Her cellmate offered her drugs if, after she got out, she'd tell some guy they'd slept together."

"Her cellmate offered her money to sleep with someone?"

"No, that's just it. She didn't actually have to sleep with the guy! Just had to *tell* him that they did."

Janet's brow furrowed. "Who's not going to remember if they had sex with someone?"

Hayley looked down at the table.

"What else did *your friend* have to do?" Janet would have bet money Hayley was talking about herself, the way her cheeks colored at the question.

"She had to drug him." She looked up through a curtain of hair and added, "But just a quick roofie in his drink one night, then get him to a hotel and undress him . . . I mean, it sounds terrible but—it's done."

"Why?"

"I don't know. I don't think my friend even knows."

Janet's eyes narrowed. "Who?"

"Some mechanic out of Island Home."

"Some mechanic?"

"The guy's name was Eric Birch."

Janet stood up from the table so quickly she banged her knee. She reached down and tugged on the other woman's elbow. "We've got to go to the police." When the other woman shrugged out of Janet's hold she added, "I've got a friend on the force, I'll stay with you while you fill out the report. What's your friend's name? Who did she share a cell with?"

Hayley's hand trembled when she reached up to tuck a stray lock of hair behind her ear. She stood up and backed to the door. "No, I can't—I'm not even supposed to be in a bar, and I'm clean now, I can't go back to the police."

Mel moved to casually stand in front of the only exit. Janet would have smiled, but she was too worried. "What did he say?"

"Who?" Hayley looked at Mel and then the door, as if calculating the distance between the two and her chances of making a break for it.

"The next morning—what did Eric say?"

Hayley rubbed her elbow, and her face became thoughtful. "He was just kind of resigned to the fact that it had happened. He said something like, 'I can't believe it,' and he just lay there on the bed, not talking." She flushed and cleared her throat. "That's what my friend said, anyway. And she just . . . she just left him there."

"To get her drugs?"

"Well, yeah. I mean, that's why—that's why she

did it." She looked up at the bar taps and after a moment of silence she said, "Only five beers on tap? What kind of place is this?"

Janet ignored her question. "Does your friend know she ruined a marriage? Eric and his wife separated right after that happened."

"I'm sure they'll work it out." Hayley waved her hand and inched toward the door again. "Marriages come together and fall apart all the time."

"But now his wife is dead."

Color drained from Hayley's face.

"She died from a bad dose of heroin. Her family thinks she was a first-time user."

"Bad luck," Hayley mumbled.

"Was it?"

The other woman frowned and pushed past Janet, who in turn shook her head at her bouncer. Mel reluctantly stepped aside.

"Hayley!" Janet held a card out to the recovering addict. "There's an investigation going on, right now. Is one of your steps to make things right? I'll come with you. Just call me, we can do it together, okay? It would be nice if the investigators had a better idea of everything that happened, you know? Hey, you never told me—who was she?"

"Who?"

"Your friend." Hayley shook her head and Janet

tried another question. "All right, who was her cell-mate? The one who offered her drugs to do that to Eric?"

"I—I should be going." She pushed the door open, then threw back one last word over her shoulder. "Sorry." Hayley walked out of the Spot and disappeared past the cones of light from the streetlamps overhead.

"You thinking what I'm thinking?" Cindy Lou sidled up next to Janet, her hands on her hips.

"Doubt it."

Cindy Lou continued as if Janet hadn't spoken. "I'm thinking that that girl seems one stressful situation away from being re*lapsed* instead of re*covered*."

Janet frowned. "Maybe. But I'm wondering who her friend is. If she even has one."

"Why would Dave want you to know that information?" Mel asked, now leaning against the end of the mop. "That's twice tonight he wanted to tell you something. Do you feel informed?"

"Hardly," Janet said. "In fact, I feel like I understand less and less about Liv's death."

"What are you going to do?" Mel asked.

Janet shrugged. "Nothing tonight. I guess I'll talk to Rivera about it tomorrow."

Mel nodded and they all walked out together.

Janet locked the door. She wasn't looking forward to going home, but she'd run out of other places to go. She swallowed hard, a chalky taste at the back of her mouth as she thought about facing Jason.

Cindy Lou smiled as she pulled on her coat. "That Kaylee sure seemed nice."

Janet shrugged. She'd hardly said two words to the other woman. But that would change tomorrow. Then she'd have an opinion based on more than the gut-clenching feeling that she was being pushed out of a spot at her father's side she'd only just come to terms with.

There life went again, giving her whiplash. She squared her shoulders. What was the point of planning when things always changed on you anyway?

CHAPTER TWENTY-FIVE

The house was dark when she drove up, save for a faint light that snaked through the front curtains. Someone was still awake—but was it Jason or his father?

Truthfully, Janet didn't feel like seeing either, but she climbed out of the car anyway.

A metallic smack from the kitchen work zone had her hustling through the house. "Hello?"

"Oh, Janet." William stopped hammering long enough to shoot her a disappointed look. "I was hoping Jason would be home soon." He turned back to a two-by-four brace and raised the hammer.

"That's a little—" The clanging of hammer on nail echoed in the small space and Janet had to wait until he stopped to speak again. "It's a little late to be working on that, William. We do have neighbors to think about!"

"Oh, I guess you're right." He sat back on his heels and looked thoughtfully at the wall they shared with the half of the duplex where Mel and Kat lived, then raised the hammer again. "They're not sleeping in the kitchen, so I think it's fine."

"William!" He dropped the hammer back down, his shoulders tight. "It's too late for hammering. You can pick back up tomorrow morning." They glared at each other until William stood and dropped the hammer heavily into his toolbox on the makeshift counter.

"Fine." He adjusted his pants and turned his back on Janet, focusing on his toolbox with unusual concentration.

Janet rolled her shoulders and turned to leave, then stopped and blew out a breath. "Why are you hammering at two thirty in the morning, William? Is everything okay?"

He tucked some stray nails into a container but didn't turn to face Janet. "Have you spoken to Jason tonight?"

It was Janet's turn to dance around an answer. "Not directly, no. We . . . well, we kind of played phone tag." Kind of, if you could call Janet's running away from Jason at every turn "tag."

"He's not very happy with me." From his profile, she saw William suck in his cheeks. "He . . . I guess he talked to his mom, and she's not very happy with how things went down. She never was, but apparently now she's ready to tell him about it. And . . ." He blew out a sigh. "Now he's not very happy."

"Why?" Janet leaned against the door frame.

"I . . . I messed up, I see that now."

"How? Was it about being in charge, like you said earlier? Was she tired of you being in charge?"

"She thinks marriage is a partnership, but it's not. It never has been. It's about managing expectations, setting boundaries for who's going to do what. I was in charge of our finances, but she wanted to change that."

He looked accusingly at Janet and she shrugged. She could hardly fault a woman for wanting to be informed of her own financial situation.

He scowled and slammed the toolbox lid. "She didn't like what she found."

"What did she find, William?"

"I cashed out our 401(k)." He picked up a rag and vigorously shined the end of a screwdriver.

Janet didn't say anything and eventually he dropped the tool and glared at her. "To buy the boathouse, okay? She was furious." He dropped his gaze and muttered, "Didn't stop her from taking half ownership of the damn thing in the divorce."

"And rightly so," Janet said. "You didn't even consult her?"

"I shouldn't have to ask permission to do something with my own money."

"*Your money?*" And there it was. William had just given voice to the exact reason she wanted to own the Spot outright. His money. William and Faith had been married for thirty-some years, but all their money was somehow *his*. She pushed off the doorjamb, feeling totally justified in her insecurities about co-owning the Spot for the first time in weeks. She wanted her own money, so there was never a question about whether she could support herself.

"No, don't go. I'm headed to bed. If you see Jason, tell him I want to talk. He can't avoid me forever, we're in the same dang house!"

She nodded stiffly and watched him walk up the stairs. After William's door closed with a muted *thunk*, Jason appeared in the basement stairwell.

"Thought he'd never leave." He stopped several

feet short of where Janet stood. "You've been avoiding me."

"Me?" She crossed her arms and leaned against the door again. "No . . ."

Jason's lopsided smile meant he recognized the lie but wasn't going to argue the point.

"I thought—well, I thought you were going to break up with me."

"And you weren't going to let me?"

She bit her lip. "Well . . . no."

His stern expression gave way and he chuckled and leaned against the plywood top of the makeshift island. "I know I could never win against you, Janet, I just wish you'd let me play the game."

"What do you mean?"

He flipped the screwdriver his father had been polishing in his hand before answering. "I mean, sometimes I need you—need to talk to you, need to hear your voice. Why would you assume I'm going to end things?"

"Well . . . you were angry with me. With good reason," she added with a frown.

"I don't like when you take unnecessary risks —yes, *unnecessary!*" he said when she started to object. "But I guess that's you, that's who you are. I won't try to change you, I just wish you'd take me into consideration when you make your choices."

"I do. Really!" she added at Jason's incredulous look. "That's why I tried to sneak out this morning, so you wouldn't worry."

He snorted but grew contemplative when he looked down at the toolbox. His phone chirped, but he didn't answer the call.

"You better get that." When he still didn't reach for the device, she added, "Didn't you say you'd be available around the clock for your new clients? What if they're testing you?"

He rolled his eyes but reached for his phone. "Get a drink. Put your feet up. We're going to talk. Tonight." He put the phone to his ear. "Brooks Security, this is Jason. Oh, hi, Nev, what can I do for you at . . . two forty-five in the morning . . ." He shot her one last look before he left the room and headed down to his office.

Janet blew out a breath but couldn't seem to release the tension holding her entire body rigid. He was coming right back—*to talk*. Though he'd said it wasn't a breakup conversation, she wasn't looking forward to taking a deep dive into their relationship just then.

The light on their home phone blinked, and Janet picked up the receiver to listen to the voicemail, happy for the distraction. The message was from Jason's dad. She almost pressed a button to save the message and hung up, but something in his tone made her stay on the line.

"J, it's your father. Blocking me on your cell phone? Really? That's what we've come to? Listen, son, I know you're upset, but this was a mutual decision between me and your mom. We both have time to be happier with other people. Don't you want that? I want to talk at the house tonight. Goodbye."

The message ended but she didn't put the phone down.

"Janet?" Jason walked back into the room, his lips pressed into a flat line.

Her poor Jason. Shaken to the core over his parents' divorce. It was a shock, of course it was. And he was reacting the only way he knew how: by locking down his own life when chaos was trying to swallow him whole. She understood the feeling. She wanted to know that life wouldn't change, too. They were just going about it in different ways.

Heat bloomed in her belly, and she walked toward him. He took in her changed demeanor and held out a hand. "Oh, no. You're not going to distract me from—"

She unbuttoned her shirt slowly and he looked

away for a moment, but then, almost against his will, he turned back and licked his lips. She wasn't trying to distract him. She finally understood where he was coming from, and she'd never felt a stronger need to be with him.

"Janet, can we please just—"

She reached out and tugged his T-shirt up from his waistband and raked her finger up his stomach as she pulled the shirt over his head. He groaned and she smiled. "We have so much to discuss. After."

He grabbed her hand and hesitated for a brief moment before he turned and led her to the bedroom.

CHAPTER TWENTY-SIX

Janet woke up on the floor, surrounded by fluffy pillows and their down comforter. Her right foot rested on the mattress above, and Jason's arm lay under her head.

"What happened here last night?" she said, her voice low and throaty.

"Well, we didn't actually talk after all," Jason said, but he smiled lazily at Janet and added, "but I remember there was a ruler, a necktie, and some new, creative cursing."

Janet chuckled and sat up, pulling the comforter to her chest. "I'm ready to talk now, if you are."

Jason traced circles on the skin of her thigh. "I could talk, or I could do other things."

"I guess we should talk first. Then do other things." Janet twined her fingers through his on her thigh. "I'm sorry about your mom. Is she okay?"

"She will be." He rubbed his free hand over his face and leaned back against his pillow. "She got tired of my dad's Han Solo act. Said she never felt like his partner. Only his secretary. I mean, if you can't be partners with your *partner*—ugh. I get it."

"And are *you* going to be partners with your dad?" Janet's brow furrowed. How would Jason feel about being his dad's secretary?

"I don't know. It's all going to come down to how much the building goes for. It's not exactly in a prime real estate area, you know? But it's probably too much. My own business, our business . . . plus another?"

Janet took a deep breath. "Well, I've been thinking about our business lately."

"How so?" Jason asked carefully. He sat up and fixed her with a steady stare.

"Well . . . I wanted to discuss buying you out of the bar."

"Buying *me* out?" he repeated slowly.

She didn't like the shadow that crossed his face and she rushed to explain away his concerns. "It's not that I don't love working with you, because I do . . . and I love how we do business together. I just think it's time for me to do something on my own, you know? And you own Brooks Security, right, I mean, we don't own that together . . . And I want to . . . I don't know, try and make it on my own."

"Do you want to be on your own in other ways?" Jason's face was a mask, expressionless.

"No! Not everything! Not anything else. I—I don't want anything else to change. At all, actually."

He let out a long breath and his brow furrowed. "So . . . Han Solo at work, but not in life?"

The corners of Janet's lips tipped up. Was this going to come out okay after all her angst about discussing it with Jason? "Right."

"Becoming a PI, meeting drug dealers . . ." Jason grinned. "That's textbook *Star Wars* stuff there."

"Oh—well the PI stuff is happening, for many reasons, but I'm going to try not to meet with that drug dealer again." She laughed lightly and snuggled into Jason's chest. "Twice was enough, *thanky-ouverymuch*."

He pulled his hand away. "What do you mean, *twice*?"

She bit her lip. *Oh, daiquiri.* "No, I mean—"

"Is that where you were last night, when you weren't answering my calls and texts?" All the warm-and-fuzzy left his expression. "Did you— were—I can't—" He spluttered incomprehensibly before clamping his jaw shut. "Janet Black. Did you meet with that drug dealer *again* last night and not even have the courtesy to tell me you might be killed?"

"I wouldn't put it that way," she answered evasively.

He stood up and threw his pillow back on the bed. "I cannot believe you. It's not even about having the manners to tell me what you're doing! How is this relationship supposed to work? If you think I won't like something, you just aren't going to tell me about it?"

"Well, it's not like you tell me everything about your business, right?"

Jason glared at Janet. "Don't turn this around on me!"

Two splotches of red at his cheeks spread across his face. Janet's breath hitched. She couldn't bear to look at the accusation in his face any longer. She picked some clothes up off the ground and stalked toward the bathroom.

Before she shut the door, Jason said, "I hope

you realize that I am *never* the one who walks away. It's always you!" She slammed the door and threw her clothes across the small room. Her bra landed halfway inside the open toilet and she swore loudly. Her heart slammed against her ribs and she could hardly catch her breath.

He had some nerve.

But she turned her back on her own reflection and twisted the shower knob on. She couldn't stand to look at herself just then, either.

———

When she got out of the shower, Jason was gone, and she harrumphed to the empty room that sometimes he *was* the one to leave.

Her phone chirped with a new message from a number she didn't recognize. Damn telemarketers. This one left her a thirty-second voicemail. Like she was going to order health insurance off the phone! Instead of ignoring the call, she sat on the edge of her bed and waited for the voicemail to play. She might even call them back just to file a complaint; that was the kind of mood she was in.

"Janet, it's Nell. I—I guess you need to get down here. To the jail, that is. I'm—I'm in jail."

"Cheese and rice!" Janet yelled at the empty room. She tapped O'Dell's name on her contact list, but the call went straight to voicemail. She shook her phone in frustration, then flew out of the bedroom and down the hall, only stopping to slip on her shoes at the door.

"Janet, can I have a word?" William stood at the kitchen door with a mug of coffee in one hand.

"No! Sorry, William, but there's an emergency downtown!"

"Everyone okay?" His brow furrowed and he lurched forward a step.

"No! I—I mean, yes, I'm sure she's fine, but no, everything's not okay!" Janet grabbed her keys and raced out of the house without a backward glance. Kat and Mel jumped in their seats on the front porch when the screen door slammed against the house. "Sorry!" she called over her shoulder, but didn't stop to check their reaction.

Her phone rang again as she parked outside the Knox County Jail. She glanced at the screen and groaned when the main line for the police department came up. Rivera! She was late for their nine o'clock meeting, but the homicide detective would have to wait.

If the jail had had more floors, the inmates

would have had a lovely view of the Tennessee River. Instead, they likely stared at the back of another building's limestone and cinder-block walls. Inside the jail, she ducked past a long line of friends and family snaking through the lobby. Tuesday was visitor's day at the jail.

Earning some angry looks as she cut to the front of the line, Janet said, "Where can I post bail?" The employee waved her over to another desk—this one without any line.

An unusually unhelpful woman refused to look up from her computer for several minutes. Just as Janet's urge to cup her hands around her mouth and yell loudly was about to take over, the clerk said, still without looking up, "Welcome to the Knox County Jail, how can I help you?"

Janet's lips pinched together at her tone. "Yes, I need to bail somebody out?"

"Inmate's name?"

"Nell Anderson."

The clerk's eyes sparked with real interest as she looked up from her monitor. "You with the old lady?"

"Uh-huh."

"She's a hoot. You her sister?"

Janet bristled and said archly, "If anything, I'd

be her daughter, but no, we're not related. I'm a friend."

"Well, friend, she'll need five thousand dollars cash or a bondsman can put down ten percent."

"Five thousand?" Janet sucked in a breath and rooted through her wallet, looking for the right credit card. "Do you take Visa?"

The woman smiled. "Cash. Or property."

"Prop—" Janet's jaw dropped. "That's highway robbery! What's the charge, anyway?"

The woman tapped her keyboard a few times. "Looks like obstruction of justice and theft."

"What'd she get caught with?"

"Let's see, theft from a motor vehicle." The clerk grinned as she read over the information on her computer screen. "Booking sheet says she stole a rabbit's foot out of a cop's car."

"Why would she do that?"

"If she was hoping for luck, it sure didn't work."

"And you're telling me that her bond is set to five thousand bucks for allegedly stealing a rabbit's foot? That's ridiculous!"

"Not to the rabbit." The woman somehow kept a straight face.

Janet blew out a sigh and heaved her purse strap over her shoulder. "Well I—I don't have enough in my account."

"I'm not surprised."

Janet scowled. "So what happens now?"

"Now your friend has to wait for a hearing tomorrow morning. Thursday at the latest."

"Didn't you say something about ten percent down?"

She passed a sheet of pink paper across the desk. "We recommend three bonds offices, and they all open at eleven." She swiveled away from Janet to answer a phone that hadn't stopped ringing since Janet stepped into the lobby. "Knox County Jail, can I help you?"

Janet stepped off to the side and added an alarm to her phone to remind her to call the bonds offices at eleven. Then she tucked her phone into her pocket and crossed her arms. The lobby was crowded, the line of people checking in for visiting hours now dispersed through the room as each person waited for their turn with their inmate. She looked at her watch, then at the check-in desk. Why not?

"Inmate name?" The man smiled politely, his hands hovering over his keyboard.

"Nell Anderson."

He dutifully typed in her name and after reading his screen said, "I'm sorry, she's not cleared for on-site visitation."

"Why not?"

"She's too new. But you can schedule a video-chat with her."

The words were so unexpected, Janet only stared at the employee while they sank in. "What do you mean? Like, from my phone?"

"Sure, or an iPad or tablet. I can schedule you fifteen minutes starting in . . . half an hour. If you pay the registration fee, and the inmate's fee, it'll be about thirty bucks. Cash or credit card. Should I proceed?"

Thirty bucks or five thousand? No question. She slid her card through the opening in the bulletproof glass. "Sure."

He held up a sheet of paper. "Instructions on how to use the system." A printer hummed to life, and he reached down and peeled a sticker off the freshly printed page and stuck it to the sheet. "This is your pin number, enter it when prompted and you'll be connected with Inmate Anderson." He pointed to an open chair across the room. "It will probably take you most of the next half hour to get registered. Wi-Fi password's on the wall if your signal's bad."

He swiveled away from Janet and she blinked a few times before heading for the open seat. She felt like she'd entered an alternate reality; she was supposed to be passing a vodka soda across the bar to Nell, but instead she was preparing to video-chat with Inmate Anderson. Her phone buzzed in her hand. She declined the call from Rivera and instead opened her Internet browser. "This should be interesting."

CHAPTER TWENTY-SEVEN

An extreme close-up of Nell's face popped on-screen in full color at exactly nine thirty. The older woman squinted over the device at someone Janet couldn't see, and Nell said, "It's not working, Anita, I— Oh, there you are!" She smiled into the camera as if she and Janet were chatting from vacation spots. "Isn't this the coolest thing?"

At the dark looks from those seated around her, Janet dug a pair of headphones out of her bag and plugged them in as she walked out of the lobby of the jail into the cool day. "Very unexpected," Janet agreed. "Like a lot of things about this day."

"What a grand day in this grand life!" Nell glanced over the camera again. "Goodbye, dear

Anita. Be good, and life will turn your lemons into grape Kool-Aid." Nell's sharp eyes followed someone Janet couldn't see for another moment, then she leaned close to the screen and said, "Anita's gone, we can talk openly now."

"Grape Kool-Aid? What was that about?"

"I'm trying to really work the senile argument. I had about four hours in the clink to convince them I'm just a sad, confused little old lady. I think it worked. I've got this guard eating out of my hand." Nell grinned. "Thanks for coming down, Janet. I knew I could count on you."

"What were you thinking, Nell? A rabbit's foot?"

Nell waved her hand dismissively. "I was distracted. I really just wanted to see if it was as soft as I thought it would be. So I jiggled the door handle for the car and it was unlocked! I wasn't going to take it, but before I knew it, it was in my pocket."

Janet snorted. As if she'd had no part in the decision to take it in the first place!

"Of course, it's unfortunate that the cop was so close. I didn't see him smoking a few doors away. I think he would have let me go but when I opened my purse to give it back he saw the wallet I'd taken from the dash." Nell sighed. "I'd left the money and cards on the seat—I just wanted the fake-croc-odile-skin wallet. You don't see that much any-more. It's a collector's item!"

"Where did this happen, anyway?" Janet settled on a bench overlooking the parking lot and angled her phone away from the sky to minimize the glare.

"I was visiting Skylar, Liv's old friend from high school. That girl has had a rough go of it, let me tell you! You and Summer were right—she's been in a bad way for some time now. But she's really trying to make her sobriety stick this time. Said that she feels like she's running out of chances and doesn't want to blow this one if it's her last. I like that!" Nell nodded decisively. "I want to support her in her quest, so I dropped off a home-cooked meal. She lives in a halfway house, and let me tell you, it was a sad, sorry little structure if ever I saw one. Full of hookers and druggies. How's anyone supposed to get clean surrounded by people like that?"

"People who've been in jail, you mean?" Janet looked meaningfully at Nell, but the other woman ignored the jab. "So let me get this straight." Janet smoothed the skin between her eyes with the middle two fingers of her right hand. "You went to a halfway house to visit a druggie friend of Liv's from high school, then stole from a cop's car on your way home?" Nell nodded. "Was it a marked car?"

"Yes, dear, that's what was so exciting. Well, at least it was when I thought I'd gotten away with it." Her lopsided smile was wistful before she shook herself. "I didn't realize this until I got here, but Skylar has a guilty feeling about her. I'm surrounded by it now, so that helped me recognize it."

"Guilty about what?"

"Well that's just it! I don't know. But she was talking about my Liv, and her family, and I couldn't put my finger on it then, but now I see that she's feeling guilty about something. Can you check on her today?"

"Before or after I bail you out?"

"Oh, good—I didn't want to pry, but is that going to happen soon?"

Janet blew out a sigh. She didn't have time to check on Skylar, her plate was already too full. "I'll have to call a bondsman—looks like most of the offices don't open until eleven."

"I'd love to be home in time for my shows. Do your best, okay, dear? What was that?" She looked over the camera again, at someone in the room with her, then looked back at Janet. "Anita says the beeping means our chat session is almost over.

Chat session, I like the sound of that, don't you? Like we're royalty or something. Oh, and Janet, I just wanted to add—"

But the screen went black, and Janet was left staring at her own reflection as she wondered what else Nell wanted to say.

She closed out the jail chat app—deciding not to delete it off her phone completely in case she needed to use it again—and dropped the device into her bag as she walked to her car.

With a sigh that bordered on a moan, Janet cranked the engine and pulled out of the lot onto the street. She drove along the river for a few blocks and then spent just as long looking for a parking spot by the police department, because like it or not, she was late for her appointment with a homicide detective.

CHAPTER TWENTY-EIGHT

Janet waited in the cold, stark lobby for what felt like a long time, and her patience was running thin.

"Janet?" She turned and found the homicide detective standing in an open doorway. "Thanks for coming."

"Sorry I'm late. I had a—a . . . well. Anyway." She ripped off her visitor badge from the jail after he'd noted it with his squinty eyes, then cursed the series of events that had started her day.

Rivera led her back into the bowels of the building. She'd visited the station before, when she and O'Dell had first met that summer, and her step faltered as they entered the maze of cubicles. She scanned the room for O'Dell.

Rivera glanced back but kept walking. "He's

not here. Called off sick, if you can believe it! Hungover is more like it." Rivera grinned and Janet tried to smile back. "You've really done a number on him, ya know?"

"What? I—"

"I've never seen him like this about a woman."

"I don't think—"

"He knows you're not available, but he really likes you. Strange."

She frowned and stopped walking.

He turned to face her, and his cheeks puffed out when he caught her reaction. "Not strange that he likes you, just strange for him to dig in on someone who's obviously unavailable."

"Are you done?" she asked. His eyebrows shot up comically as she pushed past him. "I'm not here to talk about that. I'm here to discuss a murder investigation that hasn't even begun yet."

He pulled a chair over from a desk nearby and motioned for her to sit. "No. You're here because I asked you to come in." He stood over her; they were about the same height, only—surprisingly—his attitude was bigger. "Talk."

Janet crossed her arms but eventually moved over to the chair and lowered herself down, keeping her eyes on the cop, trying to read his expression. "I have information that Liv Birch might have been purposefully poisoned with tainted heroin." She looked flatly at the cop. "And I want to know if you're looking into that as a possibility."

"Nope." She pursed her lips, but he wasn't done. "That's not how this works. You tell me things. I don't have to reciprocate."

She scowled. "And I don't *have* to tell you anything. I'm not under arrest. But I can talk to the press. I can tell them that someone poisoned a suburban mom and the cops aren't even looking into it. Let's see what happens at the next city council meeting."

A hard smile crossed his face. "You know how many crazies call those newsrooms every day? Most are ignored."

Janet leaned forward. "I have the assignment editor's cell phone number at the NBC affiliate in town. You don't think she'll take me seriously?"

"How—"

"We can do this two ways, Rivera. I'd rather keep it on the down-low so you can investigate. But only if I know you're actually investigating!"

He scrubbed a hand over his face and blew out a sigh. "Yes, we're investigating. Toxicology report came back, and Liv died from the same bad heroin that ran through town months ago. Coroner is holding off on classifying the death for now, but she says it could go two ways. Homicide or accidental death."

"What's the deciding factor?"

"The needle mark—it was in her right arm. She was right-handed, so it doesn't make sense."

Janet fell back against the seat. "It would have been in her left arm if she'd done it herself?"

He nodded. "So tell me, Janet. What do you know?"

Their eyes locked and Janet unconsciously sucked in her lips.

Rivera scrutinized her for several long moments. "Insurance company contacted us." When Janet nodded his eyebrows shot up. "You knew about that, too?"

"The million-dollar policy? Mm-hmm."

"They're withholding payment until our investigation is complete." He turned away and moved a stack of papers on his desk, then picked up a clipboard. "We think Eric—" His desk phone and cell phone rang at the same time, and he checked the screen on his device, then silenced the phone, but didn't answer either.

Janet blew out a sigh and leaned forward, resting her elbows on her knees. "Listen, I just spoke to someone at the bar last night—"

"Are you investigating this crime?" Rivera's

voice rose up a notch and he leaned in so their noses were just inches apart. "It's not your place, and, Janet, it's not safe, either! O'Dell would want me to say this—and you need to hear it. You're just a local business owner, and you need to remember that. You don't want to get in the middle of a domestic situation here, especially when there are kids involved!"

"I'm not trying to get in the middle of things, people keep putting me there! There's a difference!"

"Walk away. There's no place for you in this case. None. And I'll tell O'Dell if you can't keep some distance. He won't be happy."

Janet feigned interest in a tear in her jeans, but only so she didn't have to look Rivera in the eye. She didn't think she could keep her emotions in check for much longer.

Rivera's phones rang again, and this time he picked up the landline. "Rivera." He stared over Janet's head while he listened to whoever was on the other end, but then his eyes zeroed in on Janet with an unflinching focus that made the walls of her chest squeeze in uncomfortably. "It says what?" During the next pause, his jaw tightened, and the stare became a glare. "I'll be there in ten." He hung up the receiver and leaned back in his chair.

"Homicide call-out." He made no attempt to move.

Why was he looking at her like that? Like she was hiding something. "Who?"

"*Why* is the question I'm asking. My responding officer says he found your business card on the vic. You got anything to say about Hayley Vourhaus?"

Janet sucked in a gasp. "Hayley is dead?"

"How do you know her, and why does she have your card?"

"I—I just met her yesterday. She wanted to tell me . . ." She bit her lip. Rivera's expression told her he was one facial tic away from grabbing handcuffs and throwing her behind bars. She didn't trust him any more than she trusted Dave the drug-dealing dishwasher. "I need to go."

"Yeah, me too. I need to see about a dead woman."

Janet gulped but stood and followed Rivera out of the office.

"Don't forget, Janet. Stay out of this. I'm calling O'Dell. He'll be in touch. Soon." Rivera hopped into his unmarked car. His tires squealed as he left the parking lot, but before he disappeared, she climbed into her own car and eased out of the lot after him. A woman who'd just come to the bar to confess her crimes was dead. Janet had to know how it happened, where it happened, and when.

Keeping Rivera in her sights, she tapped Dave's number on her recent call list. With Hayley dead, Dave was either a suspect in the murder or the next potential victim. Her stomach clenched when the call went to voicemail. Which was it?

She dropped the phone down onto the seat and gripped the steering wheel tighter. First Liv, now Hayley. Who would be next? She was suddenly glad that Nell was still behind bars. Jail seemed a very safe place to be just then.

CHAPTER TWENTY-NINE

Janet followed Rivera all the way to the crime scene but stopped two blocks away and watched him brake hard at the police caution tape. She assessed the low-rent neighborhood from behind the wheel. Paint peeled off the sides of the clapboard houses, whose porches leaned precariously; it looked like there hadn't been a level building in the area for decades.

A growing crowd kept watch over the crime scene techs as they marked and bagged evidence. Rivera ducked under the caution tape and headed straight for a cluster of cops gathered on a porch. A lumpy black tarp covered a section of sidewalk between the house and street.

Janet climbed out of the car and edged into the

middle of a group of strangers, shivering slightly at the cool fall wind. When Rivera scanned the crowd, she was glad for once that her five-foot-six frame was easy to hide. She breathed out a sigh when his gaze slid past, and the man next to her chuckled.

"You on the lam, little girl?"

She grinned. "Hard to feel innocent when you're surrounded by cops."

"Preach, sister. Preach." He tucked a small hand-rolled cigarette behind his ear and swayed from side to side. His neck stretched out elegantly as he tried to see beyond the police tape before he whistled low between his teeth. "Hayley got herself into quite a mess, now. Quite a mess."

"What happened?"

The stranger was careworn, with baggy clothes and a persistent menthol smell that wafted from him as he moved. He rubbed his bald head. "No idea. I just heard it was Hayley. Shame. We all thought she was gonna make it. Just goes to show you never do know. These halfway houses—shoot. You just never know."

"Halfway house . . ." There must have been dozens in the city, but Janet squinted at the address, then pulled Nell's jail paperwork out of her purse. The arrest address on the booking sheet jumped off the page. This was where Nell had been just hours earlier, visiting Liv's old high school friend Skylar.

It was too late in the game for coincidence. She looked at the stranger with the cigarette. "Do you know someone named Skylar?"

He looked down at her with a grin. "No wonder you ain't feeling innocent! If you know Skylar, chances are you done something wrong." He whistled again and turned back to the crime scene.

"So you know her?"

"I know *of* her," he corrected with a shrug. "I know she's probably on her way back to jail now."

"Why?"

"She was Hayley's roommate. With a dead body, probie gonna do a drug test on her right now, and it ain't gonna come back good, based on how she been looking lately."

"Her probation officer?"

Her new friend nodded. "Either that or one of the cops'll just skip ahead and take her downtown themselves." He tore his eyes away from the crime scene to properly assess her. "Who are you anyway?"

"I'm—I'm nobody. I just met Hayley last night and then heard the news this morning—"

"Uh-oh, scram, girl. Cops are heading this way.

I'm out. Good luck."

She looked up and sure enough, Rivera was cutting through the crowd like scissors through paper. The strangers around her melted away.

"You." Rivera pointed at the far side of the street, to the sidewalk opposite the body. As she walked, he asked, "What's going on?"

"I don't know—"

"The victim had your business card in her hand! A gunshot wound in her chest, your business card in her hand, and then you follow me across town to get to the crime scene. Care to explain?" Rivera's voice was controlled and even, but a steely glint in his eye made her feel queasy. "What's your connection with the vic?"

"Is O'Dell here?" she hedged, wondering if she could tell her story to a friendlier ear.

Rivera frowned. "I just spoke to him—he's at home, trying to suck down enough sports drink to feel human again." He shook himself and refocused on Janet. "Talk to me, Janet. Your choice—here, or downtown."

She felt her lips purse but looked over Rivera's shoulder at the body and said, "She came in last night. She must have taken my card from the holder on the bar—what do I know?" She avoided Rivera's eyes.

"Did she get a drink?" The question was casual, but Janet knew the game: try and trap her in a lie.

"Ummm . . ." She kept her gaze forward. Would Rivera believe her?

"Carson!" he barked, and a patrol officer hurried over. "Put her in my car."

"Rivera!" Janet huffed, but he was already walking away, and the patrol officer grabbed her arms. "Cuffs?" he called. Rivera nodded and she felt the slap of cool, unforgiving metal wrapping around her wrists.

"Goddamn it, Rivera!" she yelled.

Carson jolted her and when she gasped at the shock of pain that radiated up her forearm to her shoulder socket, Rivera yelled over his shoulder, "Careful, Carson. Gently."

"Sorry, ma'am, please step this way."

Mutinous rage roared up her throat as the cop led her to Rivera's car. First of all, *ma'am*? She wasn't fifty! He opened the door and tucked her into the backseat of the unmarked car, making sure she was inside before slamming the door and standing guard by the window.

She fumed in the seat, seeing red for what felt like hours. Eventually, though, she calmed down enough to focus on the yellow evidence markers, the blue crime scene tech uniforms, and even the black of the tarp covering Hayley's body. From her new seat, she had an excellent view of the crime scene.

The coroner's office arrived and moved the body onto a stretcher, then wheeled it right past Janet's window. Perfectly painted nails poked out from under the tarp and Janet looked away, not wanting to see anything else.

As the stretcher passed by, Rivera marched toward her, another woman walking in lockstep with him, her hands behind her back. When they reached the car, he opened the back door.

"Watch your head, Skylar. Just a few more minutes and we'll head downtown." Rivera winked at Janet before he slammed the door, locking her into the back of a cop car with Liv's old high school friend, and, apparently, the roommate of the murdered woman.

She stared at Skylar and thought again of that "before" picture. Skylar's hair was no longer greasy, but dark circles under her eyes stood out starkly on her pale, drawn face.

The other woman stared down at her knees.

"Skylar, I—I'm Janet. We met at my bar a few weeks ago? At Liv's . . . at her memorial gathering?"

Skylar blinked and slowly raised her eyes to

Janet's. "I remember you. You're friends with Nell?"

Janet nodded. "What happened?"

"Is she okay? She got arrested here overnight. It must have been some weird misunderstanding, the cop said she stole from his car, but that just can't be—"

"You saw her get arrested?"

Skylar nodded.

"Why was she here?"

"Just checking in on me. I think with Liv gone she—she wants someone to take care of."

"Did she meet Hayley last night?"

"You some kind of cop?"

Janet felt one side of her mouth tip up as she held up her hands. "Cuffed in the back of a cop car? No, not a cop. Just someone the police don't trust, apparently."

Skylar snorted. "Join the club." Her fingers fidgeted, and she lowered her face to her shoulder to wipe at her cheek. "Damn handcuffs. At least yours are in front."

Janet shot her a sidelong look. "You clean?"

"Going on eight hours." She laughed bitterly and slumped against the door. "But I guess it's going to happen now, ain't it?"

Janet felt a flicker of unease and glanced out

the window, locking eyes almost immediately with Rivera, who was staring at her from the porch. She shrugged but his eyes never left hers. She squared her shoulders and turned back to Skylar. "Did you talk to the police?"

"I ain't talking to no one. I'm not some kind of narc!"

Skylar turned farther away from her and Janet pressed her lips together, then took a deep, calming breath. "You can talk to me. I'm not a cop. I'm just a friend of Nell's, trying to make sure her grandkids are taken care of. Skylar?" She waited until the other woman faced her, then decided she had nothing to lose by asking some leading questions. "I spoke to Hayley last night. She came into the bar—my bar—to tell me what happened. With Liv's husband." Skylar flinched, and the reaction bolstered Janet. Some color appeared on the other woman's cheeks, and she cast her eyes down at her feet again. "What do you know, Skylar? What do you know about what happened to Liv's husband? I think it might have to do with Hayley's death."

Skylar's eyelids pressed together and her head dropped back against the seat. She breathed out her nose and hummed something tuneless. The other woman knew something but was done talking.

CHAPTER THIRTY

"Did she say anything?" Rivera unlocked the hand-cuffs from Janet's wrists, and she rubbed her skin gently, then shook out her hands.

When she looked up, the cop was staring at her. "That wasn't cool, man. That girl is shell-shocked. And about to implode. Why'd you put her in the car with me?"

"She wouldn't talk to us. I thought she might talk to you."

"She did. She complained that she was feeling itchy and having her hands behind her back was killing her."

"She'll thank me next week. If her hands were in front, she'd be bleeding from a thousand scratch marks by now."

"Is she under arrest?"

"Janet, she's in the back of my car in handcuffs. What do you think?"

"I think that I was in the back of your car in handcuffs just a moment ago, so I'm actually thoroughly confused."

He smirked but remained otherwise silent.

"She's going to sober up in jail? That sounds fun for everyone." Janet looked back through the window at Skylar, who was now hunched over, her eyes closed, her body vibrating with an almost visible reaction to not getting her regular dose of heroin.

"You got anything to say? Anything that might help with this investigation?"

"Well . . ."

Rivera unconsciously flipped the single strand of the handcuff through the double strand with a metallic *ziiiing*.

Janet swallowed hard. Was he preparing to arrest her? She bit her lip and his face tightened almost imperceptibly. She didn't trust him at all. "Are we done here?"

"Yes. Don't say anything yet, but we're going to bring Eric in for questioning. This thing with the insurance isn't adding up. Looks like Liv didn't take the policy out on herself."

She paused halfway under the crime scene tape when her breath caught. When she stood tall she said, "How do you know?"

"The signature on the forms—it's not hers."

"But why bring him in now?"

"You questioning how I'm running this investigation?" His chest puffed out, and he flipped the handcuff again. *Ziiing.*

She turned away from him and dialed O'Dell's number as she walked down the sidewalk. She might not have wanted to tell Rivera everything she knew, but she was more than ready to let a trusted ally like O'Dell take her information and run with it. The call went straight to voicemail, and she left a message asking him to call her back.

Before she stepped off the curb, a flash of color caught her eye across the street. It was her friend from earlier, the one with the hand-rolled cigarette. She ducked across the street and stepped onto his porch.

"Now I don't know what to make of you," the careworn man said. "You looked guilty as hell when that cop came over, and I thought you were done for in the back of that unmarked car—handcuffs and everything! But then you over there walking 'round the crime scene like you at home. Which is it, little girl? You guilty or a cop? Or both?"

"I'm not a cop. I'm . . . training to be a private investigator." She knew the words were true as soon as they came out of her mouth.

"No shit?"

"No shit," she confirmed. "And today I'm looking into Hayley's death."

"I already told the cops that I don't know what happened, so you can just move on down the row, okay?"

"I'm not looking into what happened last night." He raised his eyebrows and she continued. "I'm interested in what happened all month, all year. How long have you lived here?"

"Always." He watched her for a long moment, then motioned that she should take the navy blue camp chair across from him. When Janet was settled he leaned back and said, "This block used to be nicer, you know? My grandmama raised me here, and when she passed, the house went to me. I try to keep it up, but it's hard, you know? Everything falling apart around me."

"Was that always a halfway house?"

He snorted. "Nah. Just in the last couple of years. Most of the women are nice. Really trying to make it, you know? But like I said, you just know by looking at some that it's just a quick pit stop before they head back to jail."

"I'm surprised you knew so many of them."

"Well, they here on my block, I'm gonna get to know them. My grandma always said people will treat you right if you treat them right." At Janet's expression he added, "I figure if they know me, they might rob someone else, you know? Skip my house and do the neighbor's."

She snorted. "What about Skylar?"

His lips mashed together and he shook his head. "Trouble. She didn't even look clean when she got here."

"And when was that, anyway?" Janet asked, wishing she had a notebook.

"Not long. Just a month? Maybe less?"

Janet sighed. Sounded like a dead end.

"Now, Hayley, like I said, I thought she'd make it. But you know, you try not to let anything about these residents surprise you, because you just never know."

"Yeah?"

"Yeah. Most of them try to stay under the radar. Then sometimes you got the opposite, the alpha females who act like they queen of the street. This one lady, she was here not long ago; she tried to ooze charm and sophistication, but I kinda thought she might snap your neck if you didn't keep an eye on her."

"Who was that?"

"Can't remember her name exactly. Some kind of bug. Not one of those gross ones, either, something cutesy like Ladybug, but that wasn't it, either." He scratched his jaw, then shook his head. "Anyway, never was so glad to see the back of someone as the day she left."

"And where did she go?"

"My money says she'll be back behind bars before the year's up, but I heard she was working on a new career. New job. New beginning, you know?"

"Sounds like it was a good time to make a change."

"You know what, you're right. In the end, maybe she was lucky; sometimes it's time to make a change but you don't feel like you can—don't have time, don't have the will, don't have the means. But I bet she had nothing to lose, no reason not to start over. Huh."

Janet thanked him and stepped off the porch just as an alarm beeped on her phone. The bonds office didn't open for another hour, so she looked down at the screen, confused.

PI Test. 30 minutes.

New beginnings? Her gaze hardened when she looked up and found Rivera glaring her way. She was all about them. O'Dell wouldn't answer his phone, so she decided to reprioritize her day. And she had half an hour to make it happen.

CHAPTER THIRTY-ONE

When she walked into the office building downtown, she followed the signs to the PI testing room and took a seat in the sparsely decorated space with just a minute to spare, earning her a dark look from the exam proctor.

Only one other person was ready for a life of glory as a private eye. A ragged brown hoodie obscured his face, but he grunted in acknowledgment when the test giver placed a stack of papers in front of him.

When she dropped the exam in front of Janet she stepped back and raised her voice as if addressing a room full of people. "My name is Elaine Simmons. I will be giving the exam that you must pass in order to receive a PI license in the state of

Tennessee. I am an administrative assistant"—she glared at Janet and her cohort in turn—"so do not argue with me over the fairness of the questions. I have no say whatsoever in how this exam is made!" When neither test taker spoke, her face softened and she said, "You have thirty minutes to take the exam. Notes are not allowed, nor are Internet searches on phones or computers. You may begin." She clicked a stopwatch and moved to a table at the front of the room.

Janet found a pencil buried in the depths of her bag and got to work.

The questions were taken directly from the two books she'd read, many of them from the first line or two of the main chapters. Janet looked up at the halfway point of her exam. The other would-be PI chewed the end of his pencil, staring forlornly up at the clock on the wall. Elaine scrolled restlessly through Facebook on her laptop, her eyes darting between the computer and her two charges every few minutes.

With fifteen minutes to go, Janet held the completed exam out to Elaine.

"The minute this test gets in my hand, your answers are considered final," the woman said, not taking Janet's exam. "There's no going back."

Janet nodded and laid the papers in front of

Elaine. As she headed out the door to the lobby, she couldn't help but agree. There was no going back.

———

Janet tried O'Dell's cell phone again with no luck. Her back ached from the uncomfortable plastic chair in the lobby. At the end of the half hour, the other PI candidate and the proctor walked out of the exam room.

Elaine took one look at Janet. "No. No, I just can't do anything about it, I'm afraid. I told you that once you handed in your forms, your answers are considered—"

"Yeah," Janet interrupted. "I just wondered when you grade the tests, and when we find out if we passed."

"Oh." The woman looked at Janet as if she didn't believe her. "Well. I usually grade them right away and then email the results to the county admin and—well, and you."

Not wanting to go home, Janet sidled up next to Elaine. "Can I just wait here in the lobby?" Elaine sucked in her cheeks but didn't answer. "How about this. If it's bad news, just email me. If

I passed, come on out and let me know." She looked at Elaine with a question in her eyes.

The other woman wrinkled her nose. "Well . . . I guess that would be okay . . ." She looked at the door again as if it were an escape hatch, then glanced at the man in the hoodie. "Sir—did you want to . . . ?"

The man wearing a hoodie grunted out a no, then climbed into a waiting elevator car.

"He was a little more uncertain about the test," she said, almost to herself.

Janet cleared her throat. "I'll wait right here, for the next"—she looked at her watch—"twenty minutes. If I haven't heard from you, I'll just head home."

Elaine shrugged and took the papers through a locked door.

Janet took out her phone and held in a sigh when she saw the screen was blank. No missed calls. Her stomach clenched, and she shoved the phone back into her purse. She'd been so focused on passing on the new information to O'Dell, she'd been able to ignore her fight with Jason, but now, in the sparse, quiet lobby, their fight came roaring back. She owed Jason an apology. But could she change her ways? Include him in her decisions? Or was she just like William? Feeling justified in making the right choice for her, no matter what it meant for Jason?

"No," Janet answered herself, then smiled sheepishly when a woman three seats over got up and moved to another row.

Janet stared dejectedly at the wall opposite, but not for long. Elaine was back in the lobby but she wasn't alone.

Gary Donaldson smacked a roll of paper against his opposite hand. "You passed, but that doesn't make you a PI, you know."

"Thank you, Elaine," Janet said, ignoring Donaldson completely. "It was so nice of you to fast-track the results for me."

"Janet, it was my pleasure." Elaine smiled back so broadly that Janet suspected she wasn't a fan of Donaldson either. The admin took the papers from Donaldson and handed them over. "You got one hundred percent correct! First one to do that in years, right, Gary?"

Donaldson grunted. "It's just the first step, though. Now you have to apprentice with an actual private investigator."

Janet nodded. "Yes, I've got some appointments set up already, thank you."

Gary sneered but couldn't seem to think of anything to say. He turned on his heel and marched back into the office space.

"I didn't know you knew Gary." Elaine tilted her head to the side as she took in the color rising in Janet's face.

"I don't, really," Janet replied. "He just—he's the one who inspired me to take the test."

Elaine crossed her arms and continued to stare. "He's not been the same since he and his wife divorced."

"What do you mean?"

"He—" She hesitated. "He's perfectly *polite*. But you kind of get the feeling he's not, you know?"

"He's rude?"

"No . . ." Her eyes narrowed. "Do you really have a firm to apprentice with?" she said, seeming to change subjects.

"Not yet," Janet admitted. "But I'll find one."

Elaine looked down at her hands and shuffled the papers she was holding until they were perfectly aligned. "Just stay away from Quizz Bexley," she finally said, then added with a small smile, "Apprenticing with Quizz would really piss Donaldson off. Good luck."

Janet watched her walk away. What was Elaine trying to tell her? She glanced down at her bag, resting on the floor near the chair. After digging out her phone, she found Bexley's number online. Someone answered on the first ring.

"I'd like to make an appointment with Quizz Bexley. Tell him it's about Gary Donaldson's wife."

Without a pause, the woman said, "She can see you in thirty minutes."

CHAPTER THIRTY-TWO

Quizz Bexley's office was small and exploding with *stuff*. Overflowing boxes were stacked everywhere, even under the chair the private eye offered to Janet. Towers of loose papers and file folders appeared on the verge of cascading off of tables and desks with any potential breeze. The lamp to Janet's right perched on a stack of legal notebooks the color of lemon juice.

"What do you know about Renee Donaldson?" Quizz Bexley was short, slight, and pale, with a shock of purple hair that looked like the end of a Q-tip. She wore black clothes and purple glasses.

"Not much, actually," Janet admitted. "I really wanted to know what you know about her husband." Quizz stared at her, nonplussed. Janet's gaze didn't waver and she added, "Seems like it must be a tough gig, being married to that guy."

Quizz's eyes narrowed. "I wouldn't know."

A silent standoff ensued, and Janet finally leaned forward, resting her elbows on her knees. "Listen, I just passed my PI test, and the moderator suggested I call you."

"Why?"

"I'm not really sure." When Quizz stared at her, Janet thought back to her interaction with Elaine. "She noticed Donaldson being . . . well, kind of a jerk, and she offered up your name."

"What'd you do to Donaldson?"

"No idea," Janet answered. "How about you?"

Quizz grinned and leaned back in her chair, crossing her arms behind her head. "I turned down his business a couple of years ago. Domestics can get hairy real quick, and I didn't like the feel of the guy."

"How so?"

"He came in with this big song and dance about how he thought his wife was cheating on him. These people, they think I'm just dying for their money. They're wrong," she said when Janet raised her eyebrows. "I'm not going to deliver up a woman to a violent guy—not that Gary Donaldson is violent." She raised her hands, palms out. "I don't know that. But you've gotta be careful, okay?"

Janet pushed herself back so she, too, leaned against her chair. "So what happened?"

"Turns out he and his wife were legally separated. She was dating someone. I backed out of it as soon as I saw the paperwork. Not my business."

"Who was she dating?"

"Huh?"

"Gary Donaldson's wife. Who was she dating?"

"Some cop. Guy named O'Dell."

Janet blinked with her new awareness and scrambled for a question to ask to cover her shock. "So you . . . you pick and choose which cases you'll get involved in?"

"Absolutely . . ." Quizz started to wax philosophic about which cases to take and which to pass on, but Janet couldn't hear anything except a buzz slowly building in her brain behind her right temple. O'Dell had dated Donaldson's wife when the couple was separated, and Donaldson clearly wasn't over the sting.

Was he taking his frustration out on Janet to get back at O'Dell? It seemed a stretch at the very least, but then again, O'Dell had made it clear he liked her. Was it so difficult to imagine others downtown knowing—the news slipping around the building to any interested ears? Donaldson deciding to exact his revenge on O'Dell by coming down hard on Janet?

Donaldson wasn't interested in *her*. He wanted to get back at O'Dell, through her. Was there even an anonymous complaint, or just a Donaldson complaint?

A slow grin spread across her face. O'Dell owed her. He'd have to sign off on her PI application now; she'd see to it.

"What are you smiling about?" Quizz snapped.

Janet blinked and refocused on the woman in front of her. "I'm in."

"You're in what?"

"I'm in for this apprenticeship. Just a few questions."

"Why does it seem like you're interviewing me instead of the other way around?" Quizz squinted and grabbed the arms of her chair for support.

Janet motioned to the piles of paper scattered around the office. "Looks to me like you need the help. And free help? You just hit the lottery, lady."

Quizz snorted. "True. You passed step one in the training program. Be observant."

"No offense—" Janet started.

"This'll be good."

"But what can you do as a PI that I can't do as a regular, curious person?"

"No doubt the Internet has changed the life of the private detective. I used to make half my earnings on easy background checks; now anyone can do them from the privacy of their own home. But it all takes time. And that's something a lot of people don't have these days—or at least they can't see giving up their Netflix time for something else. So they still pay up and I do the work."

"Mostly online?"

Quizz nodded. "Sure, but there's still some real-world work. Sometimes the computer only takes you so far. Then you gotta pick up the phone, go to an office."

"Huh." Sounded like just being a regular person and having someone pay you for it.

"I know. My sister is disappointed with the reality, too. When you get boots on the ground, though, you'll get much more information than the cops ever will. Certain neighborhoods, nobody's gonna talk to the police. But they don't mind talking to me. You just gotta be discreet."

Based on Janet's very limited time at the crime scene that morning, she knew Quizz's words to be true. The neighbor had told *her* about Hayley and the halfway house, not Rivera. Not the patrol officers on the scene, not the other detectives.

"All right. Let's do this." Janet checked her phone but the screen was blank.

"It's gonna cost you."

Janet's head snapped up. "Cost me? What—like money?"

"Time." The PI had an intensity about her that was exhausting. "As you can see, I'm backed up—way up. I need to know I can count on you for the duration of the apprenticeship. That I—what?" Her lips pushed out and she inhaled a long breath.

"It's just that I already have a case I want to work on."

"Why am I not surprised?" Quizz ran a hand through her hair. "Go on. Tell me about it."

"It's a murder investigation—actually, I think now a double murder investigation, and—"

"I'm going to stop you right there. That's definitely level-two apprenticeship. I was thinking I'd start you on an identity theft case that I just can't get to—"

"After the murder case, I'd be happy to take that one on." The two women stared at each other. Quizz's lips tilted up after a moment.

"I *think* I'm going to like you. Someday."

Janet grinned again. "So you'll help me?"

"Oh, *you* need help?" She tried to smother a laugh, but it chortled out, then she grabbed her belly and doubled over with a guffaw. When she sat back up she wiped a tear from her eye. "I think you just managed to hire me without a retainer and with no hope of payment for me. I guess that means you passed step two: convince and connive your way to success." Quizz locked her fingers behind her head and laughed again.

"How many steps are there?" Janet's forehead wrinkled and she wondered what exactly she was signing up for, apprenticing under this woman.

"I'll tell you when you need to know. Now, tell me about these murders."

CHAPTER THIRTY-THREE

The silence stretched so long that Janet wondered if one of Quizz's many skills was sleeping with her eyes open. She cleared her throat and Quizz grunted.

"I'm processing. Give me a minute."

It had taken Janet more than half an hour to explain everything about Liv and Hayley's deaths to the private eye, including a few trail-offs and more than once having to go back and fill in missing information. Quizz hadn't taken a single note but had fixed Janet with a nearly unblinking stare for the entire recital.

The clock behind the PI ticked, and no matter how many times she checked her phone, no new emails or text messages popped up, leaving Janet only one option: to stare at Quizz.

The other woman finally rubbed her temples. "We'll start with a background check on Dave."

"On Dave? The dishwasher?"

"The drug dealer, yes. He has a connection to both victims. Let's see if anything—or anyone— else connects them." Quizz tapped some words into her computer. "Do you know his last name?"

Janet shook her head.

"No worries." She picked up the phone on her desk and then looked at her computer screen and dialed a number. In a raspy, deeper-than-normal voice she said, "Looking for Dave. He in?" A pause while young Poppy, no doubt, gave a long, convoluted answer to a simple question. Quizz rubbed her temple again and said, "What's his last name?" Pause. The cadence of the voice on the other end of the line picked up and Quizz's eyes widened. Without another word, she slowly moved the phone away from her face and hung up; Poppy's high, chatty voice only cut off when the receiver was back in the cradle on the desk. "Jesus."

Janet smirked. "She's a teenager."

"Yeah, I got that loud and clear." She tapped some keys on the keyboard and hit enter. "Dave

Martelle apparently didn't show up for his shift this morning, and the teenager's father made her wash some of the dishes in his place."

"She wasn't a fan?"

"Mad as a hornet about the whole thing. Asked if I knew where he was, and could I go get him and bring him to Plaza Eats to do his job."

"Go get him? From where?"

"His apartment at River Crossing." She tilted her head up to look at her computer screen through her glasses. "It's nowhere near the river, by the way. Talking to her was better than reading a search results page."

"Are we going to go get him?" Janet asked, glancing at the wall clock again.

"No! But now we have his last name. I'm going to cross-search him with the other players. We'll see what comes up."

"Which other players?" Janet threw herself back against the chair. "I can't believe being a PI is all about using Google."

"Tut-tut. I'm using LexisNexis. Ever heard of it?"

Janet shook her head.

"Insanely expensive but so worth it for research. I can cross-search your buddy Dave with everyone else and a nice list of information will come up that may or may not be helpful." She sat up and moved her glasses up her face so she could properly look at the screen without hurting her neck. "I got a few hits here, let me see . . ."

Tired of waiting on Quizz to reveal anything, Janet whipped out her phone to do her own search on Dave Martelle. Over twenty thousand results, and almost all of the ones on the first page were about a baseball player. "Ugh." She bit her lip and tapped the arrow going to the second page. More baseball news.

"Bankruptcy filing about six years ago. Divorce granted the next year. Looks like some outstanding student loans and a lien filed against his car. Whew. This guy's a real winner."

Janet scrolled up and down her screen, unable to find any of Quizz's information. When she looked up, the other woman was grinning.

"I'm telling you, LexisNexis is the way to go. I pay hundreds a month for access, but it's so worth it in saved time."

Janet dropped her phone back into her bag. "Who'd he divorce?"

"Nnnn . . ." The sound issued from between Quizz's lips while she read the screen. "Woman by the name of June Martelle—née Hughes."

Janet's head went fuzzy with the information.

"What? Dishwasher Dave used to be married to a woman named *June Hughes*? Could this be a relative of Summer's?"

"Already checking." Quizz tapped more keys and a sound hummed out from between her tongue and teeth while she scrolled through the search results. "Not a relative. Summer herself. June Martelle filed for a DBA permit—'doing business as'—in Knox County about eight months ago when she opened a counseling business. Summer Hughes Family Counseling is the business name."

"That's—that's Liv's friend. The one who's been so helpful since she died." Her head spun as she tried to make sense of Quizz's words. "That can't be right—she's . . . she's so . . . refined, and professional. There must be another Summer Hughes. The Summer we're talking about would have never been married to *Dave!*"

"Another Summer Hughes who used to be named June Martelle?" Quizz looked at Janet over the rims of her glasses. "There are no coincidences in life. Only unknowns. And now we know something about Summer that we didn't a few minutes ago."

"But she told me that she, Eric, and Liv all went to college together."

"They were friends in college?" Quizz asked.

Janet started to nod but then stopped. "No. She didn't say that." She blew out a sigh. "She actually said they all went to Community, but they only recently made the connection." She jumped up from her chair to pace the small office. "I'd been assuming they were old college friends, but she made it clear that none of them graduated from Community."

"So she got her degree somewhere else." Quizz peered at Janet, nonplussed. "Let's see if she has any other aliases." *Clackety clack clack.* Quizz's fingers flew across the keyboard now. "Oh-ho! June Martelle, a.k.a. June Bug Martelle." More tapping, then, "And she did five years with the state for heroin use and possession."

"June Bug," Janet repeated slowly, thinking of her conversation with the neighbor outside the halfway house. Ladybug . . . or June Bug.

The women locked eyes over the stacks of files and legal folders.

Quizz frowned. "Quite a coincidence. And her ex still deals heroin?"

Janet nodded.

"And Liv died from a heroin overdose?"

"Yes, and Dave sent Hayley—a former customer—over to my bar to tell me about a scheme involving Liv's husband . . . and now Hayley's dead."

"Is Dave a good guy or not?" Quizz got to the heart of the matter. Janet shrugged. "What's your gut tell you?" Quizz pressed.

"That he's a good, bad guy. Does that make sense?"

Quizz tapped her chin. "Hayley was murdered this morning. Now Dave's a no-show at his job today. Are we worried?"

"No," Janet answered quickly, but prickles of unease marched up the back of her neck and settled at the base of her skull. Quizz raised her eyebrows, and Janet looked down to find her knuckles tightly balled, the skin stretched so tight it was white. "Okay, yes. I guess I'm worried."

"Then let's go." Quizz stood and grabbed a light jacket off the back of her chair. She swiped a key ring off the desk and headed toward the door. "You follow me out to his place."

Quizz opened the door and looked back at Janet, who was still sitting in the chair. "You coming?"

She jumped. "Yes. Sorry—it's just a lot to take in."

"Sounds like there's more coming, so make room."

Janet pushed up from the chair and followed Quizz out of the office, digging around in her bag for her phone.

Liv was dead from tainted heroin that she may or may not have injected herself with. A woman who knew something about an effort by a third party to break up Liv's marriage with Eric was now dead, and Dave, a person connected with everyone, hadn't shown up for his shift at work. Was she worried about Dave? Yes. But she was also worried about the other people connected to Liv.

Nell was in jail—that seemed a good, safe place for her just then. Eric? She wasn't sure about his role in anything yet, but she worried that if he was innocent, he might be targeted. And the kids—the kids were vulnerable. She tapped a name on her contact list as she walked out of Quizz's office.

Her dad answered on the second ring. "We're just leaving for the restaurant, are you already there?"

Brunch! She'd completely forgotten. "Dad, there's—well, there's kind of an emergency."

"What do you need, Janet?" Her father's gruff voice was both concerned and soothing.

"I—I need you, to check on a family for me. I —I'm worried about the kids."

After a short pause her dad said, "What's the address?"

Just like that. No questions, no grilling, just a dad willing to help out his daughter. A breath she didn't know she'd been holding whooshed out of her lungs and she slumped against the wall. "Something's going down in this murder case, Dad. Can you get to the kids, check on their dad? Just . . . stay with them until I can get to you."

"You'll meet us there?"

Us. Janet cringed. Kaylee! She'd forgotten about the other woman.

"Yes, but I have to check on something first. Be careful."

She tossed the phone back into her bag and hustled out to the parking lot behind Quizz, but her heart felt sluggish, like it couldn't push her suddenly-cold blood through her body. "You have the address?" she called.

Quizz was already behind the wheel, her window down. "Head north, away from the river." She watched Janet climb into her car, and when she'd rolled down her window Quizz shouted over the two engines. "He's probably fine. Most killers don't strike multiple locations in one night."

If the words were meant to comfort, they missed the mark. Janet's tires squealed as she peeled out of the lot after Quizz, and a horn blared as she turned onto the road with barely enough room.

Was Dave a good guy? They were about to find out.

CHAPTER THIRTY-FOUR

Quizz slowed her car and pointed at a small crowd gathered by a shabby, tattered play structure to the left of the dilapidated row houses.

Janet eased into the parking spot next to Quizz and the women walked toward the small group in time to hear someone say, "Dare you to touch him." They traded looks and sped up. Quizz held out an official-looking badge and said, "What's going on here?"

Four boys, no older than twelve, jumped and looked guiltily over their shoulders. "We didn't do it, ma'am."

Janet's nose wrinkled again at the term, but Quizz took it in stride. "Step aside, boys. Step aside." The boys parted down the middle, revealing a man lying in a heap, his feet resting awkwardly under the bottom of the slide.

Janet leaned over the body. The skin on his face and neck was tinged blue; his lips were dark purple. His eyes stared blankly to the sky. It was Dishwasher Dave.

Janet sucked in a sharp breath. "I guess he was a good guy."

Quizz's brow furrowed and she whipped out her phone and dialed 911. Janet's phone was out, too, but she dialed a different set of numbers.

"What?" O'Dell croaked into the phone. Janet hesitated, and he added, "I'm not hungover, if that's what you're thinking."

"No, I—" Uncharacteristically at a loss for words, Janet cleared her throat.

"Janet, what's wrong?"

"The, uh—" Her voice warbled, so she cleared her throat again. "Dishwasher Dave is dead."

"Whaddyamean?"

It came out as a single word, and she could feel him perking up by the second.

"Quizz and I—"

"Who's Quizz?"

"This PI I'm working with. Anyway, we got worried when Dave Martelle didn't show up at work at Plaza Eats—you remember, Liv's restaurant?"

"Yes, I remember."

"We came to talk to him at his apartment, and he's dead."

"Who's out there? Rivera?"

"No one yet, we just found him lying on the ground!" She craned her neck to see all of him and added, "Looks like a gunshot wound." A black stain bloomed out from a small opening in his chest.

"Jesus Christ."

"I know."

"Don't move. I'm calling Rivera, I'll be right there."

The underlying edge in his voice did the opposite of comfort her, but she and Quizz locked down the scene until the first police cruiser arrived. It was her old friend Happy Handcuffs, and she frowned back at him when he recognized her.

"Don't look at me like that. O'Dell and Rivera are already on their way."

His eyebrows shot up, but before he could say anything, Quizz said, "We'll wait for them by our cars. Thank you, officer."

Because more people were pouring out of the apartment complex to investigate, he was too busy controlling the crowd to stop them, but he didn't look happy as they walked away.

"You stay here to talk to the cops." Quizz jangled her keys. "I'm going to check on Eric and the kids."

"My dad should be there."

"But he doesn't know what's going on. Uninformed is the same thing as unsafe in a situation like this. I'll fill them in. What's the address?"

Janet recited it and swallowed hard.

Quizz patted her shoulder. "I'll call you when I get there."

The purple head disappeared into her car. Moments later, Quizz backed out of the lot and took off down the street. Janet's chest felt tight, and her head pounded. They said things like this happened in threes . . . Liv, Hayley, Dave—was this the end? Or was it about to start over again?

———

"So that's when you decided to check on Dave Martelle?" Rivera scribbled into his notebook, but his eyes never left Janet's face.

"Yes, we—well, I was worried about him."

"Why? Were you friends?"

"Friends? No." Janet started to laugh, the absurdity of the day wearing her defenses down. Rivera scowled and she forced the smile off her face. "I met him with O'Dell at Liv's restaurant. He . . . he seemed really down about her death, and I guess . . ." Janet stopped, not sure how to keep herself out of trouble. O'Dell drove up and she breathed out a sigh of relief—until she saw his expression as he climbed out of his car.

"Janet!" His roar echoed across the lot.

"Shit," she muttered, and Rivera moved in front of her. She peeked around his shoulder and said, "Feeling better?"

"Step aside, Rivera. I want to talk to her. Now."

"You'll have to wait. I'm in the middle of an interview. Cruise is cataloging everything found with the body. See what you can find out."

O'Dell pointed wordlessly at Janet, then at Rivera, then growled and threw his hands up before stalking off toward the body.

Janet let out a relieved breath and Rivera squinted after him. "He's worried about you, that's all."

"Well, I'm worried about him! Sheesh."

He asked a few more questions, but she dodged most of them, checking her phone screen with mounting worry.

"Something more important than this?" Rivera asked.

"It's just—" The phone buzzed in her hand and she looked down at the text from her father, then sagged against a nearby car.

Family fine. I'll stay with them for now.

"What?" Rivera cocked his head to the side.

"The kids. They're fine. Liv's kids are fine. It's fine."

"You seeing a connection here—between all of this?" He waved his hand in a circle. Before she could answer, O'Dell was back.

"Did you know about this?" He held up a silver compact in his blue-gloved hand, and Janet sucked her cheeks in. The letters L and A etched in the center of the circle identified it as Liv's. "You know the last person to have this? Eric! I released all Liv's possessions from her work locker that we didn't keep as evidence back to him. And now it's here? On a dead body? Like a calling card?"

Janet shook her head. "You think Eric did this? Then left his wife's compact on the body? O'Dell, you've got this all wrong—"

"You calling a BOLO?" Rivera asked, ignoring Janet.

O'Dell was already reaching for his radio. "Attention all units, be on the lookout for Eric Birch, white male, mid to late thirties. Suspect may be armed and dangerous. Arrest on sight, arrest on contact." He rattled off Eric's home address and his business name, glaring at Janet the whole time.

Janet stared at the ground while he repeated his message. She made a split-second decision not to set him straight. If Eric *wasn't* involved in the new murders, then he very well might be the next target. Maybe the best place for him right then was in police custody.

The cool metal slapping against her wrists was a shock. "What the—"

"Park her at my desk until I get there," O'Dell snarled. He pivoted and marched back to his unmarked car before she could articulate any words.

She stared after him, speechless, then turned to Rivera when he cleared his throat. "Am I under arrest?"

Rivera scratched his head. "No . . . not yet, anyway. Will you please accompany me downtown for questioning in the death of Dave Martelle?"

"No, thank you." She held her wrists out and raised her eyebrows.

Rivera frowned and crossed his arms. "Then, I guess you *are* under arrest—"

"Okay, fine," Janet exploded. "I'll come downtown. Don't add something to my record for kicks,

Rivera! Cheese and rice! What's O'Dell got on you, anyway?"

Rivera snickered. "'Cheese and rice'? Haven't heard that in years." He led her to his car and opened the back door. "O'Dell's got nothing on me. We're friends." He put a hand on top of her head and guided her down to the bench seat. "Just like you two are."

She scooted sideways until she was completely in the car and held her hands in front of her face, assessing the metal bracelets. "Friends? Not for long."

CHAPTER THIRTY-FIVE

For the first half hour that she was chained to O'Dell's desk, Janet sat up, alert and ready to discuss things rationally and calmly with her supposed friend.

Now, at half past two in the afternoon, she was sprawled uncomfortably back in the cushioned office chair, the fingers in her cuffed hand long since numb, her bladder uncomfortably full, and her patience incredibly thin. She'd been sitting at O'Dell's desk for going on three hours.

A commotion at the front of the detectives' section forced her upright, and she watched O'Dell walk in and deposit Eric in an interview room. Eric's wide eyes were blank, his expression empty. It wasn't panic, necessarily, more like a confusion so overwhelming his brain had decided to shut down completely.

When O'Dell reemerged and headed her way, Janet tilted her head back against the chair until she was staring up at the ceiling again. "Cheese and rice."

"You hungry?"

She refused to look at O'Dell, so she continued to stare at the exposed ductwork above. "No. Tired, uncomfortable, and irritated, but not hungry."

O'Dell pulled out his chair and unlocked her handcuffs before he sat down.

"Thank you." Janet rubbed her wrist, now looking over his head at the back wall.

"Your dad and his fiancée are with the kids, along with some woman named Quizz? I'll have to call Children's Services soon . . . but thought I'd talk to you first. Nell is in jail?"

Janet nodded but still refused to look O'Dell in the eye. He blew out a noisy sigh and rubbed his head. She lowered her gaze and took in his sweaty brow, pasty complexion, and bloodshot eyes.

"You look like shit."

"Gee, thanks," he snorted, but grabbed a sports drink from his desk and twisted off the top.

"And you've got this wrong. All wrong."

His shoulders tensed. "How so?"

She pursed her lips. "There was no calling card. Eric threw a bunch of Liv's things away at the restaurant; I don't know why, but he did. Dave took the compact out of the trash can. He showed it to me last night. Tucked it into his pocket like it was important. I think he really liked Liv and felt bad that she died."

"Felt bad, or felt guilty?"

"Okay, you're right. Guilty—but not because he killed her. I think he had an idea of who did, though." O'Dell's eyes narrowed, but before she could continue, before she could tell him all about Summer's actually being June Bug Martelle, Rivera walked in.

"You want me to start on him, or are you taking lead?"

Janet said, "Would you just wait a minute—"

O'Dell held up a rigid hand and glared at her. "Together," he said to Rivera. But before he walked away, he reached into his lower drawer and pulled out a box. He set it down gently on his desk, then glanced around the empty office and said in a quiet voice, "Whatever you do, don't look through this, Janet. Keep your prying eyes to yourself." He drilled her with a meaningful stare, then, with a smirk, he laid a set of blue latex gloves next to the box before he turned and met Rivera in the aisle. "Let's do this." The two men disappeared into the interview room without a backward glance.

Janet, however, couldn't stop looking all around the room. Her stomach clenched as she studied the box O'Dell had set out for her. Was she supposed to look inside or not? With one more sweep of the space, she stood and slid the plastic tub closer.

On regular masking tape, O'Dell's messy scrawl labeled it "Liv Birch Locker." She pried the lid off and peered inside at a jumble of makeup, papers, and notebooks. Warily, she snapped on the gloves and pawed through the evidence in a murder investigation.

She wondered how O'Dell had decided what to leave for Eric and what to keep.

She flipped through a small binder that was a piece of artwork in its own right. The fabric cover unzipped to reveal a long line of colorful gel pens, tucked into small elastic loops, and as she flipped through the planner in the front, it was clear Liv had taken great joy in scheduling her family's life. Brendon's activities were written in forest-green ink, Andrea's in deep purple, baby Bonnie's in neon pink, and Eric's in a shimmery gold. Liv's own schedule was outlined in dark blue. The planner was stuffed with old shopping lists, a few library checkout receipts, and to-do lists, and behind the planner, a spiral-bound notebook was clipped into the three-ring binder. Children's scrawls in bright blue crayon filled the front and back of a few pages. Gibberish, at first glance, but it pulled at Janet's memory. There was something familiar, something patterned about the way the letters filled the space. Not that the child couldn't spell, more that they'd deliberately put specific letters on the page in a certain order, with regular spaces and punctuation.

Flipping forward a few pages, Janet found the same code written in the sure, steady hand of an adult, with pen. It was part of the last entry in the planner. There was also a phone number and then, in a different color ink—and more hastily scrawled —were the words, "Bonnie knows everything."

Janet tapped the numbers into her device and a bored voice answered after two rings.

"Law offices of Thornton & Brown, how can I help you?"

She disconnected. A commercial featuring an ultra-serious voice talking over video of an unhappy couple came immediately to mind—in fact, the jingle would be in her head for days again:

"Need a divorce, don't stray from the course. Thornton & Brown Attorneys!"

She looked around to confirm she was alone and then took the notebook to a copy machine at the back of the room.

With the warm copies stuffed into her coat pocket and the original notebook back in the evidence box, she snapped on the lid and threw the gloves away.

She needed to find out if Liv's kids could break the code of their mom's final journal entry, but she had no car—hers was still at Dave's apartment building.

She opened O'Dell's top desk drawer and found his key ring, then walked to the edge of the office and pointed his key fob at the window. A beat-up blue Taurus winked at her when she clicked the unlock button, and she grinned and headed out the door.

CHAPTER THIRTY-SIX

"I'm headed over. Don't let anyone in but me." Janet braked hard at a light; she wasn't used to O'Dell's car, and the controls felt touchy. She eased off the brake and carefully engaged the gas pedal to turn right at the intersection.

"Quizz is here." Sampson lowered his voice. "She's a strange bird. Keeps walking from window to window, like she's expecting an invasion."

"Good."

"What does that mean?"

"Just—I'll explain when I get there."

Sampson hung up and Janet swerved as the door of a car parked on the side of the street was flung open. "Pay attention," she admonished herself. Crashing a car that was technically stolen wouldn't help anyone just then.

During the remainder of the drive she followed all the traffic laws, and at a particularly long red light, she noted how clean O'Dell kept the interior of his ride. A few gum wrappers had been shoved into an empty paper cup perched in the cup holder. The carpet was clear of dirt and leaves. Even the car manual and registration were kept neat and orderly inside the glove box.

When she finally pulled up at Liv and Eric's house, she made sure the papers she'd copied at the police department were in her pocket and headed up the front walk.

Janet shot a final glance at the street before heading in, then plastered on a smile and turned to face the room. "Brendon! Andrea!"

———

"You know how some people can speak pig latin really well?" Brendon looked at Janet, the expression on his eight-year-old, still-chubby cherubic face earnest, and she tried to nod but couldn't do it.

"Pig latin? No, I guess I've never heard anyone speak it *fluently*."

He leaned to the side and caught his older sister's eye. "Show her."

"Hat-way re-ay ou-yay alking-tay bout-ay?" Andrea said, as quickly as Janet could have said the words in English. The twelve-year-old grinned.

Janet's eyes went wide. "Are you kidding with that?"

"It was the same for me and Mom with the code." Brendon's chest puffed out. "She taught it to me when I was trying to plan a birthday surprise for my dad, but it was so cool, we spent all of last summer doing scavenger hunts around the house with it." He frowned and fell silent, then added in a quieter voice. "It was fun."

Janet gave both kids a moment to collect themselves. "So how does it work?" she asked gently, looking down at the paper. "It's not written in pig latin?" Surely she hadn't missed such an obvious pattern?

"Nah. It's way easier." He leaned forward and lowered his voice. "But it's a secret. Let me see it, and I'll read it to you."

"Um, I don't know if that's such a good idea." Janet scrutinized Liv's journal again. "What if it says something inappropriate?"

"Nah. No secrets in this house, believe me,"

Brendon said. Andrea nodded, and Janet handed the pages over to Brendon.

He studied it for several long moments, then looked up. "Excuse me, Mrs. Bexley? Can you take Bonnie to the kitchen, please? She's probably ready for a snack."

"'Nack?" their littlest sibling said, looking up from her puzzle with a smile. "'Nack!" She stood, clutching a worn and shabby stuffed animal, and wobbled into the other room. Quizz followed but shot a curious look back at Janet.

Sampson wandered closer and stood behind Kaylee, who was seated across from Janet.

Brendon recited slowly, "'Adultery is grounds for divorce, but in Tennessee must wait ninety days to file.'" He read the phone number for the law office that Janet had called earlier. Then he handed the first page over to Janet and read the line from the second page. "'Skylar says he was drugged. Don't trust Summer.'"

Brendon squinted at the final line, written in regular old English. "'Bonnie knows everything.'" He looked up. "What does that mean?" He passed the pages to Janet's outstretched hand.

Janet scrutinized the letters again and frowned. Now that she knew the message, the code became clear. Every other letter was bogus, put there to distract from the real word. In this case, "adultery" was written "ratdhuwlbtqevrry."

"Surprisingly clever." Sampson squeezed Kaylee's shoulder and smiled at Janet. Andrea reached for the paper, but Brendon smacked her hand out of the way.

"Not everyone here needs to know the code, okay?" Brendon's eyebrows rose and he grinned at his older sister.

She rolled her eyes. "Bren—you could just practice pig latin, and you'd be good at it. It's not like I'm not telling you how to do it!"

A short wrestling match between the two ensued, but Janet was too busy trying to order the events of the past several months.

Eric had confessed his affair to Liv. She had planned to file for divorce, and had started making plans to that end, but then at some point Skylar told her that Eric had been drugged. Skylar's name muddied the waters. Who'd actually drugged Eric? Hayley? Skylar? And on whose orders? Whatever Liv had heard, it was enough that she didn't trust Summer anymore. But why? Why would Summer want to force a breakup between them? She claimed to not even like Eric.

She read over the note again. How could little Bonnie have known about all of this? And just how much could an eighteen-month-old really retain?

Janet looked over at the little girl as she and Quizz walked back into the room. She had a cookie in her hand, along with drool and a smattering of crumbs trailing down her chin.

Janet turned back to the journal entry. It was dated just a day before Liv died.

One day after learning that Summer may have been trying to break up her marriage, Liv had died with drugs in her system, tumbling down the steps with a full laundry basket headed toward a broken washing machine.

Janet rubbed the back of her neck and looked up to find her father staring at her.

"What do you want to do, Janet?" he asked.

"Lock the doors! No—wait. We're leaving. Everyone, we're going to my house. Now." She whipped her phone out of her pocket and pressed a name on her contact list.

"Can you meet me at my place in twenty minutes? Bring the dummy."

"Not nice!" Bonnie looked up at Janet with wide, accusing eyes.

"You'll see," Janet said with a wink. "That's the only name for him."

The large group trooped out of the house just

as the sudden roar of an engine announced a new arrival. Summer waved as she slowed to park. Before her car came to a complete stop, though, Janet scowled and picked Bonnie up, then stood in front of the remaining two kids. Sampson, sensing the threat, stopped with a wide stance and held the kids back with his arms outstretched.

Though her heart rate quickened, Janet held Summer's gaze, her body as rigid as the sides of a keg.

The other woman's mouth pressed flat, and her eyes narrowed.

"Don't come any closer!" Janet called.

Summer's eye twitched, but she forced a smile onto her face and rolled down the window. "I brought a new book for Bonnie!" She put the car into park but didn't move to get out.

Janet frowned. "Stay right there. I'm calling the cops!"

Summer's eyes narrowed, her mouth twisted into a sneer, and she hit the gas; her car roared down the street, leaving behind the smell of burnt rubber and gasoline.

"Should I call 911?" Sampson asked, his phone out, his fingers hovering over the numbers.

Janet sighed. It was all out in the open. Dave's murder. Hayley's death. Summer's role in the entire series of events. The only missing link was whether Eric was involved, but just then, Janet didn't care. She only cared about keeping Summer away from Nell's family. Keeping Nell's grandchildren safe.

"No—the last thing we need is a beat officer getting involved." She pictured Happy Handcuffs showing up at a third incident with Janet in a single day, and knew it wouldn't end well for her. "I'll head downtown after I get you guys settled and let O'Dell know myself."

She shifted Bonnie over into her car seat—the child was nearly asleep, and even as Janet struggled with the seat belt, Bonnie blinked slower and slower until finally her eyes didn't open again. As she gently closed the door, an icicle of uncertainty rammed down her throat, making it difficult to swallow. Had she just upped the stakes? Was it enough for Summer to cut and run, or had Janet just pushed Summer to a new level of urgency? Because surely the other woman knew she was out of time. But what if she had no intention of abandoning her plan now?

CHAPTER THIRTY-SEVEN

An unexpected shriek split the air shortly after Janet opened the door for Mel. "What in God's name—"

"Bonnie, what's wrong?" Kaylee rushed over to the smallest child.

A tsk issued from Andrea, but the oldest sibling didn't look up from her perch on her chair, her nose buried in a book. Quizz and Janet locked eyes, but before Janet could offer up any solutions to quiet the noise, Mel knelt down by the little girl. When Bonnie's voice cut off in the middle of a wail, Andrea looked over the top of her book, her eyebrows raised.

"Mine?" Bonnie's lip trembled, but she swiped

her shirtsleeve past her nose and looked at what appeared to be a key chain in her hand.

"Yes, just for you!" Mel stood up with a smile and began rearranging the furniture in the main room.

Bonnie traced the pink metal outline of a cat's face with her short, stubby fingers. The cat's round eyes were sized for adult fingers to fit through, and the ears were just pointy enough to look dangerous in the right situation.

"It's not technically a weapon. It's fine." Mel pushed the couch to the back wall, then stood up and brushed her hands together. "And hey—better than listening to that scream, huh? Janet, if you lay those mats down, I'll move the dummy over here, and we can get started."

Mel had Andrea's full attention now, and Brendon's, too. "What are we doing?" He studied the naked torso of a man, perched high on a metal pole, and grinned. "Why is that thing here?"

"This is Bob, the self-defense dummy. Janet wants all of you to learn a few simple self-defense moves, and since that happens to be one of my specialties—"

"Self-defense? What about *offense*?" Janet squinted at her bouncer.

"This is not the right crowd for offense," Mel said with a frown. "Self-defense is where we start."

Mel pointed to the mat, and before Janet joined the kids, she pulled Sampson aside.

"Dad, I need another favor. Can you and Kaylee go rescue my car? I had to leave it at a crime scene . . . it's a long story," she added when his eyes lasered in on her face.

"There seem to be a lot of long stories from you today."

"I'm driving O'Dell's car now, but that won't last. Can you and Kaylee drop mine off downtown, then meet me back here?"

"No problem, kiddo. Just tell me where to go."

She gave him Dave Martelle's address. As she watched him and Kaylee drive away, a faint smile crossed her lips. He was still on her team.

"Janet? You joining us?"

She nodded and moved to the end of the line next to Brendon.

"The goal of everything you're about to learn is to get away and get to safety, so that's what we'll be working on. Say it with me: get away, get to safety."

The kids parroted the phrase back to Mel; Bonnie's small voice finished a few seconds after the others.

"We'll start with the arm chop. Kids, if

someone—now, not your nana or your dad"—Mel laughed, then, perhaps realizing both people were in police custody, she choked before recovering —"but anyone who shouldn't be is grabbing you, this is what you do." She demonstrated a swift upward swing of her arm. "That will break their hold where it's weakest, at their thumb and fingers. Now you try."

As the kids' arms swooped up and down several times, Mel secured a padded arm brace around her forearm with three Velcro straps.

"Brendon, if I grab you here, what do you do?"

Nell's middle grandchild tentatively moved his arm up, making contact with Mel's padded arm with a soft *thunk*.

"Don't hold back!" she challenged.

Brendon grinned self-consciously. "I don't want to hurt you!"

"You won't."

Brendon's eyes narrowed. "Okay. Grab me again!" When she reached out this time, he used both arms to swing up, breaking Mel's hold almost immediately.

"This is dumb," Andrea said. She sauntered over to the chair and picked up her book. But her face was red, her breathing choppy, and before

Janet could try to bring her back to the group, Mel shook her head slightly.

"Whenever you want to, jump back in, Andrea. Okay, Bonnie." She turned her attention to the smallest. "What are you going to do?"

As the little girl answered, Jason walked through the front door.

"What's—" He stepped back out of the house to check the address above the door, then tilted his head to the side as he assessed the scene. "What's going on?"

"Jason, you remember Nell's grandkids? They're going to be here for a little while."

"Here? Wh—" He broke off when he saw Janet's face and followed her into the kitchen when she excused herself from the exercises.

"What's going on?" he asked when they were alone.

"Let's see if I can sum it up . . . The kids' father is downtown, being questioned by police in two overnight homicides; Nell is in jail, accused of stealing a cop's wallet out of her car; and I think the kids are in danger, so I'm going to keep them with me until the police find and arrest Summer."

Jason managed to keep his face impassive. "So you took my advice and stayed out of it, that's good to see."

"Jason—"

"No, I get it. They needed you, that much is clear. How long do we have the kids for?"

A lump rose up in her throat and her eyes filled inexplicably. She swallowed hard and turned away. *We* . . . The single word held more meaning than an entire storybook. "Uh . . . well, I'm not sure. I'm hoping a bondsman can get Nell out with just ten percent of her five-thousand-dollar bail, but I— well, I still want them to stay with us. I don't trust Summer, and I want to make sure the kids are safe."

"Okay."

She turned to face him, and his lopsided grin widened when he saw her watery eyes. "We're going to be okay, Janet. You know that, right? Real couples have disagreements and fights. They just stick around to work through them because it's worth it."

She sniffed loudly and looked up at the ceiling.

"You're worth it. We're worth it. At least *I* think so . . ."

Her nose tingled but she forced herself to look at Jason. "I—"

"The auction was this morning." At Janet's blank look he elaborated. "The county real estate auction? My dad didn't get the restaurant."

Before Janet could hide her relief, Jason spoke again. "My mom bought it out from under him."

Janet's jaw dropped. "What? Does she have—I mean, she wants to run a restaurant?"

He chuckled. "No, I think she just doesn't want my dad to."

"Wow."

"And I've been thinking. I want you to feel secure, to know that you have options. And if that means you buy me out of the Spot, that's what we need to do. I never want you to feel trapped or stuck."

"Jason, I—" But her throat constricted again, and she had to look away.

"We'll call a lawyer as soon as this business"—he motioned toward the family room—"is settled and start the process. Because I love you, and I don't want you to feel like there are strings attached, you know?"

She couldn't speak, and when she finally looked over, Jason reached out to stroke her arm. "What?"

"You're gonna cry, darlin', and it's okay."

"I am not!" she snapped, but wiped her eyes and nose, too. She chuckled and so did Jason. "I don't deserve you." She walked forward and wrapped her arms around him.

"You do. And I deserve you. It's a good match."

Quizz popped her head through the kitchen door. "Your phone kept ringing, so I finally answered it." She held the device out and plopped Janet's purse on the plywood table between them. "It's Detective Patrick O'Dell."

Janet took the phone gingerly. "Hello?"

"Where'd you go?" Without waiting for an answer, he added, "Rivera and I are done talking to Eric, but we're gonna park him for a few hours. Give him time to think things through. Time for you to ask him some questions if you want to."

She looked at her watch. "I'll be there in ten minutes." She clicked off before O'Dell could answer.

"We'll keep an eye on the kids. You go. Sounds like there's work to do." Jason squeezed her arms and released her.

She pulled her purse across the plywood counter and plunged her phone down into the bag. Her hand hit a slick, rubbery surface. She dug around and pulled out a silicone mold she'd last seen at the bar. "What the heck?"

"Is that the ice wedge mold?" Jason asked. "Why do you have that here?"

"I have no idea. It went missing from the bar days ago." She studied the small black tray. "I just pulled this purse out of my closet this morning—

haven't used it in weeks. How . . ." Her phone rang; Detective O'Dell's name lit up across the screen. She tossed the wedge back into her bag and shrugged. "Thanks, Jason!"

As she hurried out of the room she heard him say, "So who are you?"

"I'm Quizz Bexley, PI. Janet's apprenticing under me."

"Is she, now?"

Janet caught his eye as she closed the door. He winked.

CHAPTER THIRTY-EIGHT

"What's going on?" Janet stepped between O'Dell and his desk and gently laid the keyring on the surface. O'Dell narrowed his eyes when she grinned up at him, but he couldn't seem to figure out what was making her smile.

He glanced from her to the evidence box. "I thought you'd stick around to discuss . . . things."

She crossed her arms. "I had urgent business to attend to."

"We don't have to be adversaries in here, Janet. We can work together."

"Does that mean you won't twist what I say to suit your investigation—you're actually open to listening to my well-reasoned theories about what happened?"

He stepped back, a new look on his face. "Partners?"

She flinched, knowing Jason wouldn't like the sound of that. "Colleagues, in a way, yes."

"Rivera and I already talked to Eric. You want to hear my thoughts or talk to him yourself?"

She wasn't about to give him the goods on Summer now and risk losing her chance to interview Eric. They locked eyes and he grinned.

"I'll wait out here, take as long as you like. If he asks for a lawyer, come out immediately, okay?"

"He hasn't asked for a lawyer yet?"

O'Dell shook his head. "It's what has me and Rivera so puzzled. The guilty ones either don't ask for one because they think it'll make them look guilty—then they don't really say anything of value —or they ask for one before they say hello, because they know they're screwed. But this guy . . . he doesn't seem to know what he knows." O'Dell shrugged. "Good luck."

She pulled open the door and Rivera, sitting at a desk in the corner shuffling papers, looked up, then nodded and went back to his papers. Eric half-stood from his chair and motioned to the empty one across from him; Southern hospitality, even here in the police interview room. After she'd taken the seat, he folded his hands in front of him and leaned forward. "Your dad is with my kids— thank you for that. But where's Nell? Did she make it? She wasn't answering her phone."

"Oh, ah . . . right . . ." Janet hesitated. "The kids are at my house for now. Nell is . . . well, she got busted stealing from a cop's car. But don't worry—" Eric's hands clenched and she finished quickly, "I've got a call into a bondsman, and we're just waiting on the paperwork to come through. She should be at my house and with the kids by din- nertime."

"What happens if she's not?"

Rivera spoke without looking up. "Then we'll have to call DCS. They'll place the kids in tempo- rary custody until family court takes up the matter."

"What?" Eric gasped, and half-stood, then froze uncertainly, clearly realizing he was stuck in the interview room.

Janet patted his hand reassuringly. "She'll be out. I'll make sure of it." She glared at Rivera, but the cop wasn't moved.

Eric sank back into the chair and rubbed a hand roughly across his face.

"The kids are okay. When I left them they

were playing a fun . . . game . . . with plenty of responsible adults." She guessed that learning self-
defense could be considered fun. "Anyway, I
wanted to ask you a few questions."

"You're not the only one. I keep asking how
long this is going to take, I need to check on Bonnie. I think she's getting an ear infection, the way
she was rubbing her ear." He glared at Rivera. "But
they 'don't have a timeline,' whatever that means."

Janet grimaced. It meant the cops were waiting
for Eric to trip up—get caught in a lie—so they
could arrest him. He wasn't going anywhere any
time soon. Instead of saying that, though, she said,
"I found Liv's notebook. Her planner?"

Eric's head whipped up. "Where?"

Rivera looked over, too, his eyebrows raised,
and Janet lowered her voice. "I came across it, and
found a note—written in code, actually. Did Liv do
that often?"

One side of Eric's mouth tipped up. "She and
Brendon were two of a kind." He shook his head
and stared at the wall behind her. "He's really
struggling."

Janet shifted in her seat. When Rivera cleared
his throat and tapped his wristwatch, she leaned
forward. "The note said that when—that when the
affair happened, that you were drugged."

"None of that matters now. She's dead! It doesn't matter!" Eric's anger flared and Janet flinched. Rivera's feet thunked off the desk to the floor and he reached for the handcuffs at his belt but didn't stand.

"It matters, Eric, because the note also said that Summer can't be trusted. Did Liv explain that to you? Why Summer can't be trusted?"

"N—no, I don't know what you're talking about. Summer was a good friend to her there at the end—"

"I don't think your wife overdosed on her own, just like you didn't cheat on her."

"What—what do you mean?"

"I mean there's one common person involved in all your troubles, but what the cops want to know—and what I'm here to find out—is what you knew and when."

"What are you—what are you talking about?" Bubbles of spittle collected at the corners of his mouth and his pale face turned red. "What did I know about what? My wife is dead! My kids no longer have a mother, and I'm over here drowning in decisions! Who will watch them while I'm at work? Who will read to them at night? Who will get Brendon to soccer when Andrea has to be at rehearsal at the same time? All I know is that I can't do it all! I can't do it alone! I—I never wanted to—" His voice cracked and he pinched his lips together.

Janet nonchalantly rested one foot against the flat edge of the table between them, but her focus lasered in on Liv's widower. "Eric, did you have anything to do with Liv's death?"

"How can you ask me that?"

"Answer the question!"

His hands plunged into his hair roughly. "I can't even think about it."

"That's not an answer!" she pressed.

Rivera's eyes followed the action, but he didn't move.

"It's my fault—it's all my fault that she's dead." Still grasping his head, he dropped his elbows down to his knees, his eyes closed in defeat.

Janet knew, from their earlier conversation at the Spot, that Eric thought that his affair had driven his wife to use drugs—but saying, "It's all my fault," in front of a homicide detective wasn't good. "You mean that you blame yourself, Eric?"

"Of course I do! If I hadn't had an affair, she'd still be alive."

A quick look at Rivera's face confirmed that Eric was digging a hole, and she had handed him the shovel.

She needed him to state, unequivocally, that he wasn't involved with Summer, before she dropped a bombshell on Rivera about Summer's true identity.

She cleared her throat. "Were you having an affair with Summer?"

"No—God, no! I told you, I'd only spoken to her once or twice before Liv died. I didn't want anything to do with Summer when Liv was alive. She was working against me from day one." He groaned, now staring down at the floor. "I don't know what changed when Liv died, but Summer wanted to help. She did help! Then she disappeared, too, and it was almost worse, having to figure out life again."

"Did you know—" Janet faltered, aware that this particular bit of information might be hard for Eric to hear. "Did you know that Summer spent five years in prison?"

"Pri—what? No, that can't be right." He looked at Janet, wide eyed, and when she didn't smile, when her gaze didn't waver, he gasped. "For what?"

"Drugs." Her gaze slid to Rivera. "She used to go by the name June Bug Martelle."

Rivera jerked forward in his seat and shoved his stack of papers to the side. His fingers pounded over his laptop keyboard and he groaned. "What's she got to do with this?"

Janet turned to the cop. "You know her?" He didn't answer, just stared at his computer screen.

When Rivera snapped his laptop closed and stood, she followed him out the door, leaving Eric sitting at the table muttering, his hands still roughly grabbing tufts of hair.

In the main office space, O'Dell joined them at the door. "What happened?"

"Your girl here just connected some dots I didn't even know were out there, that's what."

O'Dell turned to Janet. "Tell me." It was a command.

Rivera turned his eagle eye on Janet as well. "I'd like to hear this, too. How did you figure out this friend of the family, Summer Hughes, is actually June Bug Martelle?"

Janet dug a folded-up paper from her back pocket and held it out. O'Dell snatched it from her. "This is the DBA form she filed last year when she opened a counseling office."

"Who is this?" O'Dell scanned the paperwork, then looked back up at Janet.

"June Bug spent a few years in lockup on drug charges," Rivera answered. "Got out about a year ago." He motioned that they should follow him to his desk.

Janet's face twisted as she walked through the office. "Is that allowed? I mean, can she counsel other people without disclosing her past?"

O'Dell looked at her sharply. "How did you even know who she was? Her arrest would have happened long before you moved here. Heck, it was before I moved here, too."

"Research," Janet said simply. "I also know she lived in the same halfway house as Hayley and Skylar. I know she used to be married to Dishwasher Dave. And I know she's currently worming her way into Liv's old life."

Rivera plopped down at his desk and then turned his computer screen toward the group. "June Bug's mugshot."

Janet kept her jaw from dropping by biting her lip. There was Summer, only without the put-to-gether hair and makeup. No rosy cheeks, no perfectly applied lipstick, no sophisticated demeanor. Instead, the woman who gazed back at them from the screen was sickly thin, with smudged, blood-shot eyes and a hollow stare.

It brought to mind a similarly ravaged face she'd seen recently. "Did she ever share a jail cell with Skylar?"

"Skylar who?"

Janet looked up at the ceiling, searching her memory for a last name. "Skylar . . . Rowen, I think?"

Rivera's brow furrowed, and he attacked the keyboard, typing commands into the system. "No, they served time in different prisons."

Janet hummed out a breath. "What about Hayley? Any connection you can see in her file with Summer?" She'd never really believed Hayley's story that it was a friend involved in the drugs-for-drugging-Eric scheme anyway.

Rivera frowned and spent a few minutes poking around Hayley's records. When his frown deepened, she stood and leaned over his shoulder to read the screen with him. After a moment, Janet sucked in a loud breath. "Summer and Hayley were roommates at the halfway house?"

Rivera lifted one shoulder and dropped it. "According to the file, yes. They overlapped by a few months. Summer got out early." He rubbed his jaw and added in an undertone, "She must have had a great lawyer."

O'Dell, peering over Rivera's shoulder, said, "And Hayley clearly didn't. She was in that halfway house almost two years."

Janet's stomach clenched. Hayley had said her

supposed friend had shared a jail cell with the woman who masterminded the plan to drug Eric. Two years in a halfway house had probably felt like jail.

She crossed her arms. "So Summer's friend Liv, Summer's ex-roommate Hayley, and now Summer's ex-husband, Dave, are all dead."

"But Eric is very much alive." Rivera turned to face O'Dell. "Who's to say they're not both responsible?"

"That seems to be the last question, doesn't it? Will prosecutors want to charge them together?" O'Dell stroked his chin and looked critically at his colleague. "What do you think?"

"I think it's muddy enough that I don't want to be the one deciding. We'll present the evidence. They'll make the call."

Janet threw her hands up. "What are you talking about? Charge them with what?"

O'Dell turned to Janet. "The Knox County Prosecutor announced months ago that her office is going to go after dealers and suppliers when their customers die. If they can prove that Eric and Summer provided Liv with the drugs that killed her, they'll go to jail."

"Listen; Eric's a broken man, but broken because his wife is dead, not because he gave her the drugs!" Janet felt heat rising to her cheeks and she took a deep, steadying breath. Losing her cool now wouldn't help anyone.

"This fits a pattern." Rivera crossed his arms and scrutinized Janet. "He *said* it's his fault that his wife is dead! Prosecutors can take that and run with it. It doesn't matter if he meant for her to die. But if we're looking at the big picture here, Janet, after finding out about the affair, Liv could have thought that her life, as she knew it was over! And if drugs were in the house, it might not have been a big leap to think the only way to feel better would be to try them. And where did those drugs come from? That's the only thing prosecutors will care about! And that's homicide, second degree."

"No! Eric feels guilty—yes—but only because he thinks he drove his wife to use drugs over his affair." Rivera shot her a look that said her words were only serving to prove his point more. She groaned. "This all traces back to Summer—to June Bug! She was married to the drug dealer who was peddling bad heroin. She must have saved some— then convinced Liv to try it, and she . . . fell down the stairs? I don't know, but it has to be Summer."

O'Dell frowned. "Don't forget that Eric's skipped out on the drug test we asked him to submit to twice. Would have been an easy way to clear his name."

"So he's busy! Not a crime." She could tell by the set of both men's jaws that she wasn't going to be able to convince them of anything just then. She grabbed her bag from O'Dell's chair.

"Where are you going?" he asked.

"Home." It wasn't a lie; she would eventually get there. It just wouldn't be her first stop.

O'Dell grabbed her arm. "Stay away from Summer. I don't know if Eric's a part of this, but clearly Summer is. I'm putting an APB out on her. I want her arrested on sight. We'll bring her in, see what she knows. You leave Summer to me, got it?"

"Gladly, O'Dell. She can't be far—we saw her when we left Eric's house an hour ago."

"What?" O'Dell roared. "Why didn't you tell me?"

"I just did!"

O'Dell turned his back on her and picked up his two-way radio. Rivera shot her a disappointed look and she knew she needed to leave before she said something that would get her in trouble.

She hurried out of the police station and scanned the street. Kaylee and her dad had left her car at the edge of the public lot closest to the police department, with two crisp dollar bills tucked into the change tray that would get her through the tollbooth and on her way. She found herself reflexively looking over her shoulder and in the rearview mirror until she got out of the cramped lot. She wouldn't feel safe until Summer was behind bars.

CHAPTER THIRTY-NINE

Janet drove across downtown, to a building that was becoming all too familiar. She ducked down behind the wheel when Donaldson stalked out of the side door toward the parking lot, and she didn't climb out until she'd lost sight of his car in the side-view mirror.

O'Dell and Rivera were focused on finding and arresting Summer, but Janet wanted to get to the bottom of whether Eric was in on the plan. Only two people could help with that—and she wasn't going to go anywhere near Summer.

No, she wanted to talk to Liv's divorce lawyer. She could only guess that Liv had hired someone at Thornton & Brown; after all, Liv had scribbled the firm's number on the last page of her notebook.

She entered the building and headed up to the third floor, then walked down the hallway and pulled open the heavy oak door to the office.

A young man behind the reception desk lowered the microphone on his headset but didn't look up from his computer. "Welcome to the law offices of Thornton & Brown, how can I help you?"

"I . . ." Janet's lips pinched together. How was she going to get past the receptionist? "I just have a quick question for the lawyer who's—" Before she finished her query, the receptionist lifted one hand from his keyboard to push a stack of papers toward her.

"Here are the intake forms, we require a twenty-five-hundred-dollar retainer to open a case, and of course that doesn't guarantee a win. You can step over there to fill out the forms, or take them home with you."

Twenty-five hundred dollars was a lot of money —certainly more than Liv could have afforded . . . but since she was here, she figured she might as well ask. "*I'm* not looking for an attorney, I'm here for . . . I wanted to talk to the lawyer representing Liv Birch. Her name is, uh . . ." She suddenly knew that Liv's final note could never have referred to her young daughter. She looked down at the business card holder perched at the edge of the desk and scanned the offerings. At the top of the tiered stand were cards for Gen Thornton and Rebecca Brown. Down a level she read the names Daniel Jones and Jill Riley, she kept going down a few more levels before—ah! There it was. "Bonnie Kerben. I need to speak to Bonnie Kerben, please."

The receptionist eyed her doubtfully. "Do you have an appointment?"

"Yes." Janet turned her stare up to haughty. "I was told to come in at one o'clock."

"Well you missed that, didn't you?" He smirked.

"Funny how your time isn't your own when you're dealing with homicide detectives." She smiled archly and looked pointedly at her watch. "Is she still available?"

His lips scrunched together. He couldn't tell whether Janet was full of it, or someone more important than himself. She decided to try and tip the scales toward important.

"Listen, if she wants to call my office to reschedule, that's fine, but I'm headed to a conference tomorrow—"

"Let me just call back there and see. What's your name?"

"Janet Black. Thank you." She turned and walked to a wall of artwork and pretended to admire the cheap, reframed prints while straining to hear what the receptionist said into his headset.

"I don't know, she says—I mean yes, I asked, but. . ." There was a long pause while whoever was on the other end spoke, then, "Well, I can ask her, or you can. I mean, why don't I just send her. . . okay, good. Thanks." He disconnected and called Janet over.

"Mrs. Kerben will be right out to get you."

"Thank you."

She continued to stand, hovering by the art wall, until the door at the far end of the lobby opened several minutes later and a young, fresh faced woman walked out, a curious expression on her face.

"Mrs. Black?"

"Bonnie, thanks for seeing me."

The lawyer inclined her head slightly at Janet's confident tone, and then dropped back a step to hold the door open for Janet. "I'm the first office on the left."

Once they were both seated around Bonnie's desk, the lawyer swept her long, dark hair away from her face, and settled back into her chair. "What can I do for you, Mrs. Black?"

"Did you represent Liv Birch?"

The other woman's face tightened almost imperceptibly and her hands spread out along the desktop. "What?"

"Liv Birch? Did you represent her?"

Bonnie tilted her head to the side. "I'm sorry, but we can't give out information on any clients." She picked up a pair of glasses that had been resting next to her computer mouse and began to polish them with a cloth, her focus on the task complete. When she looked up, she'd found her poker face. "Who, exactly, are you?"

"I'm friends with Liv's mother."

"Well, like I said, we can't confirm or deny the identity of any of our clients." The woman eyed the phone console sitting inches from her right hand and then placed the glasses on her face before leveling Janet with a dismissive stare. "Was there anything else?"

"She's dead," Janet blurted out. "Liv, I mean. Did you know that?"

"What?" Bonnie's eyes widened, her fingers clenched the cloth she'd been using on her glasses.

"She died nearly a month ago under suspicious circumstances. And her family is in trouble."

Bonnie's fingers flew over the keyboard and after a moment, she flung a hand up to her throat as she read, her lips moving along with the words on her screen. "I see now. Here's her obituary—I—I had no idea."

Janet pulled the photocopied journal pages from her back pocket and unfolded them on Bonnie's desk. "Liv wrote this just before she died." The lawyer's face scrunched together as she looked over the lines of code. "I know it's hard to make out, but this right here"—she pointed to the last line—"you can read that one just fine. It says, 'Bonnie knows everything.'" Janet leaned closer. "I know a lot about what happened, but I'm not sure I know *everything*. Think we can compare notes?"

Bonnie's face paled, so that it was whiter than the paper between them. "I—I don't think that would be appropriate . . ."

Janet waited until Bonnie looked up. "We have a problem. Right now, Liv's widower is sitting across town in police custody. My friends are watching Liv's kids, because their grandmother is in jail. The police are looking for Summer Hughes, a woman who claimed to be friends with Liv but who I suspect might have had a hand in her death. And before Eric gets charged with playing a part in his wife's death, too, and Liv's kids end up in state custody, I want to know if you have any information that might help them—might help *him*."

Bonnie closed her eyes for a long moment.

When she opened them back up, her expression was pained. "I'm not sure what to do here . . . my role. . . I mean, I need to do what's in her best interest . . ."

"What's in her best interest is to make sure her kids are taken care of right now."

Bonnie looked back blankly for what felt like an eternity. She finally nodded almost to herself. "Yes . . . help the kids . . ." The lawyer studied her computer screen for a moment, collecting her thoughts. "She was supposed to come in to sign the divorce filing, but when she got here, she'd changed her mind. She told me she'd just learned new information, and wanted to stop everything."

Janet leaned forward. "Did she mention Hayley or Skylar?"

"Skylar, yes." Bonnie grimaced. "Skylar had told her what I consider to be a pretty far-fetched story about someone drugging Eric..." Bonnie rubbed at her brow roughly.

"What?" Janet asked.

"I'm a divorce lawyer! This whole thing was veering so far off course. But Liv had a name—"

"Summer?"

"Yes," Bonnie said with a frown. "We looked Summer up in the county database and discovered that she'd done time in prison under another

name." Kerben looked over. "You can imagine how
angry Liv was, I'm sure. This woman had been
babysitting her kids!"

"So...what? What happened then?"

The lawyer shook her head back and forth a
few times before speaking. "I told her she needed a
different kind of lawyer to move forward. She
wanted to talk about filing a civil suit against Summer. Calling the police and filing a criminal complaint. She said the divorce was off, and that's the
only kind of law I practice these days. I told her to
go home, discuss things with her husband. Then
I'd refer them to the appropriate kind of lawyer."

"When did you last see her?"

Kerben leaned forward and tapped her keyboard, then squinted at her screen. "September
fourteenth."

"The day she died." Janet looked down at the
paper in her hand. The last, ominous phrase was
added just hours before Liv had taken her last
breath. "When you didn't hear from her again, why
didn't you call? Check on her?"

Kerben looked over Janet's head and frowned.
When she spoke, her voice was low. "I—I guess I
was happy to think she was moving on. This was
like a bad soap opera, lots of drama, and she had
no money to pay for the next steps."

Janet narrowed her eyes at the lawyer, but before she could say anything, her phone buzzed with a new text from Quizz.

I'm out. Too much noise. Jason is here.

"I have to go—Liv's kids need me." She stood up and walked to the door, but turned back before leaving. "Her husband might be charged with killing her. You'll need to tell the police what you know." Kerben didn't react, and Janet spun on her heel and stalked out of the office and down the hall. She ignored the receptionist's syrupy, "Have a great day," her mind buzzing with information as she stepped on the elevator.

Just before Liv died, Nell's daughter had decided to call the divorce off, maybe even confront Summer with what she'd found out about Eric's supposed affair.

But what did Summer want? It was the final piece of this strange puzzle that had so far left three people dead, and from all Janet could tell, Liv's supposed friend was doing her best to blow up Nell's entire family. But why?

Janet left the elevator mentally exhausted, but there wasn't time for a break. She was late for an appointment at the jail.

CHAPTER FORTY

A crushing weight pressed down on her chest and she felt helpless standing in the jail lobby, tapping her fingers uselessly against her thigh as she waited for the bondsman to show. Kids at her house. Bodies piling up across Knoxville. And here she was, stuck downtown, waiting to spring Nell from lockup. A fourth check of her watch confirmed that the bondsman was still late.

"Janet Black?" A husky voice came from her left, and Janet smelled menthol cigarettes before she turned to find a woman in cargo pants with short brown hair. Her lips were flanked by deep wrinkles, like perfect parentheses, and the unlit cigarette dangling from them straightened when she smiled. "I'm Brighton Levine."

"Brighton Levine? You're the bondsman?"

"Bondswoman, if we're being technical. I've got the paperwork, do you have the credit card?"

Janet held out her Visa and Brighton tucked her cigarette behind her ear, then swiped the card through a reader attached to her phone.

A receipt printed from a small black plastic canister, and after tearing the paper off, Brighton placed the device back in her bag.

"Do you have an office?" Janet eyed the bag and wondered what else was in there.

"Just my car. All the action takes place out and about. Not too worried about a sixty-eight-year-old woman jumping bail, though." She reached into her bag. "Hate to tase old people, anyway. Their hearts—too fragile."

Janet frowned when the other woman caressed the Taser—she almost seemed excited by the prospect—but she took the paperwork anyway. It wasn't like she could choose someone else to do business with at this point.

"It'll take about twenty minutes. Go ahead and get comfortable."

Janet sighed and after watching Brighton head to the desk, she left the jail lobby for the cool sunshine outside.

———

"Here."

Nell sauntered out the front door of the prison as if she'd been inspecting the facility, not spending time inside of it. She held out an envelope to Janet and sat down on the bench next to her.

"What's this?"

"I'd forgotten about it until they gave me my possessions just now. You know they do a strip search even for overnight bookings? That was unexpected."

Janet grimaced and inspected the letter, still clutched in Nell's wrinkled hand. "That's for me?"

"It's from that drug dealer guy. He came to the house—"

"Dave? When?" Janet snatched the envelope out of Nell's hand and turned it over, looking at each side for clues.

"Last night. I was going to drop it off to the bar after my visit with Skylar, but obviously things came up. . ."

"What house?" Janet's stomach dropped, and she swallowed down an acidic taste, like she'd just thrown up.

"Liv's ho—Eric's house, really."

"He came to Eric's house to leave me a note?"

"Well, no. He was looking for Eric, and when I told him he wasn't there, he got all twisted out of shape. Said he had to talk to Eric, but there wasn't time. Then he asked if I was going to see you soon, and when I said yes, he left a note for you."

"What's it say?" Janet asked, a feeling of desperation creeping in.

"As if I'd read another person's note," Nell harrumphed.

"Nell."

"Okay, fine. It says, '*Watch out for Summer.*'"

Janet's chest squeezed tighter still. "Nell, Dave is dead."

"What? Such a nice young man . . . well. He could have been, at least. What happened?"

"Shot to death near his apartment."

"No!" Nell sucked a breath in through her teeth and shook her head. "What do the police say?"

"Nothing, yet. Can you think of anything else about his visit? Anything important?"

"He was real agitated when he first arrived, but he calmed considerably—almost like he'd come to accept something."

"What?"

"What am I, a psychic? I have no idea, I'm just saying he seemed calmer when he left than when he got there."

Janet slid a finger under the flap and shimmied it open, unfolded the letter, and frowned.

Watch out for Summer. Then in smaller letters at the bottom of the page, *Bitch is crazy.*

Janet looked up. The second line could have referred to Summer—or Nell.

"What else happened?"

Nell looked over Janet's head and smirked. "I took his phone."

Janet's head dropped forward into her hands. "How—you know what, never mind. He had no idea?"

"I saw him search his car in the driveway, but he didn't come back in." She shrugged. "What can I say?"

"Where is it?"

Nell unzipped her purse and pawed around in the massive bag before finally pulling out an old flip-style phone. "Drugs must not pay the bills like they used to, huh?"

"It's a prepaid phone. Cheap, disposable. That's probably why he didn't come back in for it. He probably had another ready to go." She pulled her hair back from her face with her free hand. Dave had had Hayley come talk to Janet and at the same time left a note for her, warning her about Summer. Just hours before he'd met his own death, he saw death coming—but for whom?

"Nell, a lot of things have happened since you were arrested last night. I don't think any of us will be safe until the police can track down Summer. You're coming to my house—the kids are already there."

Nell's brow furrowed, but she climbed into Janet's car without a word.

Summer Hughes had already knocked off Liv, and now she'd tried to cover her tracks by killing Dave and Hayley. What else was she planning? Were any of them safe?

Janet wasn't going to take any chances until she knew the answer.

CHAPTER FORTY-ONE

The house was as close to destroyed as Janet had ever seen it—and that included when she and Jason had torn out the old kitchen last year.

Every pillow and cushion was gathered in the family room, the sturdier pieces tilted upright against each other, forming a tunnel along the base of the couch that led to a larger fortress in front of the TV. The blanket from Janet's bed was draped over the biggest cushion-room, and regular flashes of light made their way out of the opening, along with giggling and hoots of laughter.

"You're home!" Jason rushed to hug Janet and threw an arm around Nell and gave her a squeeze, too. "I'm going to run to the . . . to the store. We're out of . . . Uh . . ." He patted his pockets and pulled out a list. "Batteries. Gotta get more batteries. And kid's Tylenol. Bonnie's been pulling on her ear . . ." He winced when a crash issued from the fort. "Your dad and Kaylee pushed back their flight —they'll stop by tomorrow on their way to the airport. Quizz left about half an hour ago. You might never see her again. And I need to—just some quiet somewhere, if I could—"

"Get out of here, Jason. Thank you so much."

Relief flooded his face, and he grabbed his keys from the hall table and backed out of the house.

After he left, Nell peered into the fort, then squinted when a flash of light hit her square in the eyes. "Hey, kids!"

Another shriek from the fort. Janet wasn't sure they'd heard their grandmother.

Nell raised her voice. "Kids! Quiet down!"

A beat of silence, then the loudest burst of laughter yet. A cushion tilted, dangerously close to falling in, but it was quickly straightened from inside, and the laughing resumed.

Nell stepped back and sagged against the door frame, her face red, her breath labored. Janet had filled her in on her suspicions about Summer on the drive over, and rather than galvanizing her, the news seemed to have drained Nell of her remaining energy.

Janet stopped picking up puzzle pieces—where had they come from, anyway?—and walked over. "It's okay. Let them wear themselves out now, maybe everyone'll sleep better tonight."

Nell tried to smile, but it died about halfway to her lips. She pushed herself away from the door frame and took a step forward, then stumbled.

Janet caught her arms and steered Nell over to the couch, then stopped short. There was nowhere to sit.

Amid loud protesting, she picked up the two closest cushions from the tunnel and added them back to the furniture, then she helped Nell sit slowly.

"You need a break!"

"Well I can't take one, and neither can you! Not until O'Dell finds *that woman*."

"Nell, you're exhausted. Go lie down in the guest room. I'll take them to get ice cream." Janet held up a hand to stop Nell's protesting. The other woman was wilting right in front of her. She needed to rest, and even if it was only an hour of silence, it would do Nell good. "I insist. You take a break, and we'll bring back dinner, too."

Nell raised another feeble protest, but Janet already had the keys in her hand. "Come on, kids. Let's go get some ice cream!" The cushions broke apart, falling flat as the blanket sailed overhead. A herd of children galloped to the front door. Bonnie burst into tears and before Janet could ask what was wrong, Brendon stopped and ran back. "You're not last, Bonnie, see, I'm behind you now!" The youngest Birch child immediately cheered and the group trooped out the door ahead of Janet.

"They're amazing, aren't they?" Nell asked weakly from the couch. "I'm not going to be able to do my daughter justice. I just don't have the energy."

"You're here," Janet said, a lump rising in her throat. "That's all that matters. You're here, and you'll do your best. Can't ask for more."

"Of course I can. But it doesn't do any good." Nell leaned back heavily against the newly restored sofa cushion. "Bring me back some mint chocolate chip, huh?"

"Sure." Janet locked the door behind her, then, after making sure Bonnie was latched in, she got behind the wheel. "All right, kids. My mom used to take me to get ice cream on special occasions. What should our special occasion be today?"

"Childhood, as we know it, is over?" Andrea crossed her arms and looked mulishly at Janet through the rearview mirror.

Brendon groaned. "Nice, Andy. Nice." He

turned to Janet. "We get to miss school tomorrow?"

Before Janet could tell them that there was no way they were staying home from school, Bonnie piped up from behind her.

"It's Thursday?"

"It's not—you know what?" Janet decided correcting the toddler was pointless. "Yes!" She cranked over the engine and grinned. "Yes! Ice cream for Thursdays!" She slowed to turn at the corner and glanced at Andrea. "And you're still a child. Despite what you've been through this last month, there is lots of fun ahead for you."

But Janet's optimism was short-lived. She hadn't planned well, and the first ice-cream store they went to was closed. Bonnie threw up in the backseat before they got to the second. Janet climbed out of the car at a light and found a full roll of paper towels in the diaper bag. She ignored the honks and did her best to soak the vomit up off the carpet.

By the time she turned the car into the parking lot of a convenience store, she separated a fifty-dollar bill from her stack of cash and set it aside for a full auto detail. That left them with ten bucks for ice cream.

Andrea watched her brother and sister while

Janet washed her hands in the bathroom, plastering on the sunniest smile she could muster as she headed back out to the main store. "Did everyone order?"

Bonnie wailed unexpectedly, and the sound drilled right down into Janet's brain, pulsing behind her right ear. "What's the matter with her?" Janet asked.

Bonnie's sobs ratcheted up to a new, unheard-of level, and she crumpled slowly to the floor. Janet's eyes widened, even as she wanted to plug her ears with her fingers. The child was saying something, but the words were muddy; they sounded like a coffee machine in the last gurgles before the brew is ready.

"Andrea?" Janet looked to the eldest sibling.

She was already checking under tables. "It's Baby Turtle."

Sure enough, the super-soft, extremely well-loved blanket with a head was not attached to Bonnie's right hand.

Janet picked up the stack of coats and searched through them. Bonnie's wailing grew louder, punctuated by occasional hiccups and coughing fits that left the child breathless. Snot ran down her nose and into her mouth. Before Janet could find a napkin, the little girl ran her sleeve across her face, smearing it into her hair. Janet's face contorted with disgust.

"It must be in the car!" Andrea said, glaring at Janet.

"It's not in the car, I just cleaned it from top to bottom!"

"Uh-oh," Brendon said, sitting on a chair with his feet propped on another.

"What?"

"I think it's at home."

"In the fort?" Janet asked, a sudden lightness in her chest. "Bonnie, honey, we'll just eat our ice cream and go right back home to get him."

"Her."

"Her. We'll go right back home and get her."

"Not *your* home," Brendon said. "Our home. I haven't seen Baby Turtle since we left our home this morning!"

They all thought back to the packing and leaving. Bonnie had fallen asleep as they left the house, and had slept in her car seat right though the ride to Janet's. The little girl had become upset right as they'd arrived at Janet's house, but Mel had come to the rescue with the self-defense key chain. Bonnie must have been so enthralled with the strangers and the pillow fort that she'd forgotten Baby Turtle. Until now.

Bonnie had stopped crying, but only to catch her breath. As if on cue, she opened her mouth wide and started screaming again.

"Did you guys want to order something or . . . ," the girl behind the counter said, and looked accusingly at Janet.

She rushed the group through ordering, but it was all wrong. The ice cream was too cold, Brendon's fell off the cone and splattered onto the floor, and Bonnie continued to lie rigid on the floor, her hair wet from the tears that streamed down her face.

"Let's go."

"We'll need a scoop of mint chocolate chip to go." Janet handed the employee her credit card.

"And then we'll stop by the house to get Baby Turtle?" Andrea asked.

"No, we'll just have to distract her. Look, she's already quieted down." Bonnie struggled to sit up and looked around, her eyes wide and glassy from the recent tears. "I think she's going to be okay."

Andrea crossed her arms over her chest. "Three. Two." Janet wrinkled her nose. What was up with this kid? "One," she finished, and Bonnie wailed anew.

Janet jumped at the onslaught of noise. "We can't go to your house. You know that."

"I heard you tell Grandma Nell that the police are out there looking for Summer, and she knows it. She's not going to show up at our house. Besides, we only need to grab Baby Turtle and leave, then we'll be gone."

Janet took another look at Bonnie, who'd flung her little chubby arms over her eyes and stopped yelling to take another deep breath. "She'll calm down, won't she?"

"She'll keep going until she passes out. Then she'll wake back up and start all over again."

Janet crossed her arms and stared out the window. It was still daylight, and they could be in and out of the house in five minutes. Probably better to do it now than wish she'd done it at three in the morning.

"Okay, guys. Let's go get Baby Turtle."

CHAPTER FORTY-TWO

A gust of wind pushed them up the front walk, and Janet scrambled to find the key, buried in the depths of her bag. When she finally opened the door, she turned to block the kids from entering.

"We have five minutes. I want you to spread out and find Baby Turtle. The one who does gets . . ." She scrunched up her nose, trying to think of a fitting reward, until Brendon interrupted.

"Extra TV time tonight?"

"Yes! Extra TV time," Janet agreed. She held the door open for the children, then twisted the dead bolt after they were all inside. She wasn't going to take any chances, even if they *were* only going to be in the house for five minutes.

Bonnie tottered next to Janet, then used one leg to lever herself up onto the couch. She'd stopped crying as soon as she'd learned they were going to get Baby Turtle, but her face was still streaked with tears and snot, and the little girl was clearly exhausted.

"Baby Turtle," she whimpered.

"Shh, hush, baby. We're going to find it." Janet crouched low to look under the couch. When she stood up, she rubbed her hands up and down her arms. The cold weather outside had followed them in. She glanced around the room and found the thermostat. Though it was set to seventy-eight degrees, the room only registered at sixty-two.

A chill snuck up her spine that had nothing to do with the temperature. She walked back to the couch and picked up Bonnie. "Come on. Let's go find your brother and sister."

Janet walked up the stairs slowly, shifting the baby's weight so that she could see the steps. Just as she reached the upper level of the home, Brendon rushed out of a room, a triumphant grin on his face. "Got it!"

Bonnie took the stuffed animal and laid it out carefully on Janet's shoulder before snuggling in. A small, happy purr hummed from her chest.

Brendon stuck his tongue out and Janet turned to see his older sister. Andrea rolled her eyes. "You get more TV. Big deal."

It was warmer up here, and the house seemed secure. A quick check confirmed that all the windows were closed. So why was she still feeling so jumpy? Janet tried to shrug off the sense of unease. "Okay, great job. Let's get going."

She led the way back downstairs, and on the latest pass through the family room, the gaping black hole of the basement door beckoned her closer. Cold air blew up the steps and smacked her in the face when she reached across the opening to close the door. Her heart beat faster and she bit her lip. "Hello?" She set Bonnie down and turned to the older children. "Andrea, Brendon, keep an eye on Bonnie while I go and check the basement."

The baby howled anew, and Janet jumped at the sudden noise. "What now?"

"Take me!" she wailed.

Janet swallowed hard. "Fine! Just, shush, now. You two go get buckled up. We'll be right out." Bonnie waddled closer and Janet picked her up, then flicked on the overhead light in the stairwell and headed down. It was like entering the walk-in cooler at the bar, and Bonnie snuggled in closer, her hot breath leaving a trail of goose bumps along Janet's neck and down her back. She shivered and Bonnie giggled.

"'Gain!" She breathed hard onto Janet's neck.

Janet shivered again for pretend this time, and the little girl's peal of laughter ricocheted around the enclosed staircase. One final step, and the space opened up to the large rec room.

"Mom-mom." The little girl pointed solemnly to a spot on the floor.

Janet gulped and sidestepped where Liv's body would have lain weeks earlier. Her eyes moved around the basement, then zeroed in on the problem. The door to the backyard, beyond the laundry machines, stood wide open.

As soon as her fingers made contact with the wooden door, it whooshed closed with a terrifyingly loud *bang*. Bonnie whimpered and Janet twisted the dead bolt and the small lock on the doorknob for good measure, then whirled around to face the room. It was still empty. Nothing seemed to be out of place, but as she stood there, the feeling of dread she'd had since walking into the home came into sharper focus.

In the cool, open basement, she realized what was missing. A floral scent had been at the tip of her nose upstairs. Her brain hadn't even really registered it until she got to the cool, clear air in the basement.

"We need to leave right now." She tried to keep the panic out of her voice, but that smell distinctly reminded her of the disgusting rose-scented fragrance Summer had been wearing when they went to lunch, and Janet hurried across the room.

The staircase was ominously dark, and Janet hesitated before putting her foot on the first step. She'd turned that overhead light on just minutes earlier. Now it was off.

Perhaps sensing her strain, Bonnie was quiet. The child's grip around her neck was borderline uncomfortable. Breathing hard under the effort of carrying her, Janet hustled up the stairs, only to skid to a stop on the top landing when she sensed a flash of movement. She gasped and fell back a step as pain sliced down her free arm, her mind simultaneously processing the pain, calculating the closeness of the top of the stairs behind her, and scrambling to figure out how she could protect Bonnie from whatever threat lurked.

Summer stood to the side of the basement door, a tiny pocketknife in her outstretched hand. It might as well have been a machete. Janet had nothing in her arms but a child, and she knew then, with a conviction that surprised her, that she'd do anything at all to protect Bonnie.

Summer sneered and slashed the knife closer to Janet's midsection. "Give me Bonnie," she said, looking greedily at the child, "and I won't hurt you." When Janet glanced at the blood dripping down her arm, Summer added, "Any more than I already have."

Janet tightened her grip on the child. Summer's ensuing laugh was the least cheerful thing she'd ever heard.

"You don't even like kids!" Summer turned her attention to Bonnie. "Come here, sweet pea!" she crooned. "I will take care of you." She held her hand out and her eyes sparkled as she looked at Liv's youngest daughter.

Bonnie stuck her tongue out and the cooing that had died on Summer's lips turned into a howl as her knife slashed forward.

"I will not lose now!" Summer's nostrils flared as she faced Janet again. "I have worked too hard for this to end now, when I'm so close to what I want."

Janet couldn't tear her eyes away from the other woman, but she needed to know—where were Andrea and Brendon? Safe? Dead? Oh, God, why hadn't she listened to Jason? To O'Dell? "Why are you here?"

"I came to get what's mine. What I've worked so hard to get for these past six months."

"What did you do? What did you do to Liv?"

Summer's eyes glittered dangerously as her fingers tapped against the knife. "Don't we all deserve to be happy? To enjoy life?"

"I think we get what we deserve." Janet turned her body to the side to shield Bonnie in case Summer struck again. But her arm throbbed, and the fingers in her right hand were starting to tingle. Her eyes darted around; the living room seemed empty. Had the other kids made it outside to safety? Would they stay there?

"You're right, we *do* get what we deserve." Summer nodded, and the crazy spark in her eyes intensified.

"Liv trusted you with her kids—at least, she did for a while. But she was on to you at the end. Did you know that?"

"No!" Summer snapped. "She didn't know what to believe at the end, she was confused. But she was too close to the truth. Just like you are now!"

The counselor was veering off the rails, and

Janet didn't want to end up at the bottom of the stairs like Liv. She needed to calm the situation. "What happened to you, Summer? You seemed to have it all together when I first met you, but I know you served time in prison. What happened that got you so far off track all those years ago?"

Summer backed away, stopping when she bumped into the back of the couch behind her. "What happened?" She bit her lip. "I've spent a lot of time thinking about that over the years. What happened." She laughed, but there wasn't any humor in the sound. "It was... it was a dumb, run of the mill car accident. A broken ankle. No big deal. But the doctor prescribed morphine for the pain." Summer shook her head, still unable to believe her luck so many years later. "Morphine, for a sore ankle! That was it. I was done."

"What do you mean? You got—addicted to the pain meds?"

"Yes, and once the prescription ran out, I got my fix other ways."

"Is that how you met Dave?"

"That's exactly how I met Dave." She spit out his name like a swear word. "So he was my undoing —and in the end, what saved me." At Janet's questioning look she elaborated. "He sold me out to the cops to avoid going to jail himself. I sobered up behind bars—had no other choice, obviously...but still, he owed me. I guess now we're even." Her grim smile made Janet shiver.

"What does that have to do with Liv? With her kids?" Janet asked, trying to keep Summer talking. She needed time—time to find a way out of this mess.

"My sentence was almost over, I was almost free after serving my time." Summer's eyes glazed over, as if in her mind she was back in the court-room—back in jail. "My counselor told me I needed to visualize where life went wrong so I could fix it."

"And what did you come up with?" Janet's eyes darted around the room, looking for something to use as a weapon.

"A date. It was the last normal thing in my, at that time, normal life. A date with Eric. We'd met up at a coffee shop. The accident happened as I drove myself home. So, obviously, Eric was the answer. When I got out, I found him. Of course by then he was married. Liv remembered me from our time at Community. But Eric? He didn't remember me.

"Here he was, the key to the last time I was

happy—*and he didn't remember me at all?*" She blinked
back to the present day, back to the room, the
knife, the baby. "That's when I realized, I didn't
want *him*—just a chance to start over with a family
I missed out on having. Of course Liv was in the
way of that. Eric was, too."

She folded the knife in and out of its handle;
the repeated click seemed to count off the number
of people Summer had killed.

Click. Liv.

Click. Hayley.

Click. Dave.

Click. Brendon? Andrea? Janet took in a shaky
breath. Maybe herself?

"You worked for a long time on this plan, didn't
you? But how did you work things out with Hayley? To set the divorce in motion?"

Summer frowned. If Janet knew, it was possible
that others did, too. Police. Prosecutors. She shook
her head and refocused on her current prey.

"You forget what a small town this is. I don't
know how I forgot that, but I did." She rubbed
her eyes. "Hayley was my roommate in that hellish
halfway house. I was ready to be on my own, but
not everyone there was. When we met, Hayley
was still drooling at the memory of drugs. I just
planted the idea that I could help her if she

helped me. She jumped at the chance, okay? Jumped.

"But I didn't realize—how could I have?—that Hayley would get assigned a new roommate who'd been friends with Liv in high school. Hayley must have told her what she'd done for me. And Skylar was going to ruin everything! Tell Liv. And I had Liv eating out of my hand by then! I'd convinced her to get the life insurance policy that will make this new way of living so much easier after Eric goes to jail and I become the children's guardian. You should have seen the way she was sobbing when she signed the forms. 'My life is over.'" Summer's face contorted into an awful rendition of crying. "She was weak, and she knew it."

"So that's why the signature looked like a forgery." Janet's head pounded in time with her oozing wound. Liv was so devastated to be planning her new divorced life, she could hardly sign the form.

Summer's eyes glinted, the knife glittered, and she kept talking, almost in a trance. "Some people never get rid of that hungry look. I thought Hayley wouldn't. But apparently her small errand for me left a bad taste in her mouth. Made her want to take the high road later. I couldn't have that! It wouldn't work!"

"Where did you get the drugs?"

Summer snorted. "You can get a roofie on just about any street corner—"

"Not the roofie for Eric. The bad heroin for Liv."

"I told you, some people are desperate to believe in second chances. Dave and I met after I got out. He'd been holding on to the tainted drugs for ages—debating whether he should go to the police and confess after those men died. I told him not to be ridiculous and that I would get rid of it for him. And really, in a way, I did."

"In the end, all of you knew too much."

Janet didn't like how Summer was referring to her in the past tense already, but before she could correct the other woman, Summer flicked the knife back to attention and advanced on Janet.

"Was Eric in on the plan?"

Summer halted. Her face scrunched distastefully. "Eric's too dumb to know anything. And he never will." The lines around her eyes smoothed out and she smiled. "He'll be in jail taking the blame for Liv's death. And little Bonnie is too young to understand what's happening."

"What about Brendon? Andrea?" Janet asked, holding her breath.

"Why would they know anything? I'll walk out

of here with Bonnie and they'll never know what happened to you. Never."

Janet sagged against the door frame. Summer didn't know that the other children had come to the house with her that day. That meant they were safe—for now. So what was Janet going to do to keep them that way?

CHAPTER FORTY-THREE

Janet slowly lowered Bonnie to the ground and stepped in front of the child. Her arm throbbed; she felt each beat in her head, in her chest, even in her toes. She unclenched her jaw and tried to speak as if they were back at the restaurant in Market Square. Maybe if she remained calm, Summer would, too. "So what happened? Liv didn't suddenly decide to shoot up heroin, did she?"

"No, of course not." The other woman studied the knife handle, the mad humor gone.

"Did you just—" Janet looked sideways at the basement staircase and her stomach turned as hollow as the opening behind her. It was too terrible to think of doing that to another person . . .

and yet. "Did you push her down the stairs in her own house?"

Summer looked up, her expression clinical. "She was making wild accusations after talking to Skylar. Liv was threatening to call the police! But Skylar's a user, and I told Liv she'd be crazy to listen to someone like that. I asked her to meet with me, to give me a chance to tell my side of the story." She snorted. "See? Second chances again." She glanced at the stairwell. "It was quick. I made sure of it. One little shove, then I followed her down with a syringe. It should have worked. A terrible accident. Such a tragedy."

Janet would have laughed at the gross miscalculation if her life wasn't on the line. "You didn't know the washer was broken, did you?"

"You plan something for weeks—months even —and something as dumb as a broken washing machine sends things spiraling out of control!" Summer groaned. "It was supposed to have looked like an accident—a missed step, sad but understandable when she was carrying all that laundry. How in the hell would I have known the machine was broken—or that a mother of three didn't deign to do laundry in her own house? But because of the damn broken machine, the police looked into things more thoroughly, and they noticed that little puncture in her arm, and I knew my plan was in trouble."

A flicker of something fired in the back recesses of Janet's brain. "And you planted the syringe in the bathroom trash can later, didn't you?"

"I got rid of the original—no one was supposed to know about it. But when they launched an investigation, I couldn't have the police think that Liv shot up on her own, could I? So I planted the idea with Nell that Eric could go to jail for giving Liv drugs. I had to make sure they locked on to Eric. So I put another needle in the trash can when I saw you and Nell drive up that day. Made up that lie about Crayons clogging the downstairs toilet, so Nell would have to go upstairs. It couldn't have been easier." Her smile made Janet's skin crawl. "With Nell's history of stealing, I knew *she'd* never get the kids, and there I was, being so helpful to Eric after his wife died. I was the one he'd turn to when he needed somewhere safe for the children. Me."

"There is no happily ever after for you. You must have realized that by now." Bonnie clung to Janet's legs, and she took a small shuffle step forward, to put some distance between the girl and the steep staircase. Unfortunately, that move also took her closer to a deranged woman with a knife.

Summer nodded, almost to herself. Her expression cleared, and she gripped the knife firmly again. "I am making my own happily ever after. No one is going to do it for me. I've learned that much since going to prison." Her tongue folded against the back of her teeth as she stared at the ultimate prize. Bonnie peeked out from behind Janet's leg and whimpered as Summer took a step forward.

Janet knew she had to act now and decisively, just like Mel had taught her. This wasn't self-defense; this was all about going on the offensive, and she'd only get one chance to keep Bonnie safe. To keep the other kids safe. She lunged forward. Summer's eyes widened slightly as Janet's arm struck out toward the other woman's windpipe.

Summer was fast—faster than a drunk customer ever would have been—and Janet's hand missed the other woman completely. She lost her footing and sprawled clumsily over the couch and rolled onto the floor.

Bonnie cried out, startled, and in the moment Janet looked back to check on her, Summer whirled around and kicked her in the ribs. Air whooshed out of her chest as if it were a burst balloon and she scrambled to get up, her injured arm affording her zero help as she tried to push off the floor.

Her brain felt fuzzy, the pain pulsing in time with her heartbeat, but she braced her feet and prepared to kick out, using all the power left in her body. Instead she jerked back when the knife whizzed by her face, so closely she could feel it graze her hair.

"Jesus!" Janet yelled. Anger bubbled up over her fear. Going for the face seemed well out of bounds.

Summer's miss meant she was the unsteady one now, and Janet's foot aimed for the inside of the other woman's knee. But again, Summer was too fast. She sidestepped the kick and swiped her elbow down on Janet's already injured arm. A crack echoed through the room—or maybe just in her head—like a gunshot. She dropped to the floor between the couch and coffee table, unable to move.

Summer threw her head back and laughed. The sound was unbalanced, raw, and ugly.

Janet moved her head, trying to find Bonnie, but from her vantage point, she could only see under the coffee table. The four legs—one with a sizable crack where the joint met the table—jutted down like tent poles, buried into the dirty shag carpet.

Liv's murderer leaned down, only stopping when her face was inches from Janet's. Her smile grew wide. She drew the knife back for one final blow but stopped when Janet said, "Was Dave angry when he found out what you used the drugs for? Is that why you killed him?"

Her eye twitched and the grin froze on her face.

"He liked Liv," Janet continued. "He wasn't happy that she died from his bad batch. The police know, Summer. They know. I made sure of it."

Summer's smile drooped until her lips finally pressed together in a flat line, and she stood up tall again, putting some physical distance between them. She raised one eyebrow and shrugged, forcing a slight smile back onto her face. "The police won't find any phone records connecting me and Dave in the last decade. You, on the other hand?" She grinned again. "You'll be the suspect, Janet. Not me. Don't you see? I've set it all up perfectly. You bought drugs from Dave, then met him on your own in a dark alley. Days later, he's dead?" She tutted. "Very suspicious, I think." She pushed her hair away from her forehead and stared hard at Janet. "I admit the police finding your body at Liv's house won't be ideal. But this can still work, I can still make this happen. You'll be dead and I can write the narrative! You . . ." Her wild eyes brightened as she tried to come up with a new plan. "You felt so guilty about Dave's death that you killed yourself! Yes, that's exactly what happened. I'll make sure of it."

Summer's over-bright eyes were hard to look at, and instead, Janet focused on her lips, trembling with excitement. Liv's former friend had gone off the deep end, and the only thing that cheered Janet, albeit slightly, was that Summer was now entering *her* realm of expertise; subduing drunk and otherwise impaired people. One thing kept repeating over and over in her brain; *keep her talking.*

"How do you even know I met Dave—" As the pain numbed, Janet's brain started firing again, and she looked at Summer with new respect. "You planted his phone number in Eric's wallet, didn't you?"

"In his wallet?" Another peal of crazy town laugher split the air and from somewhere in the distance, Bonnie whimpered again. "I put Dave's number everywhere for *Eric* to find—I needed him to have a connection to a drug dealer for my plan to work. I wrote that phone number on the whiteboard on the refrigerator, a Post-it note next to the TV. And then somehow—Nell intercepts the one that was in Eric's wallet? Oh, that's just too perfect.

"Another unforeseen hitch in the plan. But in the end, it was still going to work out. I followed

Dave to your parking lot, saw Nell make the buy. It was just more ammo to keep her away from the kids. *My plan can still work!*" Her eyes were bright; she leaned back down close to Janet's face again. "I'm sorry it has to come to this." There was real regret in her voice, and for a moment, Janet felt sorry for her. Sorry that she lived such a sad life, her happiness based on taking away from others instead of making her own. "Do you have any last words?" Summer looked down solemnly, her fingers twitching on the knife again.

"You won't be happy, Summer. You can't be. Not by forcing yourself into someone else's life. That's just not how it works. You can't make all the rules and hope that everyone just falls in line! You can only be happy by coming up with the rules together." Janet rested her head back against the carpet and turned away from the woman who was about to kill her. Bonnie's feet peeked out from the far side of the couch—the little girl was hiding. No matter what happened, she'd have nightmares for years to come from this day. Janet closed her eyes. "Life is change, Summer." She thought of Nell's words from weeks ago, and knew with surprising clarity that the older woman had been right. "You have to be ready to make those changes work for you, or make more changes until you get it right. What you're doing here? It will never work. You won't be happy, and neither will the kids."

Janet thought about Jason, about her dad and his new fiancée. She thought about Andrea and Brendon and hoped they were hiding or had left the house altogether. She thought about her bar, and her customers and employees there, who all felt like family. Cindy Lou, Nell, Elizabeth, Mel. And now here she was, lying prone on the floor in a dead woman's house, about to die on dirty shag carpeting next to a broken coffee table.

A spark of hope kindled in her gut as she studied the coffee table's cracked leg. She chanced a look at Summer, then, easily allowing the real fear she felt to color her voice, asked, "Where did Bonnie go?" When Summer's head whipped around, Janet reached up. Using her good arm, she grabbed the nearest leg of the coffee table and pulled with all her might. She'd heard it crack apart at the house a week earlier, and sure enough, as she gasped through another stab of pain, it snapped off in her hand. Summer turned back just as Janet stood and smashed the makeshift club down on her head. Hard.

Summer's last, predatory expression slid off her face as fast as her body dropped to the ground.

The carpet muffled the sound of the fall, except when her head hit the unsteady coffee table with a thump. Summer lay on the floor, not moving.

"Better than a windpipe smash, and just as good as a goddamn beer bottle." Janet dropped the club next to Summer's unconscious form and slumped against the nearest wall. A smear of blood cut a sharp contrast against the white paint, and a steady stream still oozed out of the gash in her arm. She pressed on the wound, but the pain that seared up her arm left her breathless.

The front door blasted open on a gust of wind and faraway sirens sliced through the quiet room. Andrea stood at the threshold, holding a baseball bat in trembling arms.

Janet slid down the wall. "It's okay. We're going to be okay."

"I called the police," she said, still holding the bat aloft. "They're on their way."

Brendon appeared from behind her, just as a gentle snore came from the far side of the couch. Andrea bent down and laid a hand across Bonnie's forehead. "Baby Turtle works every time."

Brendon walked forward and leaned over Summer's inert body. His hand snaked out toward her coat pocket and he shoved something inside it before he backed up to his sisters.

"What are you doing?" Janet squinted, her vision blurry from pain.

"Just returning her pen. Grandma Nell took it by mistake a while ago, and I wanted to give it back."

Nell had said that one of the children had been putting items she took back in their rightful places —it looked like Brendon was that kid. He must have seen Nell take the pen and had just been waiting for the right moment to return it. Janet's head dropped back and she closed her eyes, and as her heart rate slowed, she listened to the wail of the sirens get closer.

CHAPTER FORTY-FOUR

The doctor frowned as her fingers probed the irritated and swollen flesh near the wound on Janet's left arm.

"Does this hurt?"

"Yessss," Janet hissed.

"Well, you're definitely lucky. The knife missed your major arteries, and the bones aren't broken." She snapped her gloves off and picked a tablet up off the table, then studied the readout from an X-ray image again. "The radiologist says we're looking at bone contusions on your distal ulna. That's going to be very sore for two to four weeks." She turned back to face Janet. "And it looks like you've got a pretty recent scar on the pointer finger of that hand. I'm sending our social worker in to talk to you, but you can talk to me, too, if you need help." She raised her eyebrows and waited for Janet to speak.

"Oh no—nothing like that—"

They both turned at a gentle tap on the door.

"You done in here, doc?"

The doctor looked between O'Dell and Janet, then tucked the tablet under her arm. "Maureen is very nice—trustworthy. She'll be in to talk in about fifteen minutes. Detective, she's all yours."

O'Dell stared out into the hallway for a moment after they were alone. "You've got quite a crew waiting for you out there. Your father's trying to get a court order to get past the nurses' station. I thought he was going to deck me out there."

Janet had to tamp down a grin. It was nice to have a father agitated on your behalf. The feeling died, though, when O'Dell moved closer and perched on the edge of the hospital bed.

"Summer is under guard at UT Medical Center across town. Grade-three concussion and a broken elbow. A judge is coming in to arraign her from her hospital bed on three counts of first-degree murder."

"The kids?" Janet winced when she tried to adjust her position and fell back against the bed with a groan. O'Dell jumped up and fluffed her pillow awkwardly before stepping back.

"They're going to be okay. Andrea and Brendon had just climbed into your car when they saw Summer walk around from the backyard. They ducked down to the floorboards to hide, and when Summer entered the house, they ran to a neighbor's to call 911. They had to try five different houses before someone answered the door, and even then, it took a minute for the stranger to believe that there was a crisis. Our cruisers were there within four minutes of getting the call for help. But if you hadn't been able to take care of yourself and Bonnie, we would have been too late." O'Dell's pale face looked haggard. Janet remembered that he'd started the day hungover, and things had gone downhill from there.

"Those kids are amazing."

"So are you."

When she glanced up at O'Dell, his cheeks turned pink.

Janet reached for a large Styrofoam cup of water on her table, but O'Dell got there first and gently guided the straw to her lips. She took a long sip and sighed as the icy water slid down her throat. "How is Skylar?"

"Skylar?" O'Dell placed the cup back on the

table and perched at the edge of the mattress. "I'm working on getting her into an inpatient drug treatment facility. She says she's ready, for real this time, to try and get clean. I think everything that happened might just scare her straight this time around."

"What about Eric?"

"Released with no charges, after we got a call from a Bonnie Kerben." He plucked a small notebook from his pocket and studied the cover. "We should have—*I* should have listened to you from the start."

"You can make it up to me easily."

"Oh, yeah? How?" O'Dell leaned close, and even through her pain, Janet's heart rate increased.

"By supporting my PI candidacy in the next board meeting for the Tennessee Department of Commerce and Insurance."

O'Dell sat back and nodded slowly. "Yeah. I can see that. I'll do it."

———

After a week of recovery at home, Janet fled back to work, delighted to return to the Spot. She'd had too much of William, and his hammering and yammering. She was only going in for an hour, to see how the stitches in her arm would feel during a shift of bartending.

Janet slammed the car door, and as she approached the bar, a warm sense of belonging filled her soul. But when she opened the door, that feeling evaporated.

Cindy Lou stood next to Mel, both women grinning ridiculously at her. What was wrong with them? Then she saw William sitting next to Nell at the bar. Both with absurdly cheerful, brightly colored frozen cocktails at hand.

Janet scowled when she caught sight of the frozen margarita machine churning on the bar, taking up prime seating spots. She had been gone a week and someone had seen fit to change the very nature of her business into one that served happy little frozen drinks? What was the world coming to?

"Janet?"

Jason dropped down to one knee as soon as she looked toward the sound of his voice. Her father and Kaylee stood off to his left, smiling too. The blood froze in her veins, and her jaw dropped.

"Janet," he repeated earnestly from down low. He held something small in one hand, and even as she gasped, he lifted the blue velvet box up toward her.

Her heart felt weak, like she might faint. She shot an accusing look at Cindy Lou, who had the gall to smile bigger.

She didn't want to do this, not in front of a crowd, but if Jason was going to force the issue, she had no problem pushing right back. "Jason, stop right there!"

"Darlin'," he said, ignoring her completely, but before she could object again, he opened the box. A folded up piece of white paper was inside.

"What is that?"

He smoothed it flat against his bent leg. "Will you sign this, completing the sale of my half of our business over to you, and pay me one cent to make it official?" She didn't answer, just stared blankly into his eyes. "Will you continue to be your own goddamn obnoxiously independent woman, who also occasionally allows me to be the chivalrous, loving, and caring boyfriend I long to be?"

"Wh—" The sound puffed out of her mouth, but she didn't have enough breath to sustain an entire word.

"And when the bar is all yours, will you still let me drink here for free?"

She laughed, then gasped when the movement rocked her body and the wound in her arm protested the unexpected jolt. Jason looked expectantly at her, a pen in one hand, the sale paperwork in the other. She bit her lip and stepped forward, a wide smile spread across her face. "Yes! Yes, I will, Jason!"

He stood and slid the paper across the closest table. She signed with a flourish, then Mel signed on the witness line.

After the initial congratulations had passed, Mel pulled her aside. "This came for you in the mail today." She held out a white business envelope.

"Can you just throw it in the office? I'll deal with all the bills when I'm back full-time next week."

"I think you should take a look at this one now."

Mel held it up and the sender's address leapt off the page. Tennessee Department of Commerce and Insurance. She raised her eyebrows at Mel, who shrugged in return. "Want me to open it?"

Janet snatched it away and grumbled that she could open her own damn mail, *thankyouverymuch*.

She unfolded the letter and then smiled. "I've been awarded a temporary license to operate as a private investigator while I continue my apprenticeship with Quizz Bexley."

A small slip of paper fell out of the envelope.

Janet bent to pick it up and gaped when she read the handwritten note. "This is from Gary Donaldson's admin." She scanned the note once and then a second time.

"Well?" Mel prompted.

"It says he's been placed on administrative leave for not following department procedures in my case." She looked up. "She says Donaldson made the anonymous complaint against me himself, based on a personal issue." She chortled out a laugh. "O'Dell owes me so big."

Before Mel could react, Janet's father walked over. He and Kaylee had hung back after Jason's "proposal."

"Congratulations, Janet," her father said, one arm still wrapped around his fiancée.

Janet grinned at Mel, then turned to smile at her father and Kaylee, too. "New beginnings for all of us this year." Jason hugged her carefully on her good side and she felt at home. "But let's not go crazy here. The margarita machine has to go."

Jason squeezed her tight. "Obviously."

Cindy Lou filled a rocks glass with the frozen drink and passed it over. Janet took a sip. "I mean, that's just terrible." She took another, longer drink, then a third. "Really, really bad."

Cindy Lou grinned. "Sure, boss. I can tell how much you hate it."

"Oh, fine. It can stay—as long as you do, Cindy Lou."

"Then we're good." Cindy Lou smiled.

"Yes we are." Janet scowled. "Now get back to work, everyone!" As her employees—*her* employees—headed to different parts of the room, Janet couldn't keep the happy grin from her face. All was right with the world again—or at least her little corner of it.

Turn the page to preview *Last Chance*, book 3 in the *Janet Black Mystery Series*.

ALSO BY LIBBY KIRSCH

For updates on new releases or to connect with the author, go to www.LibbyKirschBooks.com

ABOUT THE AUTHOR

Libby Kirsch is an Emmy award winning journalist with over ten years of experience working in television newsrooms of all sizes. She draws on her rich history of making embarrassing mistakes on live TV, and is happy to finally indulge her creative writing side, instead of always having to stick to the facts.

Libby lives in Michigan with her husband, three young children, and Sam the dog.

Connect with Libby
www.LibbyKirschBooks.com
Libby@LibbyKirschBooks.com

A JANET BLACK MYSTERY

LAST CHANCE

LIBBY KIRSCH

LAST CHANCE - PREVIEW

The office was, predictably, a mess. The manila file folders stacked halfway up the wall listed precariously off center, and Janet Black carelessly rifled through one stack after another until she found what she was looking for and groaned.

"Really? Another identity theft case?"

Quizz Bexley adjusted her ball cap and grinned, her hair puffing out from the sides of her hat like purple wings. "Don't knock it. Those cases are our bread and butter." She adjusted the purple frames of her glasses. When Janet looked at her watch, Quizz said, "Oh no you don't. You owe me another hour today. Thirty minutes, at least!" she added hastily when Janet groaned again.

Janet threw herself down onto the couch and

winced. The cushions might as well have been made of concrete for how much they gave when her body hit. She bounced more than sunk. She should be at her bar, the Spot, getting ready for a busy night. She *should* be preparing for her boyfriend's mother to arrive in Knoxville from Memphis for what was sure to be an exhaustingly revealing visit, crowding into the home they also shared with Jason's father—who they couldn't seem to shake after his parents had divorced and he'd moved in with them months ago for what was supposed to have been a week—maybe two—max.

Instead, she tucked her brown hair behind her ears and crossed one leg over the other, then flipped the file open across her lap and leaned back to scan the forms inside.

"Who investigates ID theft anyway? I mean, you just get your money back from the bank, close that credit card and move on with your life, right?"

"Sometimes. But what happens when the thief continues to use your social security number to get new credit cards?" Quizz asked.

"Jerks."

"Exactly. Jerks that we investigate and turn over to police."

"If we can stay awake long enough." Janet rubbed her neck and then grabbed a highlighter

LAST CHANCE - PREVIEW

from the table and passed the bright yellow ink over the most salient information on the papers in front of her. When she'd gleaned all she could from the credit form, she headed to her own computer to type up some notes on the case.

Soon the only sounds inside the small, cramped office were keys tapping and Janet's stomach grumbling.

She jumped when the shrill ringing of the phone cut through the air. Quizz swiveled away from her extension, her laptop balancing on her knees, so Janet reached across the small space to pick up the receiver.

"Hello, Bexley and Associates."

Quizz snorted. The company name was actually Bexley Investigations, but Janet was in the early stages of her apprenticeship to become a PI, and the approval of her permanent license hung on her finishing the required hours with a qualified pro. If she was going to be here, working for free, she hated to feel like a secretary answering the phone, so she embellished the name when she answered.

She grinned at Quizz while the person on the other end of the line stumbled through their own greeting.

"Yes, hi. Uh—umm, hi. I'm looking for Janet?"

"This is Janet with Bexley and Associates. How can I help you?"

Quizz smirked and got up, then motioned to the door, and likely the bathroom at the end of the hall.

Janet settled into her uncomfortable seat. Whatever was waiting on the other end of the line had to be more compelling than a two-week-old identity theft case. After all, some of the most interesting things in life were difficult to explain succinctly. This could be good.

———

Quizz walked back into the office twenty minutes later to find the phone still pressed firmly to Janet's ear. She had three pages of notes scrawled on a yellow steno pad on the desk.

"Yes ma'am. I think we can really hit the ground running on this one and make a difference for you."

Quizz's brow furrowed and her eyes narrowed. Her nose wrinkled; in fact, her whole face shrunk by two inches in circumference as Janet watched, bemused.

"How many missing persons cases have we

solved?" Janet repeated the client's question and looked at Quizz, her eyebrows raised.

Her mentor's eyes widened comically and she groaned. "None. We don't take missing persons cases."

Janet turned away. "Not many, ma'am, but we're a small firm and devoted to helping in cases like yours."

"Cases like whose?"

Janet peeked over her shoulder and saw Quizz advancing on her.

"We don't do missing persons cases. Period. We don't have the manpower."

Janet covered the mouthpiece, but it was too late. The woman on the other end of the line sniffled and said, "Who is that? Is that true? No—n-n-no missing persons cases?"

"It *was* true," Janet said. "But our firm recently doubled in size, and we're now more than happy to take on this kind of case."

"Oh, thank you." The woman blew her nose, and when she came back on the line her voice was steadier. "And you'd like which documents again?"

"We'll need anything you think might be relevant. Medical records, police reports, just bring copies of it all to me by close of business today, okay?" Janet glared back at Quizz when her boss popped a hand on her hip. She kept her voice soft, though, when she addressed the grieving mother. "I look forward to meeting you in person. Hopefully we can bring Lola back home."

"Lola?" Quizz said when Janet had hung up. "We don't do missing persons cases, especially not for girls named *Lola*." She shuddered visibly and dropped into her seat with a *thunk*. "You may be slowly taking over, but I do still get a say in some things."

"This case is special."

"Why? Because the mother sounds sad?" Quizz shook her head. "Well, I hate to burst your bubble, but they're all sad. The mothers, the fathers, the brothers. Even the dogs—you've never seen a sadder set of relatives than those of a missing girl."

"Yeah, but this is completely out of character for her! She's a star student, not some girl who'd up and take off with a boyfriend! I think she's in trouble."

Quizz's brow wrinkled again. "No one can sell a case like a mother, Janet. You don't know what's true yet and what the mother only *hopes* is true. So, I'm sorry, no dice. We're not taking the case."

Janet packed up her bag silently but turned back to Quizz before leaving the office. "I want to help."

"Missing persons cases are lose-lose," Quizz groaned. "Always have been. Most missing people don't want to be found. Also, there's no money in it! ID thefts—they pay the bills."

"But a solved missing persons case could put us on the map."

"But only if we find her!"

"And we will!

Quizz blew out a sigh as Janet twisted the knob and walked through the door. "I know you're not used to it, but I am the boss in this office. My word is the word. I know *that*, at least, is something you understand. And I'll tell the mother that myself when she comes in later today."

"No you won't!" Janet grinned. "I'm having her meet me at the bar. That's my domain."

The last sound Janet heard before the door slammed shut was Quizz laughing incredulously, and Janet thought, admiringly. Maybe.

www.ingramcontent.com/pod-product-compliance
Lightning Source LLC
Chambersburg PA
CBHW051936240626
47153CB00005B/1513